THE
PHOTO

BOOKS BY A J MCDINE

The Baby

When She Finds You
Should Have Known Better
No One I Knew
The Promise You Made
The Invite

THE
PHOTO

A J MCDINE

bookouture

Published by Bookouture in 2024

An imprint of Storyfire Ltd.
Carmelite House
50 Victoria Embankment
London EC4Y 0DZ

www.bookouture.com

ISBN: 978-1-83525-010-5
eBook ISBN: 978-1-83525-009-9

The wedding was, predictably, hell.

I'd known it would be the moment I met the bride-to-be, a thirty-something City banker called Arabella with a plum in her mouth, cold blue eyes and very fixed ideas about what she wanted from her wedding photographer.

'Informal. Candid. No posed shots. And no family portraits,' she'd announced at our initial meeting.

'A documentary, photojournalist style?' I checked. It's what all my couples wanted. Fly-on-the-wall photos that captured the magic of the day as it unfolded.

She nodded. 'What I don't want is all our relatives lined up as if they're standing in front of a firing squad.'

'Reportage is my speciality,' I said, because even though I knew she would be a complete pain in the arse, I needed this job. 'I used to be a press photographer.'

She looked up from my portfolio, one eyebrow arched. 'So why are you taking pictures of couples getting hitched?'

It was a fair question. Wedding photography never featured in my career plan. I wanted to be a famous news photographer, capturing pivotal moments in time, winning awards. But my appetite for news evaporated the day tragedy came knocking on my door. That was the moment I realised every picture I'd been chasing was someone else's misery and I no longer had the stomach for it.

'Because I love being a part of one of the most important days in someone's life,' I said with as much sincerity as I could muster.

Luckily, Arabella seemed to buy it.

The wedding was every bit as terrible as I'd feared. Having categorically told me she didn't want a single group shot, Arabella did a complete volte-face ten minutes before the ceremony, handing me a list of over twenty different family line-ups it was 'utterly imperative' I take.

The groom, an Old Harrovian called Barnaby, sipped surreptitiously from a hip flask as he waited outside the church. By the time the speeches started he was slurring his words.

Barnaby's best man was too busy trying to pull the married maid of honour to wrangle the guests into any semblance of order for the group shots, and Arabella's uncle was a keen amateur photographer who followed me around all day, mansplaining how and when I needed to adjust my ISO and shutter speeds and asking if I'd taken into account the wind direction for the confetti shot.

My shirt is sticking to my back as I let myself into my flat. I dump my camera bag by my desk, kick off my shoes and grab a bottle of Peroni from the fridge. It is almost ten o'clock, too late to eat, so I make do with a bag of crisps and a KitKat.

Knowing I won't be able to relax until I've checked the photos, I open my laptop, pop the memory card into the reader and hit download.

As I scan the photos with a practised eye, my anxiety lifts. They'll benefit from editing, but all the shots are there. Arabella and Barnaby walking up the aisle. Their first kiss. Signing the register. The obligatory confetti shot and arriving at the reception. Cutting the cake and the first dance. She may have been a nightmare client, but Arabella photographs well, her haughty, angular face capturing the light beautifully. And if the bride looks good, she'll be happy. Job done.

I take a deep draught of beer and remember my harbour shots from this morning, when the light in the post-dawn golden hour was soft and red. I click on the first. Something about the composition is off, and I scroll through a few more, discounting them, until I find one I like. I'd used the harbour wall as a leading line to draw the viewer's eye towards an old Thames sailing barge. Its peeling blue hull is perfectly reflected in the water, and a beady-eyed seagull perches on a mooring post to its right as if by design. I take another sip of beer and begin playing with the contrast and highlights.

And that's when I see him.

At first, he is just a random man on a balcony who's slipped into my photo uninvited. But as I squint at the screen I realise there's something familiar about the heft of his shoulders, the shape of his head.

He has a thick beard now and his close-cropped hair is peppered with silver. Curly, dark-brown hair skimmed his collar when I last saw him a decade ago. But even as I tell myself it can't be him, I know in my gut that it is.

The man we all thought was dead.

My brother-in-law, Jason Carello, the lowlife who stabbed my sister and her two little boys to death.

I'm hit by a wave of loss so intense I have to grab hold of the table to stop myself from buckling under the weight of it. But I don't have time to fall apart. I need to work out what the hell is going on.

Ten years have passed since Jason fled. Ten years since the bloodied bodies of my sister, Isabelle, and my nephews, Jack and Milo, were discovered in their beachside home near Tidehaven.

Within hours of their murders, police named Jason as their prime suspect, but despite one of the biggest manhunts in the force's history, he was never caught.

He simply disappeared.

Some people assumed he fled abroad; others claimed he had plastic surgery to change his appearance. We always believed the police's theory that it was a murder-suicide, but no one could tell us why an apparently loving husband and father butchered his own family.

I push the laptop away and bury my face in my hands. Memories are crowding into my head, coming thick and fast like a downpour after a prolonged drought. And no matter how much I try, I can't stop the deluge.

It was raining that night too. Coming down in stair-rods, swirling in the gutters, turning the dry roads slick. Treacherous.

I was leaving the newsroom when I heard the sirens.

It was gone seven o'clock, two hours after I should have finished for the day, but I was still stewing over the dressing down Ralph, *The Post*'s picture editor, had given me earlier.

I'd just got back from covering a visit by a minor member of the royal family, who was in town opening a new community garden. It was the biggest job I'd been asked to cover since I started at *The Post* and I wouldn't have been given the gig at all if Len, our most experienced snapper, hadn't broken his ankle tripping over the kerb in his haste to get to the pub. Since Jed, the third of our three photographers, had been struck down with flu, Ralph had no choice but to send me.

'We're all counting on you, Lara,' he said, as I checked my camera bag for lenses and spare battery packs. 'So, for Christ's sake, don't fuck it up.'

No pressure then.

And it had been going so well. I arrived at the garden with time to spare and found the perfect spot right by the sapling the duke was due to plant.

I felt a fizz of nerves as his black Daimler arrived. But nerves were good, I reminded myself as I checked my battery for the hundredth time. Complacency was a photographer's enemy.

I trained my camera on the Daimler and watched through the lens as the car door swung open, my nerves turning to excitement. I'd show Ralph I had what it took.

But I hadn't factored in the sharp elbows of the sallow-faced photographer from *The Post*'s rival paper, who jostled me the moment the duke exited the car. Nor the sun, which came out from behind a cloud just as he planted the tree, leaving me with half a dozen overexposed shots. Or that he spent most of the visit talking to the well-wishers on the opposite side of the garden, giving me a lovely view of his bald spot.

I was beginning to panic that I would be going back to the office empty-handed when the duke strode towards us and accepted a posy of wildflowers from a little girl dressed as a bumble bee at the precise moment my rival photographer was changing his lens. I squeezed the shutter as the pair beamed at each other, glanced at the back of my camera and grinned. I had the money shot and Ralph could go to hell.

It was only when I was back at the office and had pulled the picture up on Photoshop that I realised the duke's eyes were shut.

Ralph had gone ballistic.

'In here, now!' he yelled, standing by the door to the old darkroom, nicknamed The Bollocking Room by the older staffers.

'What the fuck d'you call this?' he said, pointing to the screen of his laptop.

'It's not my fault he closed his eyes,' I grumbled.

'*Not my fault?*' Ralph mimicked. 'Whose fault was it, then?' He shook his head despairingly. 'You had one job, Lara. One bloody job. And now I've got Pete on my back asking why his chief reporter took a better photo on his bloody phone.'

Typical, I thought. I was in the doghouse while Johnny Nelson was employee of the month. Again.

'You do know we're one advertorial away from another round of redundancies?' Ralph raged. 'How am I supposed to win the fight to keep three staff photographers when the reporters can get better photos on their frigging iPhones?'

'Actually, I think Johnny has a Samsung Galaxy—' I began, but Ralph cut across me.

'I don't care what bloody phone the cocky little bastard has.

The fact is, it's his photo that'll be gracing the front page tomorrow, not yours. And I'm not happy.'

'Really? You should have said.'

He fixed me with a look. 'That's the trouble with you kids. You come out of university with your fancy-pants photography degrees thinking you know it all, just because you can find your way around Photoshop. A good photographer is proactive and tenacious. You need to be one step ahead, Lara, not on the back bloody foot. Have I made myself clear?'

Ralph's words were still ringing in my ears as I shrugged on my coat and slung my camera bag over one shoulder. I'd left university with a first in photography and a belief that a successful career was mine for the taking. But the leap from uni to newspapers was way bigger than I could have imagined, and there were days I wondered if I'd made a huge mistake.

Wearily, I trudged across the newsroom to the stairs. The place was empty bar Pam the cleaner, who was staring out of the window as another siren echoed around the building.

'That's the third in as many minutes,' she said, her expression glum. Pam's glass was always half-empty. 'Two police cars and an ambulance.' She tutted. 'Someone's evening's just gone pear-shaped.'

'Mmm,' I agreed, but my brain was working overtime. Ralph thought I was a useless snowflake. Could this be a chance to redeem myself?

'Did you see which way they went?' I asked Pam, hitching my camera bag further up my shoulder.

She flapped a duster ineffectually over the chief sports reporter's desk. 'Towards the station.' Her eyebrows screwed up suspiciously. 'Why? You're not going to follow them, are you?'

I smiled. 'You bet I am.'

Ten years later, it's hard to recall how I felt as I held my camera bag over my head and splashed through the puddles to my car which was, inevitably, parked in the far corner of the car park.

I know I felt a surge of excitement as another ambulance raced past and I slammed the car into first and pulled out behind it. Getting the pictures was my only concern. I had no idea what was to come.

I kept a respectable distance behind the ambulance, but it was half past seven on a wet Thursday night and the roads were so quiet it was easy to keep it in my sights.

The windscreen wipers ticked left and right like the pendulum of a grandfather clock. Ahead, the ambulance pulled onto the main A-road that cleaved through the town, slicing it in two. I knew the road well. It was the route I took when I visited my sister, Isabelle.

The ambulance swerved right, and I flicked my indicator, glanced in the rear-view mirror and followed. It was almost certainly on its way to a crash. Some idiot driving too fast for the conditions.

My excitement gave way to anxiety. I'd never covered a

collision before, at least not in the immediate aftermath. I'd taken pictures of cars in ditches and wrapped around lamp posts. I'd even taken a photo of a classic car which ended up on its roof in the middle of a roundabout after the owner skidded on a patch of ice. Jason, my brother-in-law, had joked that he was going to contact the owner to see if they couldn't come to some agreement over the insurance claim. At least, I'd thought he was joking.

There were sirens behind me, and I checked the mirror again. A police car was hurtling towards me in the middle of the road. It flashed its headlights and I slowed to let it pass.

Perhaps it was a house fire, or something even bigger. A gas explosion. It could be the scoop I'd been waiting for. I ran through the list of things I'd need to do when I arrived. Assess the situation. Get the shots. Call Ralph so he could alert the editor. Pete would want to scramble a couple of reporters to the scene as soon as possible.

An image of a burly firefighter carrying a small child down a ladder, flames dancing behind him, formed in my mind. I Photoshopped the scene in my head, swapping the burly guy for a female firefighter, the child for a small dog. Something cute, like a cockapoo. Did pets sell more newspapers than kids? Probably. My shots were bound to be picked up by the nationals. I pictured one of my photos on the front page of the *Daily Mail*, my byline below it.

I'd driven the last couple of miles on autopilot, my head too full of the accolades coming my way to concentrate on the road ahead, so I was taken by surprise when the patrol car in front of me turned into Isabelle and Jason's swanky estate.

They'd moved there when Isabelle was pregnant with their twins, Jack and Milo, and their daughter, Lily, was three.

Next to a famous links golf course and overlooking a pebbly beach, the Sandy Lane Bay Estate was a mishmash of house styles. Shabby chic weatherboarded bungalows rubbed shoulders with grand 1920s Arts and Crafts country homes. The closer to the beach, the higher the price tag. Isabelle and Jason's new home, Sea Gem, cost a cool £1.75 million.

The first time I saw the place I was blown away. The house exuded 1920s glamour. With its gracefully curved white walls, dark walnut parquet flooring and floor-to-ceiling Crittall-style windows that perfectly framed the panoramic beach view, it was an architectural triumph. A sweeping staircase, reminiscent of an ocean liner, drifted lazily up to the first floor. The open-plan kitchen, with its veined marble worktops and huge central island, was bigger than my entire flat.

True to form, Isabelle had landed on her feet. Ever since we were kids, she'd led a charmed life. I used to joke that if she fell into a bucket of shit she'd come out smelling of roses. But I never envied her. The prospect of marriage and kids left me cold. I was too focused on my fledgling career.

'I have to keep pinching myself,' Isabelle admitted as she gave me a guided tour. We paused on the landing, gazing out of yet another vast window that offered a breathtaking view of the beach. 'I just hope Jason hasn't stretched us too thin. You know how impulsive he can be.'

Jason had always been a risk-taker, but I suspected Isabelle had no idea of the lengths to which he'd gone to fund their lavish lifestyle. It was the perfect opportunity to tell her, but she was the happiest I'd seen her in a long time, and I didn't want to burst her bubble.

'I'm sure he hasn't,' I said, starting for the stairs. 'You know Jason.'

Yet therein lay the problem. Everyone thought they knew Jason. He was the type of person who wore his heart on his sleeve. He was an open book.

But, as it turned out, he was a stranger to us all.

I rub my eyes, trying to chase the memories away, but they fill my head, insistent and complete. I can almost taste the salt in the air as the patrol car I'd been tailing careened through Isabelle's estate and hurtled towards the beach.

What then?

White knuckles gripping the steering wheel, sirens wailing and one question playing on a loop inside my head.

What if they're heading for Sea Gem?

But there were over a hundred houses on the estate. The chances were negligible. And, anyway, Isabelle, Jason and the kids weren't even in the country. They were in France on holiday, staying in a plush hotel on the Côte d'Azur, eight hundred miles away.

It's fine. Don't panic.

The odds narrowed dramatically when the police car swung into Isabelle's road. There were only a dozen houses in Chetwynd Avenue. But I ignored the first flutters of anxiety that dried my throat, because the odds were still stacked in my favour.

The police car slowed and pulled up alongside a white van

with the words *Forensic Investigation* on the side. I eased my foot off the accelerator and peered through the windscreen at the flickering blue lights. The heavy rain made it almost impossible to judge distances, but the emergency vehicles seemed to have stopped outside the 1970s chalet bungalow next to Isabelle and Jason's house.

I'd only met Dave and Maureen, the couple who lived there, a handful of times. In their early seventies, they'd moved to the bay from Hertfordshire when they retired. According to Isabelle they were the perfect neighbours: quiet, considerate and happy to water her patio plants when she and Jason were away.

Two officers wearing hi-vis jackets burst out of the patrol car and raced towards the bungalow, their heads bent against the sheet-like rain. My anxiety tipped into compassion. Perhaps Dave had suffered a stroke or heart attack, poor thing.

But the officers ran straight past their bungalow to Sea Gem.

I remember pulling my phone from my bag and calling my sister, my eyes trained on the scene unfolding in front of me.

After a couple of rings, her voicemail kicked in.

'Hi, Iz, it's me,' I said breathlessly. 'I just wanted to let you know...' I faltered. What did I want to let her know? That two ambulances and four police cars were parked outside her house, blue lights flashing and sirens blaring? She was in France. There was nothing she could do. Did I really want to worry her while she was on holiday?

It was probably a false alarm anyway. A malfunctioning burglar alarm or a malicious call from some nutter who got a thrill from summoning the emergency services. I resolved to find out exactly what was going on and then decide whether it could wait until she and Jason were home.

I realised my phone was still pressed to my ear. I cleared my throat. 'I just wanted to let you know that I'm missing you tons and hope you're having a great holiday. Give Lily and the boys a big kiss from their favourite auntie and tell them I can't wait to see them. Bye, Iz. Love you.'

I ended the call, grabbed my camera bag from the passenger seat, pulled my hood up and let myself out of the car. Spying an officer talking into his phone outside Dave and Maureen's front gate, I scurried over, catching snippets of his conversation.

'Extra resources... secure the scene... duty DI's on his way.'

My heart beat a little faster.

Seeing me, the officer held up a pre-emptive hand. Then his gaze fell on my camera bag, and he frowned. 'The media's just turned up,' he muttered into his phone. 'Yep, will do. I'll call you back when the DI arrives.'

He stepped into my path. 'I'm afraid you can't come any further, miss.'

'Why, what's happened?'

'We're dealing with a serious ongoing incident,' he said officiously.

'What kind of incident?' I tried to peer around his bulky frame but he stepped to one side, blocking my view.

'I'm not at liberty to say. You'll have to ring the on-call press officer.'

'But my sister lives here.'

His head snapped round. 'Your sister?'

'Isabelle Carello. I need to tell her if something's happened. She, Jason and the kids are away.'

'Away?'

'In France. They drove down last week.' My gaze flitted to the house. Jason's silver BMW estate was parked on the drive, which threw me, as I could have sworn Isabelle said they were taking his car because it had more room in the boot for all the kids' paraphernalia than her Volvo. But I must have been mistaken.

'Stay there,' the officer said, pointing to the pavement. He started talking into his radio. 'Sarge, I have someone here who says she's Isabelle Carello's sister.' He nods once, then barks at me, 'Name?'

'Lara Beckett.'

Two paramedics rushed past us, carrying a stretcher.

'What's going on?' I cried. 'Where are they going?'

No one answered. The paramedics conferred with another officer standing outside Sea Gem's double front doors, then disappeared into the house.

'When did you last see your sister?' the officer asked.

'I don't know. About a fortnight ago. Why are you asking?'

Before he could reply, his radio crackled and, as he turned away to answer it, I hurried past him.

Perhaps I already knew by then that something terrible had happened, but my fears were confirmed when a young officer rushed out of the house, his face the colour of putty. He staggered over to a flowerbed and vomited. A second officer left his post by the front door to check his colleague was OK. It was the distraction I needed and, with a quick glance over my shoulder to make sure no one was looking, I slipped into the house.

If I was expecting to find evidence of a break-in – furniture upended, drawers tipped out – I was disappointed. Everything looked normal. I ran up the stairs two at a time before anyone could spot me. As I crossed the landing to Isabelle and Jason's bedroom, the two paramedics I'd seen earlier emerged from the twins' room carrying a stretcher. Tousled blond hair poked out from under a blanket. Milo's hair; Jack's was a shade darker. But the twins were supposed to be in France. It didn't make sense.

I was gripped by a suffocating panic that squeezed the air from my lungs and I stumbled backwards, slamming into the curved landing wall. *Nothing* was making any sense.

'What's happened?' I asked the paramedics but they didn't reply. It was as if I was invisible. I knew Isabelle must be in the house somewhere. She would never leave the kids. I tried her bedroom. The door was ajar and, ignoring the police officer standing like a sentry outside, I pushed it open.

There were rust-coloured stains on the walls, with more darkening the carpet and Isabelle's expensive Egyptian cotton bedsheets. But my eyes were drawn to the figure on the bed. It was Isabelle. She was wearing denim shorts and an olive-green vest top. It took a moment for me to notice the blueish tinge to her skin, the unnatural angle of her neck, her glazed expression. And the blood. It was on her pillows, her top, her shorts. My eyes darted around the room.

So much blood.

I felt myself pitching forwards when a hand grasped my shoulder and jerked me back.

Someone screamed, the harsh sound reverberating around Isabelle's elegant, understated, bloodied bedroom like a klaxon, on and on. It continued as the police officer spun me round and frogmarched me out of the room. It was still echoing off the walls when we reached the landing.

It was only as I clutched the banisters and stared, unseeing, into the stairwell, that I realised the person screaming was me.

5

I am seized by a sudden sense of urgency and spring from the chair with such force that it tips back and clatters to the floor. I don't stop to right it. There isn't time. I need to see if my imagination's playing tricks on me, or if I really have taken a photo of my missing brother-in-law.

In my bedroom, I fall to my knees and reach for the shoebox under my bed. I can't remember when I last looked through it, and there's a thick layer of dust on the top that tickles my nose when I brush it off.

I sit cross-legged on the floor, the open box in front of me, and peer inside. Everything is as it should be. The plastic sleeve filled with newspaper cuttings; Isabelle's platinum wedding band and matching diamond engagement ring in their navy velvet ring boxes; a faded photo of Isabelle and me clutching ice creams on a windswept Cornish beach when she was ten and I was three; the silk scarf I gave her for her thirtieth birthday. I hold it to my face and inhale. Tears prick my eyes when I catch the faintest trace of her perfume. I put the scarf to one side and continue to sift through the half a dozen other mementos of my sister I squirrelled away after she died.

I don't know why I keep this stuff. I suppose I always thought I'd give it to Lily when she was old enough. She's fifteen now. Is that too soon? It's hard to tell. Lily rarely talks about her mother, which I know concerns Mum. But I get it. She's locked her grief in a box. It would swallow her whole otherwise. She'll take it out and deal with it when she's good and ready.

Maybe I'll unlock my box of grief one day too.

I tip the plastic sleeve of cuttings onto the carpet and flick through them. I'm looking for a picture of Jason. A decade has passed since I last saw my brother-in-law, and if there's the slightest chance I've got this wrong, I need to know.

The headline on one of the cuttings from *The Post* catches my eye.

Police launch murder enquiry after mother and two children found dead in 'house of horrors'

The Post was the first paper to break the story, but that had nothing to do with me. I didn't take a single picture that night, or think to phone my boss to warn him something big was happening and he needed to get people over pronto. My earlier intention, to show Ralph I had what it took to be a hard-nosed news photographer, was forgotten the moment I realised my sister was dead.

I remember a paramedic gently guiding me out of the house and settling me on the low wall outside Dave and Maureen's bungalow before disappearing in search of a glass of water. I sat for a while with my head in my hands, trying to erase the images of Isabelle and the boys that had already imprinted on my memory. When I eventually glanced up, a breath caught in my throat.

Johnny Nelson, *The Post*'s chief reporter, was standing

outside Sea Gem talking to a tall, broad-shouldered man in a charcoal-grey suit, cool as a cucumber.

Even in the fog of grief, white-hot anger consumed me.

How dare he turn up here, at my sister's house, with his notebook and his cocky swagger?

I knew he'd think nothing of it, of course. He was on the trail of a story, following the scent with the single-mindedness of a bloodhound. I could almost hear him justifying his presence. Some bollocks about showing the human face of tragedy. His thoughtless pursuit of my sister left me winded, as if he'd walked straight up to me and delivered a gut punch. Because Isabelle had never courted publicity, and she sure as hell didn't deserve to have reporters turning up on her doorstep baying for a scoop. It was a betrayal of the worst kind and I knew I would never forgive him.

Ten years on, I still have no idea how Johnny knew what had happened. He was a good reporter, but he wasn't psychic. There were rumours he used a scanner to listen in to police radio frequencies, an illegal – though not unheard of – practice among some journalists. Perhaps he'd heard the sirens and followed them, just as I had. Perhaps he'd had a tip-off from one of his many contacts in CID. Johnny's contacts book was legendary. He had a knack for forging friendships with everyone from politicians to police, usually over a few pints at the pub.

I'd wanted to march over and confront him, but what was the point? I knew from bitter experience that Johnny would do anything for a story.

I didn't know it then, but the murder of my sister and nephews would launch his career and he was poached by *The Daily Tribune* a couple of months later. Word was he couldn't leave *The Post* fast enough, even though our editor, Pete, had given him his first break. It didn't surprise me. Johnny was only ever interested in feathering his own nest.

The man in the charcoal-grey suit broke away when he saw me and strode over.

'You must be Lara,' he said. 'I'm Detective Inspector Curtis Frampton. I'm sorry for your loss.'

I nodded and tried to say, 'That's OK,' but the words stuck in my throat. And, anyway, it wasn't OK. My sister and nephews had been stabbed in their beds. My niece was hanging onto her life by a thread and my brother-in-law was missing. My whole world had imploded.

DI Frampton took my elbow and guided me towards a waiting patrol car. 'I'll find someone to drive you home.'

'Thank you.' My voice was barely a croak.

'You're very welcome.' He paused, a muscle twitching in his jaw. What must it be like to walk in his shoes, I'd wondered. Dealing with the worst of humanity every day. Making life-and-death decisions. Working round the clock to bring the bad guys to justice. As if reading my mind, he said, 'I will catch the bastard who did this.'

'You will?'

His expression tightened. 'If it's the last thing I do,' he promised.

6

The newspaper cutting flutters in my trembling fingers. Published a week after the attack, it not only names Isabelle, Jason and the children, but also, crucially, has photos of them all, pilfered by Johnny from Jason's Facebook account.

Jason's profile picture is of him suited and booted and standing next to a sleek silver Jaguar E-Type on the forecourt of his vintage car showroom, JC Classics.

I study his face, comparing it to the photo I took this morning. The last ten years have not been kind to him, but if you look past the puffy eyes and the saggy jowls, the likeness is unmistakable. His paternal grandfather was from southern Italy and Jason inherited his olive skin and wavy, dark brown hair. Brown eyes, a strong jawline and generous, almost girlish lips. He could have been a model... apart from the fact that he was only five foot six. My sister, a willowy five foot ten without shoes, had towered over him.

That hadn't stopped Isabelle falling head over heels in love with Jason the first time they met. Nor did the fact that she was engaged to a newly qualified barrister called Harry, who was buying a classic Porsche 911 from Jason's garage to celebrate passing the Bar.

Isabelle, who thrived on drama and was never happier than when in the midst of a crisis – existential or otherwise – dumped Harry on the drive home. That evening she met Jason for a drink. Six months later she was pregnant with Lily. Three months after that we were throwing confetti over them as they left the register office as newlyweds.

I always felt sorry for Harry, who was a nice guy and had worshipped Isabelle. But at least he had his new car to console him, and the thirty-year-old Porsche 911 was less high-maintenance than my sister.

I pick up another article and just like that, I'm transported back to the dark days following the attack, when Mum and I kept vigil at Lily's bedside, waiting for her to emerge from her medically induced coma.

Police have released the name of a man they are seeking in connection with the murder of a woman and two children at an exclusive beachside property.

Detectives are keen to trace Jason Carello after the bodies of his wife Isabelle and their twin sons Jack and Milo, aged two, were discovered by officers at their £1.75 million home on the Sandy Lane Bay Estate near Tidehaven on Thursday.

The couple's five-year-old daughter Lily remains in a critical condition in hospital.

Officers have yet to confirm how Mrs Carello and her sons died, but have taken the unusual step of naming Mr Carello as a person of interest in the investigation.

At a press conference yesterday, the detective leading the murder inquiry, DCI Phil Glover of Tidehaven Police, said: 'We are keen to speak to Mr Carello to establish the circum-

stances surrounding the tragic death of his wife and two
young sons.

'We urge anyone who thinks they might have seen him or
who knows of his whereabouts to contact the incident room
or Crimestoppers immediately. We also ask anyone who was
in or around the Sandy Lane Bay Estate between Thursday, 17 July, and Thursday, 24 July, and saw or heard anyone
acting suspiciously to please get in touch.'

When asked if police were seeking anyone else in
connection with the murders, DCI Glover said: 'As you can
imagine, this is a complex and fast-moving investigation. But
while we are, of course, keeping an open mind, our priority
and all our resources are focused on locating Jason Carello
at this time.'

Police attended the beachside property in Chetwynd
Avenue following a call from a concerned neighbour.

The woman, who asked not to be named, said she
became worried when she noticed that the Carellos' front
door was ajar.

'It was strange, because as far as we knew, Isabelle,
Jason and the children were in France on holiday. My
husband went inside to check everything was all right, and
when he saw what had happened he came straight home
and called the police,' she told reporters.

'We're absolutely devastated. They were a lovely family.
Isabelle and Jason doted on those children. We just can't
make sense of it.'

The unnamed woman in the article was Maureen, Isabelle's
next-door neighbour. She found me huddled in the police patrol
car the night the bodies were found and ushered me into her
bungalow, making me cup after cup of sweet tea until a police
officer could be spared to drive me home.

Much of that night is a blur, but I will never forget the

anguish on Mum's face as I sat her down hours later and told her what had happened. She aged ten years in as many minutes. To lose a child is unthinkable, especially in such a violent, unnecessary way. But she also lost two of her grandchildren that day. Between one beat of their hearts and the next, they were gone. Three lives, snuffed out at the hands of the man who was supposed to protect them.

If it hadn't been for Lily, I don't know what would have happened. Lily gave us both a reason to live.

Another newspaper cutting catches my eye. It's from *The Daily Tribune* and was published on the fifth anniversary of the murders. Johnny Nelson was the *Tribune's* crime correspondent by then and this was one story he couldn't let go.

Police have admitted they are 'no nearer the truth', five years after the notorious Carello Killings.

Isabelle Carello, her five-year-old daughter Lily and her twin sons, Jack and Milo, aged two, were found with stab wounds at their beachside home near Tidehaven in July 2014.

Only Lily, now aged ten, survived the brutal attack.

Early in the police investigation, detectives named Mrs Carello's husband Jason, a classic car dealer, as their prime suspect.

But despite a manhunt that at one point involved over fifty officers, the thirty-eight-year-old has never been located.

Police held a press conference today to issue a fresh appeal for information about the murders and the whereabouts of Jason Carello.

The case has puzzled both police and amateur detectives for the past five years.

Post-mortem examinations showed that Isabelle Carello died from a vicious knife attack. Her sons Jack and Milo each died from a single stab wound to the heart.

The only witness to the murders, ten-year-old Lily Carello, has no memory of the night her mother and brothers were killed.

Her father remains the prime suspect and a police source, speaking exclusively to *The Daily Tribune*, said the most likely scenario was that Jason Carello killed himself after slaughtering his family.

This theory is further fuelled by the discovery in the days after the attack of a framed family photograph of the Carellos on the cliffs at Beachy Head. Despite a search of the shoreline, his remains have never been found.

'I can't begin to imagine what it must have been like for Isabelle's family, not knowing what happened to her, Jack and Milo,' said DCI Phil Glover, who will continue to head the investigation until his retirement later this year.

'For the last five years my officers have followed every reasonable line of enquiry. We have reviewed over a thousand hours of CCTV and have conducted over a hundred house-to-house enquiries. The entire team is dedicated to exposing the truth for Isabelle's family.'

Since 2014, more than three hundred potential sightings of Carello have been received by the police, with people claiming to have seen him in mainland Europe, America, and even Bangkok. None of the sightings have proved credible.

Carello, who was described by neighbours as 'the life and soul of the party' and 'a dedicated father who doted on his children', owned a classic car showroom, JC Classics, in Tidehaven.

He remains the subject of an international arrest warrant.

In the early days, the police used to be in touch every couple of weeks to update us on the investigation. These days we consider ourselves fortunate if someone remembers to call on the anniversary.

Although the investigation has never formally been closed, Mum and I came to terms with the fact that we would never see justice for Isabelle, Jack and Milo a long time ago.

Every police force was looking for Jason; every man, woman and child in the country must have seen his face staring at them from a newspaper or the television news. Yet he still managed to disappear off the face of the earth for ten whole years.

That's why I'd always suspected the police were right, and that Jason – for whatever reason – killed Isabelle and the boys before killing himself.

But the police were wrong all along, and so was I. Jason is alive, and he is here in Tidehaven.

And I have the evidence to prove it.

Seventeen hours have passed since I took Jason's photograph. He could be in another county – another country – by now. I stare at my phone, my finger hovering over the keypad, ready to call 999, when I pause. What if I'm mistaken and it isn't him at all? You read about people having a doppelgänger. It's conceivable Jason has a lookalike out there. And then I catch myself. A lookalike that just happens to turn up in Tidehaven close to the tenth anniversary of the murders of his wife and sons? It's too much of a coincidence. I should trust my gut, and my gut says the man in the photo is Jason.

Then I'm hit by a fresh worry. What if the police don't take me seriously and my reported sighting is filed away, never to be seen again? I can't take that chance. I need to take this information to someone on the original murder team. Someone who gives a damn.

On a whim, I try the number of the incident room, but the line has been disconnected. I could approach Johnny, ask if he still has any contacts on the team, but pride stops me. He probably wouldn't share them with me anyway.

And then I remember DI Curtis Frampton, the detective

who'd sought me out the night Isabelle and the boys died. Three weeks later, he'd pressed his card into my hand at their funeral and told me to call if I ever needed anything. A couple of years after that, I bumped into him in town. I was touched when the first thing he did was to check I still had his number in my contacts.

I hit the call button before I have a chance to change my mind. He answers on the third ring.

'DCI Frampton,' he says brusquely.

A detective chief inspector now, I think, and my courage almost deserts me, but I take a breath and force myself to speak.

'My name's Lara Beckett. I'm—' I begin, but he cuts across me.

'Lara,' he says warmly. 'It's so good to hear from you. How's Maggie? And Lily? She's what, fifteen now?'

I'm so pleased he remembers who I am that I forget to censor myself. 'Mum's good, thanks. And Lily's a stroppy little madam. Surgically attached to her phone, but I suppose it'd be weird if she wasn't.'

He laughs, then says, 'Teens, eh? Who'd have 'em? It's funny you should call. I've been thinking of you all, what with the tenth anniversary almost upon us. I assume you're phoning to see if there's any update?'

'Well, actually—'

'I wish I had something concrete to tell you but I'm afraid there are no new developments. I expect you know I took over the investigation after Phil Glover retired. We still have a small team assigned to the case, of course, but their remit is to act on any new information that comes in and, well, there hasn't been any in a long time.'

'That's why I'm phoning, actually.' I clear my throat. 'The thing is, I've seen Jason.'

'Jason Carello?' His voice is razor-sharp. 'Where?'

'Well,' I say, backtracking. 'I've not *seen* him as such. I took a photo of him. To be accurate, he was in a photo I took.'

'A photo? What of? Where?'

I can hear the rustle of paper and picture Frampton thumbing through his notebook, his policeman's nose aquiver.

'Down at the harbour.'

'Tidehaven?'

'Yes. I often go down there to take photos of the fishing boats. I went this morning. I wanted to catch the golden hour. I suppose it must have been about half past five.'

There's an intake of breath. 'You didn't think to call at the time?'

My cheeks colour. 'I only noticed him when I was looking at the photos tonight. He was on the balcony of one of the fishermen's huts. You know, the weatherboarded ones they've converted into holiday accommodation?'

'I know the ones you mean. And you're sure it's him?'

'As sure as I can be. I'm sorry, I shouldn't have bothered you, especially this late on a Saturday night. I can phone the non-emergency number in the morning if you like?'

'No, you've done exactly the right thing. No offence to my colleagues in the force control room, but intel like this has a habit of disappearing into the abyss.'

'That's what I was worried about.'

'Then we're on the same page. Can you email me the photo? I'll get my best guys onto it pronto.' He reels off his email address. 'And, Lara?'

'Yes?'

'I'm sure I can rely on your discretion. Firstly, it would be irresponsible for us to worry the public before we're in a position to confirm the man in the photograph is indeed Jason Carello. But, secondly, and more importantly, the last thing we want is to alert him to the fact that we know he's back.'

'Of course. I won't breathe a word.'

'Thank you.' He pauses. 'I know you said you didn't notice Carello at the time, but is it possible he saw you?'

I think back to this morning. I'd stood on the quayside for a while, working out how to best capture the barge in the early morning light. Apart from a couple of fishermen unloading their catch, the harbour was empty. Normally when I'm working I like to stay on the sidelines, as inconspicuous as possible, so people forget the camera is even there. But it's different with landscape photography, of course, and I'd have been impossible to miss as I played around with lenses and shutter speeds.

'It's possible,' I admit. My stomach clenches because there's something else. In the photos I took this morning, Jason is staring right at the camera, right at me.

There's no way he didn't see me.

'More than possible, actually.'

After the murders, Mum and I stayed in Tidehaven, even though many in our position would have moved away, keen for a fresh start. But Jason had already taken so much from us that we weren't prepared to let him take our home, our history. It means that anyone who googles me will find my website in a couple of clicks and see that I am still living in the town I grew up in, still taking photos.

'You don't think he'll try to contact us, do you?' I ask Frampton.

The line falls silent as he considers this. 'I don't know,' he says eventually. 'But it's worth staying vigilant, in case he does.'

9

'Lara!' Mum says, when she sees me on the doorstep the next morning. 'You didn't tell me you were coming.'

'I was just passing,' I lie, dropping a kiss on her cheek. I can't tell her the truth: that I'm here to check she and Lily are all right.

'Well, it's perfect timing,' she says. 'I was just explaining to Lily why lip fillers are a terrible idea.'

'Lip fillers? Seriously?' I look at her in horror. But the tight knot of anxiety in the pit of my stomach loosens a little. If all Mum's worried about is lip fillers, Jason obviously hasn't made an appearance.

I hand her the box I picked up from the DIY store on my way over.

'What's this?'

'It's a video doorbell. We can link it to your Alexa and you can see who's at the door even when you're not at home.'

'Why on earth would I need a video doorbell?'

'So you can keep tabs on all Lily's ASOS deliveries, for a start.'

'True,' Mum says, inspecting the box. 'It looks a bit complicated.'

'Don't worry, I'll set it up for you.'

'I thought you were broke?'

'It was a Black Friday deal. Cheap as chips,' I assure her, even though the sixty quid the doorbell cost will send me over my overdraft limit. 'Where's Lily?'

'In here,' calls a voice, and I follow Mum inside. She moved here a year or so after Isabelle and the twins died. Downsizing from a spacious Victorian villa to an anonymous-looking three-bedroom new-build on a sprawling housing development on the other side of Tidehaven meant she could afford to hand in her notice at the bank and devote all her time to Lily.

I helped where I could, and Mum has never once complained about her change in circumstances. After losing Dad to a heart attack twelve years ago and Isabelle, Jack and Milo two years later, she is desperate to cling onto the few remaining fragments of our family.

Lily is sprawled on the sofa in the living room watching a YouTube make-up tutorial on the TV. There's a can of Coke on the coffee table and a packet of crisps in her lap.

'All right, duckface?' I ask, leaning forwards to pinch a crisp.

'Oi!' she says, smacking my hand away. 'They're mine. And don't call me that.'

'It's what everyone'll be calling you if you have lip fillers,' I say, pressing my lips together, mimicking an Insta-worthy pout. 'I had a bride a couple of weeks ago who couldn't close her mouth because her pre-wedding lip filler went wrong. She had to drink her champagne through a straw. I've had to Photoshop her lips in all the photos.'

Lily sighs dramatically. 'All right, point taken. You don't have to go on about it.' She brightens. 'I'll get a tattoo instead.'

I follow Mum into the kitchen, and she flicks on the kettle. Lily's a good kid, even if she spends half her life online. Unfortunately, when she told her careers teacher she wanted to be an influencer when she left school, she wasn't joking.

I take the mug of coffee Mum gives me and we sit at the kitchen table.

'How was parents' evening?'

'Frustrating,' Mum says, shaking her head. 'All Lily's teachers say she's bright. She just doesn't apply herself. She's her mother's daughter all right.'

'Iz didn't do so badly for herself,' I point out. After dropping out of art school in the middle of her final year, Isabelle put her love of charity clothes shopping to good use, sourcing retro and vintage clothes and flipping them for a profit on eBay. When she let me, I'd tag along with her and we'd spend hours rootling through the rails together, scrutinising labels and rummaging for hidden treasures.

Once, I found a Vivienne Westwood corset top buried in the bargain bin at our local hospice shop. Isabelle sold it on eBay a week later for five hundred quid and wrote me a cheque for the full amount, airily waving my protestations away.

'You earned it,' she said. 'You can buy yourself that camera you've been mooning over for months.'

I took photos of Isabelle's finds with my new Nikon: the Dior clutch bag, the Max Mara wool jacket, the Ossie Clark dress, the Prada shoes. I played around with lighting and composition, backdrops and mannequins. Isabelle used my pictures online and started making more than just pin money.

I couldn't have been prouder when she set up her own online store. By the time she met Jason, The Vintage Vault was turning over more than fifty thousand pounds a year.

'Lily's been recording videos of herself and putting them on the internet,' Mum says.

I raise an eyebrow. 'For Instagram?'

'No, the other one. Like the mint.'

'TikTok?'

'That's the one. I don't know what she talks about, she won't tell me. But it worries me, Lara. She thinks she's streetwise, but she really isn't, and there are monsters out there preying on pretty girls like her. If I say anything she tells me I'm overreacting. Will you have a word with her?'

'I can try, but I don't suppose she'll listen to me either.'

'Don't be silly. She worships you.'

I laugh at that but Mum folds her arms across her chest, signalling the matter is closed.

I push my chair back. 'I'll fit this doorbell then, shall I?' I'm attaching the doorbell to the side of Mum's uPVC front door when I see a reflection in the porch window of a dark-coloured car crawling past the house. I turn to see who it is, but the car accelerates away, roaring out of the estate with a squeal of its tyres. If it had been a souped-up hot hatch, I wouldn't have given it a second thought, but it was a saloon, not the kind of car boy racers drive.

The door's on the latch and I push it open.

'Did you see that?' I call to Mum.

She appears from the kitchen, drying her hands on a tea towel. 'See what, love?'

'The idiot who just shot past in his car. Is he one of your neighbours?'

She shakes her head. 'Probably a delivery driver.' But the hairs on my arms stand on end as an unwelcome possibility occurs to me.

What if I've unwittingly led Jason to Mum and Lily's front door?

10

I wake on Monday morning with a woozy head after tossing and turning for much of the night. When I did sleep, my dreams were full of faceless men in dark saloon cars, lurking, watching, waiting to pounce.

It's only when I pick up my phone to check the time that I notice it's the twenty-fourth of June. Jack and Milo would have been – *should* have been – twelve today.

The twins were so young when they died, it's hard to imagine what they would have been like had their lives been spared. But there were clues, even at two. Born by caesarean section, Jack was the oldest and more extrovert. Milo, eight minutes younger, was the quiet, affectionate counterpart to his louder, cheekier brother.

While Lily inherited her father's dark curls and olive skin, the boys took after our side of the family. Fair and freckly. Although they looked alike, they weren't identical twins. Milo was sturdier and his hair was almost white-blond and poker straight. Jack had a mop of dark blond curls and was taller than his brother by a couple of inches.

The twins were only a few hours old when Mum and I took

an overexcited Lily to the hospital to meet them for the first time.

We arrived at the maternity unit clutching teddies and blue helium balloons for Jack and Milo and a bouquet of blue irises, lisianthus and delphiniums for Isabelle.

My sister looked exhausted, her face chalky white bar the purple shadows ringing her eyes, but I'd never seen her more serene as she gazed at the sleeping babies in the cots either side of her bed.

'Aren't they gorgeous?' she murmured, as we trooped into the room.

Lily peered into each cot before wrinkling her snub nose and asking, 'When can they play with me?'

'Not for a little while yet, angel,' Jason said, scooping her up in his arms. He looked knackered too, but he couldn't disguise the pride in his voice.

As I hovered by the bed watching them, I viewed the scene through a photographer's eye. The handsome father, his beautiful wife and their three gorgeous children. Perfection in a freeze-frame. And then Jack – or was it Milo? – started wailing, and his brother joined in, their plaintive mewling in stereo. As everyone's attention turned to the twins, Lily, feeling left out, wriggled out of her father's arms and launched herself at Isabelle, who howled in pain as her daughter landed on her recently stitched abdomen.

Mum and I rushed to soothe tears and offer comfort, and I'd felt a flicker of disquiet at just how quickly Eden could crumble to dust.

* * *

Sunlight floods into the flat as I sip my first coffee of the day. A restlessness crawls over my skin like a rash. Mondays and Tuesdays are my editing and admin days and I have a heap of work to get through, but before I make a start, I grab my purse and phone and leave the flat. Although it's early, it's already warm, and the sun beats down on the back of my neck as I tramp along the street towards the cemetery.

Mum visits a couple of times a month to tidy Isabelle and the boys' grave, often leaving a hand-tied bunch of flowers from her garden. I haven't been for a couple of years, but my memories are pulling me there this morning.

Their grave is in the far right-hand corner in the shade of a large yew tree. I'd forgotten how peaceful it is here. Even the distant rumble of the bypass is drowned out by birdsong.

Ten years may have passed but a hard lump still forms in my throat as I stare at the inscription on their gravestone.

IN LOVING MEMORY OF ISABELLE CARELLO, BELOVED
MOTHER, DAUGHTER AND SISTER, AND JACK AND
MILO CARELLO, OUR BEAUTIFUL BOYS, GONE BUT
NEVER FORGOTTEN

When the stonemason asked if we wanted to include the word wife in the inscription, we'd been adamant. Jason didn't exist as far as we were concerned.

I crouch down by the grave, tracing the letters with my finger. The Portland stone feels cool to the touch. Mum must have been here in the last couple of days because there's a huge bunch of sunflowers – Isabelle's favourite – by the grave, and the grass around it is neatly tended.

I count the stems. There are twelve. The thought that Mum must have gone into her local florist and asked for twelve sunflowers, one for every year since the twins were born, makes me unexpectedly tearful, and I retire to the bench under the yew, my hands clasped in my lap.

The cemetery may be bathed in sunshine, but it's impossible to stop the dark memories flooding in. Sea Gem's white-rendered walls pulsing with blue lights; the wail of the sirens; the stricken faces of the police and paramedics.

Did Isabelle, Jack and Milo know they were going to die? It's a question I have obsessed over for the last ten years.

During Isabelle's post-mortem examination, the pathologist discovered several defensive wounds on her body. Not on her hands and forearms, where they're often found if a victim fights back, but on her feet and shins.

'What does that mean?' Mum had asked PC Josie Fletcher, our police family liaison officer.

'It suggests she was conscious when she was attacked,' Josie explained.

'You mean she knew what was going on?'

'I'm afraid she did.' Josie reached out to squeeze Mum's hand. 'The injuries show she was trying to protect herself.'

'But why her feet? I don't get it.'

I met Josie's eye, and a look of understanding passed between us.

'It's because she was lying down when she was attacked, Mum,' I blurted. 'She must have kicked out at Jason when he was... when he...' I couldn't finish the sentence, but I didn't need to. We were all picturing Isabelle's last moments, whether we wanted to or not.

Mercifully, there were no defensive wounds on the boys' bodies, which the pathologist said indicated they were asleep when they died. Lily had a small cut on the palm of her right hand, which suggested she wasn't.

I've been on the verge of asking Lily about that night so many times, but I never have. There's absolutely no point. During the hours of gentle questioning by a specially trained police officer when she came home from hospital, Lily was always adamant she couldn't remember anything. In fact, her memories are a blank from the moment Isabelle picked her up from her primary school that Friday afternoon.

A child psychologist explained to me and Mum that even if Lily did witness all or part of Jason's frenzied attack, blocking the memories was a natural coping mechanism. They might, he said, be triggered next week, or some distant day in the future. And they might never be triggered at all.

11

Back home, I lose myself in the edits of Arabella and Barnaby's wedding photos. A lot of people assume my job is done once the photos have been taken, but the post-production editing is where the hard work begins.

My goal is to get the best out of every image, manipulating them to make sure they look as good as they possibly can.

I'm adjusting the contrast on a shot of Arabella and her dad arriving at the church when my mobile buzzes.

'My phone keeps pinging every five minutes with notifications from the doorbell camera,' Mum huffs.

'Have you been checking them?' I ask, thinking of the dark-coloured saloon I saw crawling past the house yesterday.

'Of course I have. First it was the postman, then it was a delivery driver leaving a parcel for Colin two doors down, and every time since it's been next door's cats. How do I disarm the damn thing?'

'I think you mean disable.' I stifle a smile. 'I suppose you could turn off the notifications on your phone. But it's good to have it, Mum. Just in case.'

'In case of what?' She snorts. 'A burglar turns up on the

doorstep and rings the bell to ask if I can let him in? Honestly, Lara, it's driving me round the bend.'

'Perhaps I can tweak the camera so it only picks up people and not cats. I'll sort it when I'm over tomorrow.'

I have been going to Mum's for tea every Tuesday without fail since I left home. It's never a chore. I love spending time with both her and Lily. Plus, I get my dinner cooked for me.

'They were nice flowers you left for Iz and the boys,' I say, changing the subject.

'The sweet peas? I've got a glut at the moment. I'll pick some for you to take home tomorrow.'

'No,' I say, confused. 'The sunflowers.'

'I didn't leave any sunflowers.'

'Are you sure? There were some by the headstone. I assumed you'd left them for the twins' birthday.'

'Oh, hell. Is it the twenty-fourth?'

'All day,' I confirm.

There's a long exhale of breath. 'How could I have forgotten their birthday?'

'You're busy, Mum. Don't beat yourself up. It's not a big deal.'

'But I've never missed it before. I'll pop down this afternoon. I'll ask Lily if she wants to come with me.'

We both know what the answer will be. Lily stopped visiting the cemetery when she started secondary school. She said it was morbid, and she'd rather remember her mum and brothers as they were, which is fair enough. But Mum always asks her, just in case.

'So, who left the sunflowers?' I say.

'Perhaps they blew over from another grave.'

I cast my mind back to earlier. The flowers looked as though they had been placed in front of the headstone deliberately.

'Was there a card?' Mum asks.

'I don't know.' I'd been so certain she left the flowers that I hadn't thought to check.

'It was probably Frank and Viv. Jack and Milo were their grandsons too, remember.'

'But they live in Bexley.'

'Maybe they're visiting.'

'Visiting who?' I say, my voice rising. 'Jason and Isabelle were their only family down here.'

'I don't know why you're getting so worked up about a bunch of flowers,' Mum says, finally losing patience. 'Why does it matter who left them?'

It matters, I want to yell at her, because Jason is back. The man who murdered her daughter and grandsons in their beds. The man who fled the scene, too much of a coward to face up to his own actions.

Jason knows sunflowers were Isabelle's favourites. He knows today is the day his sons would have turned twelve. If not Mum, who else would have left exactly twelve stems on their grave, today of all days?

It can only be him.

* * *

I turn back to the computer but it's no good. I can't think about wedding photos until I've spoken to DCI Curtis Frampton. The phone barely rings before he answers.

'Lara,' he says. 'Is everything all right?' I can hear the concern in his voice and feel a stab of guilt. I'm probably over-reacting.

'Everything's fine,' I assure him. 'I just wondered if you'd arrested Jason?'

'Not yet, but we're working on it. He's left the holiday accommodation at the harbour, that much we do know,' Frampton continues. 'But he gave a false name and paid in cash when he booked, and the mobile number he left is fake, so we have no way of knowing where he's gone.'

'Oh, right.' I don't even try to hide my disappointment. 'Can you put out a public appeal?'

'As I explained yesterday, at this point we don't want to alert Jason to the fact that we know he's in the area because it's probable he would abscond. He's done it once before, remember.'

'You're right,' I say. 'I'm sorry. I know you're doing everything you can to find him.'

'We are.' Frampton exhales. 'And we haven't ruled out a media appeal. Just not yet. Is that all?'

'Actually, there is something else. Something I thought you'd want to know. It might help you find Jason.'

'Shoot.'

'I think he left a bunch of flowers on Isabelle and the boys' grave. Sunflowers. Twelve of them.'

'What makes you think it was him?'

'Sunflowers were Isabelle's favourite, and the boys would have been twelve today.'

'Ah, I see.' He is silent for a moment. A police radio crackles in the background. 'And it wasn't your mother who left them? Another family member?'

'No, I've checked. It can only have been Jason. And they looked fresh. They must have been left there this morning. It's been so hot they would have wilted by now otherwise.'

'Are they still there?'

'As far as I know. I left there about ten.'

'I'll send someone over and we'll check them for prints. I'll also get the team to look at CCTV in the area. The cemetery is covered by a couple of cameras if my memory serves me right.'

'Thank you,' I say, glad I called.

'Don't mention it. And, Lara?'

'Yes?'

'You don't need to worry about Jason Carello. The net's closing in. We'll find him before you know it. And when we do, you can rest assured he's going to prison for a very long time.'

'Are you sure there's nothing else I can do to help?'

'There is one thing.' The DCI's voice is grave.

'Name it,' I say, leaning forwards, my elbows on the desk.

'Forget all about Jason Carello, OK? We have it covered.'

12

I spend the rest of the day at my desk, only getting up at lunchtime to make myself Marmite on toast and drink a pint of tap water. By half past four my eyes are gritty and my back is aching. It's time to stretch my legs.

I head for the beach, the cries of the gulls growing louder as I near the sea. Tidehaven is one of the few towns along this stretch of the south coast to still have a working harbour, and it's something the locals are proud of. There's a small fishing fleet, and shallow-hulled coasters dock several times a week to unload their cargos of aggregates and timber. A paddle steamer offers day trips to see the colony of common seals that bask on a nearby sand bar at low tide. An art gallery, coffee shop and artisanal bakery, the converted fishermen's huts, a wine shop and a fishmonger add to the atmosphere.

I pop into the gallery, which is run by my friend, Ruth. I was working at the local supermarket when we met, my days at *The Post* a distant memory, my camera languishing in its bag under my bed.

I liked the routine, the monotonous predictability of life as a checkout girl. I no longer wanted a job where every day was different, when you never knew what was round the corner. I wanted tedium because tedium was safe.

Mum had told me countless times I was wasting my degree, my life, but I didn't care. I was still hollow with grief, stripped bare like a tree in midwinter, its branches stark against a bleached-out sky. I missed my sister and nephews with an almost visceral longing.

For a while, hatred smouldered in the vacuum they'd left. I loathed Jason for what he did with every fibre of my being. But, eventually, even my hatred faded, to be replaced by apathy. Because what was the point of anything when your life could be blown apart in the blink of an eye? You might as well sit at a checkout all day, scanning other people's shopping, earning just enough to keep your head above water, one day the same as the next.

I was walking home after a shift one evening when I took a detour through the harbour. It was summer and a fishing boat had just arrived. As two men in yellow oilskins tipped fish into large plastic containers, the golden sunlight turned their scales silver, and for the first time in years I felt an urgency to capture the moment. I reached instinctively for my camera before I remembered it was collecting dust back at the flat.

I went straight back and cleaned it up, returning the following evening, and when the same fishing boat chugged into the harbour, its baskets heaving with shimmering fish, it felt like a sign. I spent the next hour clicking away, so absorbed in my work that I didn't notice the woman a little further along the quayside, watching me.

'It's a lovely light,' she remarked. 'Did you get the shot you wanted?'

'I think so. Although you're never sure until you see them on-screen.'

'Painting's my thing,' she said, nodding her head towards Harbour Arts, the small gallery sandwiched between the fish shop and coffee shop. 'Watercolours, mainly. But I want to branch out into photographic prints and greetings cards. I don't suppose you have a portfolio?'

'Not any more. It's been a while since I picked up my camera,' I admitted.

'Not to worry.' She rootled around in her handbag, pulled out a card and offered it to me. 'My name's Ruth. I liked the way you worked; send me some shots from today if you're interested.'

I was about to explain that although I was grateful for her kind offer, I wouldn't be taking her up on it, when I paused. I'd missed the feel of the camera in my hands, the pleasure of creating something beautiful from the mundane, sharing the world I saw with others. Photography had been the way I'd expressed myself ever since Dad gave me his old Kodak Insta-matic camera when I was seven. I felt incomplete without my Nikon, like I'd lost an arm. And taking pretty photos of boats bobbing in the harbour was a far cry from the news photography I'd turned my back on.

'Thank you,' I said instead, flashing her a smile. 'That would be great.'

Ruth loved the shots I sent her and within a few weeks my pictures were gracing photographic canvases and greetings cards in her gallery. The pictures sold well but were only ever a side hustle. It was Ruth who'd suggested I take up wedding photography five years ago.

The bell on the gallery door rings as I push it open, and Ruth comes out from behind her desk and gives me a hug.

'Cuppa?' she asks.

'Thought you'd never ask.'

She disappears into her tiny studio at the back of the gallery, reappearing a few minutes later with two mugs of tea. We chat about sales and I show Ruth a few of the photos of the sailing barge I took yesterday, although I'm careful to scroll past the ones with Jason in.

'Stunning,' she says. 'You're wasted on weddings.'

'You're the one who suggested I do them.'

'Only as a sideline. I suppose you haven't contacted my friend at the gallery in New Cross?'

'I've been run off my feet,' I tell her.

It's true the weddings are a full-time job and I'm fully booked for the next two years, but it's also true that I'm too scared to reach out to Ruth's friend. What if she takes one look at my landscape work and says it's not good enough? At least if I don't ask, I can't be rejected. It's the coward's way out. I know it and Ruth knows it, but she is too good a friend to say so.

She pats my hand. 'You do what's right for you.'

I change the subject. 'Is Sue still taking the bookings for the fishermen's huts? A friend was asking about them and I said I'd check availability for her.'

'She is. She normally shuts up shop about half five. If you go now, you should catch her.'

I drain the last of my tea, tell Ruth I'll have some new prints with her by the end of the week, and head back onto the quay.

Sue owns the coffee shop next door and she's cleaning her huge chrome and black Gaggia coffee machine when I let myself in. 'Hello, Lara. What can I get you?'

'Ruth's just made me a cup of tea, thanks. I popped in to ask about someone who was staying at the fishermen's huts at the weekend.'

She stops wiping and tilts her head to one side.

'Mum bumped into an old university friend of mine from way back when she was in town on Saturday,' I improvise. 'We lost touch years ago. He told Mum he was staying at the huts.'

Sue glances down at the counter, where a well-thumbed A4 desk diary sits next to a charity box collecting for the RNLI, then resumes wiping. I smile brightly at her. 'I just wondered how he was doing. He's been living abroad for years, you see.'

Her brow wrinkles. 'I thought you said your mum saw him. Didn't she ask him how he was?'

'She was rushing to get to the dry cleaner's before they shut. She didn't gather any useful intel. Hopeless.' I roll my eyes, then shut up, leaving a silence I hope Sue'll feel obliged to fill. Eventually, she does.

'Saturday, you say? There was a chap staying in Hut Six that night. It's funny, you're the second person to ask about him.'

My pulse quickens. 'Am I?'

She nods. 'The police phoned yesterday asking for his contact details.'

'The police?' I feign concern. 'Did they say why?'

'Nothing to worry about. He witnessed an accident on the bypass and they needed a statement from him, apparently. Mind you, I hope they had better luck than I did getting anything out of him.'

'He never was the talkative type,' I tell her, glad that DCI Frampton's on the case. But my relief is short-lived.

'The only information I was able to glean was that he was down visiting family,' Sue says.

My stomach clenches. The only family Jason has left here is Lily. What if he's come back to finish what he started on that terrible night ten years ago?

A phone rings in the kitchen and Sue drops her J Cloth on the counter. 'Won't be a sec.'

Alone in the cafe, my gaze travels to the diary. Without stopping to think, I flick through it to the weekend, running my finger down the lines of names and phone numbers. One name stands out. I shake my head. If I was in any doubt that the man I saw in the photograph was my brother-in-law, I'm not any more.

13

I reread the name scrawled in the desk diary next to Hut 6 just to reassure myself I haven't imagined it.

Austin Healey.

Only someone who knew Jason would get the joke. It was the first classic car he bought himself when his used-car dealership in Lewisham turned profitable. It was the car that inspired him to ditch the second-hand Fords and Vauxhalls in favour of classic British, German and American icons.

It was a risky move, but it paid off in spades. The classic and specialist car market was flourishing, and Jason rode the wave. And it all began with his Austin Healey 3000.

In Healey blue and ivory, the car was in an immaculate condition, having been shipped over from South Africa.

'The dry climate means she doesn't have a single spot of rust,' Jason explained proudly, the first time he took me for a spin in it.

'Cars aren't women,' I wanted to say, but I didn't, because I was a little in awe of Jason. We all were. He had a charisma you couldn't ignore. It's what made him such a great salesman.

The Healey only ever came out on high days and holidays.

The rest of the time it had pride of place in Jason's showroom, where it worked its magic on visitors, turning them from window shoppers into customers. Not that the Healey was for sale. Jason claimed he wouldn't part with it for a million pounds.

Isabelle sometimes joked that he loved that car more than he loved her and the kids. I think it was more that the Healey represented everything Jason had worked so hard to achieve. Evidence – if he needed it – that the boy who started with nothing on a Hackney council estate had made it.

Where is the car now, I wonder, as I slip my phone out of my bag and snap a picture of the page. As far as I know, it was sold along with the business after a presumption of death certificate was granted by the courts seven years after Jason went missing. The proceeds went into a trust fund for Lily, a fund for which Mum and I are the trustees. She'll be a wealthy woman when she turns twenty-one.

'Thanks, Sue,' I call, and she sticks her head round the door and waves. I set off for home, glancing up at Hut 6 as I pass. There's no one on the balcony and the curtains are drawn.

Truth is, I couldn't care less where Jason's cherished Healey is. Only one thing matters. Where the hell is he?

* * *

Mum has made a salmon and broccoli quiche for dinner on Tuesday and it's such a warm evening we eat on the patio.

Lily lays the table while I dress the salad and sort drinks. Coke for Lily and a glass of Pinot Grigio for Mum and me.

'How's school?' I ask Lily as we take our places.

She doesn't look up from her plate. 'Boring as.'

'Have you decided what A levels you're going to do?'

'Nah. There's no point.' She takes a slug of Coke. 'School's a complete waste of time. I've decided I'm going to college instead.'

This is news to me, and I raise an eyebrow at Mum, who shakes her head as if to say, 'Don't get me started'.

It's twenty years since she's had a teenager in the house and it's taking its toll, judging by the new crop of worry lines grooving her forehead.

'College? I thought you wanted to do business studies at uni.'

'As I keep telling Gran, you don't need a degree to be an influencer,' she says patiently.

'Christ, I thought you were joking when you said that's what you wanted to do. Please tell me it's not really your dream job?'

'Says the wedding photographer,' Lily retorts. 'You know what they say about people in glass houses, Auntie Lara.'

She only ever calls me that when she's point-scoring, and even though I know I'm the adult here, I can't let it go.

'You know why I left the paper,' I say, through gritted teeth. 'And the weddings are a stopgap while I make a name for myself as a landscape photographer.'

'Ah, yes, how *are* the birthday cards selling?' she says sweetly.

I press my lips together. I love my niece, but sometimes I could throttle her.

'For heaven's sake, will you two stop bickering?' Mum splutters, setting her knife and fork on the plate with more force than necessary. 'Lily, don't be disrespectful, and as for you, Lara, will you please act your age? You're thirty-three, not thirteen.'

'Actually, I'm not thirty-three until September,' I mutter under my breath. 'You should know that, *Mother*.'

'Yeah, Gran,' Lily agrees. 'Get your facts right.' She catches my eye and giggles. It's infectious, and I swallow a snigger.

'Honestly, you two are worse than you and Isabelle used to

be,' Mum complains, placing her palms on the table as she prepares to stand.

'It's all right, Mum, you stay where you are. We'll clear up, won't we, Lils?'

'Course,' Lily says, pushing her chair back.

Mum's right. Isabelle and I used to fight like wildcats when we were growing up, Isabelle needling me until I invariably bit back. Lily and I have fallen into the same pattern. But I don't mind. In fact, I find it kind of comforting.

In the kitchen, as Lily stacks plates in the dishwasher and I wash the wine glasses, I ask her about her sudden change of heart.

'I've been thinking about it for ages,' she admits. 'You know I'm not very academic.'

'Don't put yourself down,' I say loyally.

'I'm not.' She sighs. 'Let's face it, I took after Dad in the brains department.'

I catch a breath. Lily rarely talks about her father, and she hasn't called him Dad since the day she woke from her coma and discovered what he'd done. I let it go unchallenged. I'm just glad she's talking to me properly.

'What d'you want to do at college?'

'Digital marketing. The course is brilliant, Lara. It covers everything from producing content and how the algorithms work to video editing and Photoshop.'

'I can teach you that,' I say.

'I know. But you can't teach the rest.' Her eyes are shining. 'I'm not stupid. I know I probably won't make it as an influencer, but every business in the country needs someone who understands how to sell stuff online.'

'True,' I say, realising that maybe Mum and I have got it wrong, and Lily's more pragmatic than we give her credit for. Because she's right. Digital marketing is a growth industry, and the career potential must be huge. And she might yet decide to go to university to do her business degree after she's finished college.

I hand her a tea towel. 'It sounds great. I'll have a word with Gran if you like. Help explain it to her.'

'Would you?'

'Of course.'

'Thanks.' She stands on her tiptoes and pecks me on the cheek. 'Love you, Lara.'

I inhale the floral notes of her perfume, Ari by Ariana Grande. I bought her a bottle last Christmas and she's already halfway through it.

'Love you too, Lils,' I say.

14

After dinner Lily mutters something about having an English project to finish and disappears upstairs. Mum and I sit in the garden chatting while swifts swoop around us, catching insects on the wing. It's hard to imagine they have flown more than three thousand miles over land and sea to spend their summer here, and that soon they'll be off again, Africa-bound.

Mum is in the middle of a long, convoluted story about a pair of trousers she's going to have to take back to Marks & Spencer because she only realised once she was home that they were black and not navy, and I sit back in my chair and let her words wash over me as my mind wanders.

Swifts mate for life, returning year after year to the same nest site. Perhaps Jason's back because he felt a similar pull to return home. Why else would he risk arrest after ten years on the run?

My brother-in-law's what some people would describe as a wide boy. Someone for whom the line between right and wrong is a little blurry. And they would be right. Underneath the sharp suit and veneer of respectability, he was a wheeler dealer at heart, always happy to bend the rules to make a fast buck.

I was still at university when Jason and Isabelle started dating. Mum told me during one of my weekly calls home that Isabelle had dumped Harry the Barrister and was seeing a guy who owned a car showroom.

'What's he like?'

'Jason? Well, he's not Isabelle's usual type,' Mum had said cryptically. 'But he obviously thinks the world of her, which is all you can ask for, really, isn't it?'

My curiosity roused, I caught the train home the following weekend so I could meet my sister's new boyfriend. And Mum was right – Jason was nothing like the young professionals Isabelle usually dated.

'It's so nice to finally meet you, Lara,' he said, enveloping me in a bear hug when he arrived for Sunday lunch. 'I've heard so much about you.'

'All good, I hope?' I said, inwardly wincing. How banal could you get?

'Mostly good,' he said with a disarming wink. And I'd found myself grinning back.

Over lunch, Jason regaled us with stories of his childhood growing up in Hackney. He talked football with Dad, chatted about gardening with Mum, and quizzed me about my course and what I wanted to do when I left uni. By the time he finished helping us with the washing-up, I felt like I'd known him for years.

'Well?' Isabelle asked once he'd gone. 'What d'you think?'

'Since when have you worried what I thought about your boyfriends?' I asked, surprised.

'Since I knew Jason was going to be your brother-in-law,' she said.

I gaped. 'Bloody hell, Iz. Has he asked you to marry him?'

'Not yet,' she replied. 'But he will. So I need to know if you approve.'

I thought about it for a moment. Jason was a hustler, one

of those loud, larger-than-life charmers who usually left me cold. But I liked him. Perhaps it was his innate ability to put people at their ease, or the way he gave everyone his full attention, as if everything they said mattered. Perhaps it was because he'd slotted into our family like he'd always been a part of it.

Isabelle was watching me anxiously.

'I approve,' I said, grinning. 'As long as I don't have to be a bridesmaid.'

Isabelle grinned back. I'd never seen her so happy. She waggled her finger at me. 'You are so totally going to be my bridesmaid, Lara Beckett. Whether you like it or not.'

A week later, Jason rang me.

'Isabelle gave me your number. I hope you don't mind.'

'Course not,' I said, wondering why on earth he was calling.

'Fancy a summer job?' he asked. 'I've been meaning to get a professional photographer in to take photos of the cars, but you fit the bill. I'll pay you fifty quid a day. Cash.'

It seemed an obscene amount of money for doing something I loved, and I bit his hand off.

On my first day, I turned up at the showroom, butterflies in my stomach, unsure what Jason expected of me. He led me over to the workshop and introduced me to his mechanic, a guy in his late forties called Trev.

Trev liked posters featuring topless women draped over classic cars. He liked chocolate digestives and his coffee strong and sweet. Trev also liked to talk.

'Trev and I go way back,' Jason said. 'If you need to know anything about the cars, he's your man.'

That day, I took photos of every car in the showroom for the JC Classics website. Interior and exterior shots, close-ups of dashboards and chrome bumpers, walnut steering wheels and leather seats. Jason declared himself thrilled with the results and I was back the next day photographing Trev's current restoration project, a 1969 Mercedes-Benz Jason had picked up on one of his buying trips up north.

I spent most of that summer at the showroom and in the workshop next door, taking arty shots for adverts and features in classic car magazines.

'Course, it wasn't always Astons and Austins,' Trev said cryptically one lunchtime, as we sat on an old bench eating our sandwiches. Jason was in the showroom, showing a wealthy-looking couple around a silver Ferrari with a cool £89,000 price tag.

'What, when Jason started out?'

'It was old bangers in them days. Anything he could lay his hands on. My job was to tart them up so we could shift 'em quick, before Trading Standards or the police came sniffing.' Trev looked sidelong at me. 'If you know what I mean.'

I didn't, but I was intrigued, so I made him another coffee, offered him one of my biscuits and waited for him to elaborate.

15

'Ever 'eard of a cut and shut?' Trev asked as we sat in the workshop eating our lunch all those years ago.

'Nope.'

'It's when you get two identical cars that have both been pranged, one at the front, the other rear-ended, and you fix 'em together to make one brand-new car.' He clasped his fingers together to demonstrate. 'It's one of the oldest tricks in the book.'

'Jason used to do that?'

'You didn't hear it from me,' he said with a wink. 'Clocking cars, overinflating tyres, filling dents, using air fresheners to hide the smell of a burnt-out clutch. He did it all. But only in the early days, mind. He'd cleaned up his act by the time he met your sister.'

'Isn't it all illegal?'

'Just a bit.'

'But he doesn't do it any more?' I checked.

'Just the odd cash only sale that doesn't go through the books. How else d'you think he funds that jet-setting lifestyle of theirs?'

I chewed my sandwich thoughtfully. 'How did he manage not to get caught?'

Trev scratched his chin. 'Search me. Knowing our Jase, he had a few mates on the force.'

'Are you saying he was bunging the police money so they turned a blind eye?'

'I couldn't possibly comment.' Trev rolled the clingfilm from his sandwich into a ball and threw it in the general direction of the bin. 'Anyhoo, best get back to work. That exhaust won't fix itself.'

That afternoon, as I took pictures of a classic Ford Mustang Jason had shipped over from the US, I digested Trev's revelations. I wasn't that shocked, not really. It had always puzzled me how a boy from an inner London sink estate had ended up owning one of the most successful classic car showrooms on the south coast. Not that Jason wasn't a grafter – he was – but you needed money to start a business like that. I'd often wondered where it had come from.

Now I knew.

'Lara, are you listening to me?' Mum says, dragging me back to the present.

'Sorry. What?'

'Will you have a look at those trousers? The last thing I want is for some smart Alec till girl to tell me they're navy after all. They're hanging from the door of my wardrobe.'

'Need anything else while I'm up?'

'Tea would be nice.'

I stick the kettle on before I head upstairs. Lily's door's closed, which is unusual. Usually she leaves it propped open with a pile of textbooks so she can see the landing light. She can't sleep in the dark – a legacy of the attack.

I stop outside, my hand on the doorknob, about to let myself in to ask if she wants a cup of tea, when I hear her talking to someone on the phone. Not wanting to interrupt, I cross the landing to Mum's bedroom. The trousers, tailored polyester with a crease down the front and an elasticated waistband, are definitely navy, so it's just as well I checked. At least it'll save her a trip into town.

On Mum's bedside table is a photo of Isabelle and the kids picnicking on the beach by Sea Gem.

When we were little, Mum made strawberry jam and Marmite sandwiches for our picnics. There would be ice pops to keep everything cold and – if we were lucky – a packet of Fox's Party Rings for pudding.

Isabelle's picnic, decidedly more upmarket, consists of cherry tomatoes and carrot sticks, hummus and a couscous salad. There's a French stick and Scotch eggs, Babybels and yoghurt, all washed down with a bottle of Evian.

The photo was taken by Jason a couple of weeks before they were due to leave for the Côte d'Azur. Mum found it on Isabelle's phone when the police returned it to us months later.

Isabelle had been looking forward to spending some quality time together as a family, away from the pressures of work. She never gave so much as a hint that things were anything less than perfect.

I pick up the photo and study her face, searching for clues, but no matter how hard I look, all I see is a happy, smiley mum spending a sunny summer's day at the beach with her family.

But deadly currents can exist beneath the calmest of seas.

Did Isabelle have any idea that within her seemingly perfect life, evil was lurking?

16

Lily's still talking when I pass her room. I open the door a crack, about to mouth, 'Want a cuppa?' when I freeze.

My niece is sitting on her dressing table chair in the middle of the room, a spotlight angled towards her. A tiny mic is fitted to her T-shirt and she's holding her phone on a selfie stick.

She springs to her feet when she sees me and stops recording. Expecting her to launch into a rant about respecting her privacy, I'm surprised to see colour blooming up her neck and across her cheeks, as if I've just caught her with her hand in the biscuit tin.

'Sorry to interrupt,' I say. 'I just wondered if you wanted a cup of tea.'

'No, you're all right, thanks.'

'What were you recording?'

'Nothing,' she says, her gaze sliding to the floor. 'Just practising camera angles and stuff.'

'I can help you with framing.' I step into the room. 'Can I see?'

'No!' Lily swipes the phone and presses it against her chest. 'For God's sake, Lara, stop interfering. I can do it myself.'

'Keep your knickers on, I'm only trying to help.'

She finally looks up. There's a flash of defiance in her eyes, a challenge in the angle of her chin that reminds me of her mother so acutely that for a moment I can't speak.

'How many times have I told you I don't need your help?' Lily snaps. She flings open the door. 'So if you don't mind...'

'All right, I'm going.' Frowning, I head back downstairs.

'Can you bring the biscuits?' Mum calls from the garden.

I place the mugs on a tray with a packet of chocolate-chip cookies. I'm pretty sure Lily's up to something. Why else would she overreact like that? I just hope to God she's not about to start flaunting herself on social media.

I want to storm back upstairs, snatch her phone and place it under lock and key, but there's no point. She'll only go underground. All I can do is watch and wait, ready to step in the moment things get out of hand.

After I've helped Mum clear up, I head home. There aren't any parking spaces in my street, and I cruise up and down nearby roads until I finally find a space a ten-minute walk from the flat. It's a clear night and the sky glitters with stars. It's the perfect night to capture a star trail and I ought to pick up my camera and tripod and head down to the beach to get some shots for Ruth's gallery, but fatigue weighs me down as I trudge towards my flat. The star trails can wait. My bed can't.

As I turn into the road two streets from mine, I notice a rhythmic sound behind me. Footsteps. Not the click-clack of high heels, but the muffled pad of trainers.

I stifle an urge to look over my shoulder to see who's there, telling myself there's no need to be anxious. It's a quarter to ten on a Tuesday evening in a quiet seaside town in the south of England. Bad things don't happen here.

Only they do, a little voice in my head whispers. *You of all people should know that.*

I can't help myself. I glance back. A man is following me. He's wearing dark clothes and a baseball cap, the peak low over his face. He's holding a mobile in one hand, the other is thrust deep into his pocket. I tighten my grip on the strap of my bag and quicken my pace. Behind me, the man hawks up phlegm and spits. The sound is unnaturally loud in the quiet street.

Who is he?

He's too tall to be Jason, but that doesn't mean Jason hasn't sent him. My brother-in-law employed a motley gaggle of undesirables at the showroom. Acne-scarred, hard-bitten men who were happy to clean cars all day providing they were paid cash in hand. Men who would have been willing to keep Jason's secrets because they had plenty of their own.

I stop and pretend to retie my shoelace. The man stops too, slouching against a lamp post halfway down the street. As I take my time tying a double knot, he pulls something from his pocket. I hold my breath, only releasing it when I recognise the bag of tobacco in his hand. He proceeds to roll himself a cigarette. The tip of the roll-up flares red as he lights it and takes a long drag. Looking up, he sees me staring and his posture stiffens.

He's one of Jason's men, I'm sure of it. Sent to keep tabs on me... or worse. But it doesn't make sense. If Jason sent him to hurt me, surely he'd have done it by now?

I slip my hand into my bag, my fingers closing around my phone. The smooth familiarity of it is comforting, as is the knowledge that I can summon the police the moment I need to.

I stop at the kerb and glance back again. The man is still lounging against the lamp post, smoking. Just as I'm about to step into the road there's a squeal of brakes and a bike swerves round me.

'Oi! Look where you're going, crazy bitch!' the boy on the

bike yells, giving me the finger. He can't be any older than twelve, shouldn't even be out this late, let alone on a bike with no lights. It's so dangerous.

'Jesus!' I mutter, retreating between the parked cars to catch my breath. There's another squeal and I look back. The bike's skidded to a halt beside the lamp post. The man in the baseball cap takes a final drag of his cigarette, drops it on the pavement and grinds the stub with the heel of his trainer before pulling a couple of notes from his wallet and handing them to the kid.

In return the boy presses something into the man's hand, then wheels off into the darkness, his body crouched low over the handlebars.

I shake my head. The man wasn't following me at all. He was here to score drugs.

I check left and right, then cross the road. When I'm on the other side, I look back. The man is sauntering off in the direction he came.

I scoop the post up from the doormat and trudge up the stairs to my front door, feeling a little sheepish. It's stuffy in the flat and I open the kitchen window before sifting through the post. There's a reminder from HMRC to pay my tax before the end of July, and a menu for a new Chinese restaurant that opened recently at the end of the road. As I flick through the menu a piece of paper flutters to the floor. I stoop down to pick it up, wincing as my shoulder twinges. Hefting a camera bag around all day plays havoc with your back.

The sheet of paper has been folded in four. I open it and smooth it flat. A message has been scrawled across the paper in thick black marker pen.

QUIT WHILE YOU STILL HAVE A CHOICE.

17

Minutes pass as I stare at the note, trying to make sense of the message. *Quit while you still have a choice.*

What does it mean? Quit taking wedding photos? I rack my brains, trying to think of anyone who might have a grudge against me, but the only person who comes to mind is a disgruntled bride who claimed my photos made her look fat and asked for a twenty per cent discount. But that was a couple of years ago. There's no reason for her to suddenly contact me now.

The note can only be from Jason, confirming my fears that he saw me taking his picture at the harbour and is warning me off. Little does he know that it's already too late, and Tidehaven Police are even now scouring CCTV footage in an effort to track him down.

I moved to this flat four years ago, long after he disappeared. My email address and phone number are on my website, but my address isn't. I rarely invite couples here to discuss their weddings: I usually go to theirs. Which means I might have been wrong about the man in the baseball cap, but I was right to worry that Jason has been following me. How else would he know where I live?

My fingers itch to call DCI Frampton and tell him Jason's made contact. His team would be able to test the letter for fingerprints and check cameras in the area. But it's almost ten o'clock. I can't bother him this late again. I resolve to call him first thing.

I find a pair of rubber gloves under the sink and a plastic wallet from a drawer, slip the gloves on and drop the letter into the wallet.

An unwelcome thought strikes me. If Jason has tracked me down, has he found Mum and Lily too? The possibility flips my stomach. I should phone Mum to warn her. But a call at this time of night will send her into a blind panic. I'll call her in the morning, too. In the meantime, the doorbell camera will keep its beady eye on anyone coming to the house.

Even though my head's buzzing, I get ready for bed. I have a wedding in the morning. Fortunately it's not a big do. Just thirty guests for the ceremony, which is being held at the register office in town, followed by a meal at an Italian restaurant nearby. In their early sixties, Marian and Bob are both widowed and met while volunteering at the local hospice. They are the sweetest couple and I want to do them justice. I should at least try to get some sleep.

* * *

I wake with a start, my heart racing. I must have forgotten to pull the curtains last night because sunlight is streaming into the flat. I grab my phone and peer blearily at the screen. It's ten to nine.

Shit. *Shit.*

Marian and Bob's wedding is at eleven, and I'm supposed to be at their house taking photos of Marian getting ready at ten o'clock.

I leap out of bed, wondering how the hell I forgot to set an alarm. I suppose I'd been so focused on the man in the baseball cap and Jason's note that I clean forgot. And despite my fears that I'd spend all night awake, I'd fallen into a dreamless sleep moments after my head touched the pillow.

Once I've showered, I pull on a pair of stone-coloured capri pants and a fitted white shirt. Paired with a navy blazer and navy Converse, this is my go-to wedding 'uniform', comfortable enough to spend all day in, while smart enough not to look out of place among the wedding guests in all their finery.

I race around the flat gathering everything I need, stopping every now and again to take a slurp of coffee. For breakfast, I shovel in three digestive biscuits and bung an apple in my camera bag for later.

I make it to Marian and Bob's bungalow a couple of minutes after ten. Marian is still in her dressing gown with her hair in rollers. She beckons me in with a smile and offers me a glass of Prosecco.

'Not while I'm working, thanks,' I say, following her along the hallway to her bedroom, where her two bridesmaids – her daughter and stepdaughter – are having their hair blow-dried.

I check the right memory card is in the camera. I always use two: one for the formal ceremony and one for the reception. It makes things easier to organise when it comes to editing the photos later.

At first, Marian and her bridesmaids are self-conscious as I dart around the room with my Nikon. But as the Prosecco flows, they start to forget I'm there, which is exactly what I want. The light in the bedroom is fantastic, and when I scroll through the photos while Marian's daughter helps her into her stylish, ivory lace shift dress, I feel a dart of pride. They're among the best I've ever taken.

Marian is travelling to the ceremony in an open-topped Beauford, and once it's left, I jump into my car and race across town. Outside the register office Bob greets me like a long-lost daughter, introducing me to his two sons and his best man.

He runs a hand around his collar and checks his watch.

'Don't worry.' I smile. 'She's on her way.' Minutes later the Beauford draws up and Marian joins Bob on the steps of the register office. Her smile is radiant. His eyes shine with pride. I lift my camera and snap away as they kiss briefly, then disappear through the double doors, hand in hand.

* * *

I have a breathing space of about twenty minutes between the ceremony and the wedding breakfast, and I pass the time in my car. Once I've put new batteries in the camera and switched the memory cards, I check my phone. There's a notification that I have a new review and, curious, I open the app.

'Disappointed Bride' has left a one-star review. My eyes widen as I quickly scan it.

Unprofessional... didn't seem invested in our wedding... poor communication... key shots missed or botched... lack of effort... dismissive and arrogant attitude...

If that wasn't damning enough, it ends with, 'Hiring Lara Beckett was the worst decision we have ever made. If you want a reliable and professional photographer, I strongly advise you to look elsewhere.'

If there's one thing I've learnt from my time at *The Post*, it's to take criticism on the chin, constructive or otherwise, but this review is particularly hard to swallow, especially as I have no idea who 'Disappointed Bride' could be, and if she was so disappointed, why didn't she say something to me at the time?

I mentally list all the couples whose weddings I have covered this year. No one has complained about the standard of my work. To the contrary, they've all seemed delighted. I know that responding would be a mistake, so I decide to chalk it up to experience, close the app and check my emails.

There's one from Arabella, and when I see her name I wonder if she's my 'Disappointed Bride'. She certainly was very exacting. But I couldn't be more wrong. She's giving me the go-ahead to upload a little behind-the-scenes video I made of her and Barnaby's wedding to TikTok. It's a great way to promote my business, and their wedding was such a sumptuous affair it'll go down a storm with my followers.

Feeling more cheerful, I upload the video, add half a dozen hashtags, then check my notifications. A video I put together on the dos and don'ts of choosing a wedding photographer is getting a lot of love, and I quickly thumb replies to a few of the comments.

I click back to the home page and swipe half-heartedly through a couple of videos. A tabby cat who miaows on demand. A drunk bride and groom singing 'Islands in the Stream' – badly. A *Love Island* celeb demonstrating how to apply fake eyelashes.

And then Lily's face appears on my screen. She is talking but is on mute so I can't hear what she's saying. My heart lurches, and I close my eyes briefly before clicking on the video.

18

I can see the corner of Lily's corkboard on the wall behind her. Her hair looks newly washed and falls over her shoulders in long, wavy curls. She's wearing make-up. Cat flicks and cherry-red lip gloss. She looks about eighteen, not fifteen.

I turn the volume up and hold the phone against the steering wheel with trembling fingers.

Lily gives a small smile, then starts to speak.

'To most of you, I'm a nobody, but to all you true crime fans out there, I am a victim, searching for the truth.'

Lily reaches down for something on her bed, then shows it to the camera. I recognise it immediately. It's the scrapbook of cuttings our Auntie Jenny, Mum's older sister, kept after the murders. Auntie Jen religiously cut out every story the papers ran about Isabelle and the twins and the subsequent police investigation.

'Someone should keep a record of what happened in case Lily ever wants to know,' she said at the time.

Mum told her it was macabre, and they didn't speak for a while. Over the years, the argument was forgotten. So was

Auntie Jenny's scrapbook. I'd forgotten about it, at any rate. But it seems not everyone had. It also seems she was right. Lily did want to know.

'These,' Lily says, flicking through the pages, 'are newspaper stories about a triple murder in Tidehaven ten years ago. The Carello Killings, the headline writers called them, because three members of the Carello family, Isabelle Carello and her twin sons, Jack and Milo, were murdered in their beds that night. Only Isabelle's five-year-old daughter, Lily, survived the attack. That's me, if you hadn't already guessed.'

Her voice is as steady as her hands as she holds the scrapbook closer to the camera. A headline swims into focus.

Three killed in beach home bloodbath

Lily lowers the scrapbook and gazes into the lens. Her brown eyes are clear and there is a defiant tilt to her chin.

'Stick around to join me on my search for answers as I reveal what I remember of the night my mum and brothers were killed.

'Next time, I'll share unseen footage of my family and describe what I remember about the days before the attack. Until then, take care out there.'

The screen goes to black.

I throw my phone onto the passenger seat and rest my forehead on the steering wheel as the enormity of what I've just watched sinks in. When Lily said she wanted to become an influencer, I assumed she'd be making lifestyle vlogs or beauty tutorials. I didn't for one minute think she'd be sharing her past – *our* past – all over social bloody media.

What is she thinking, turning the spotlight on our family's darkest hour without even discussing it with me and Mum? Doesn't she realise that by releasing this video she's opened herself up to all sorts of weirdos and trolls? Never mind the legions of conspiracy theorists who led the rumour-mongering after Isabelle and the twins died.

There were whole forums on the internet dedicated to solving the Carello Killings. Most people agreed with the police and pointed the finger at Jason. Some were convinced that the evidence suggested a burglary gone wrong. A few decided Isabelle must have suffered a psychotic episode and murdered the twins and attacked Lily before turning the knife on herself.

She died from over twenty stab wounds, for fuck's sake.

And then there were the out-and-out nutters who claimed their deaths were Russian executions in retaliation for perceived slights by the British Government, or that Isabelle was a member of a cult and had been planning to expose the leader.

So many lies and falsehoods. Did the people who dreamt this nonsense up ever stop to think how the stories they were peddling affected the victims' families?

Of course they didn't.

And now Lily has given them the perfect excuse to start all over again.

'Christ, Lily, what have you done,' I mutter. It's a betrayal of the worst kind. Mum, who has done so much for Lily, who put her own life on hold to bring her up, is going to be devastated.

I reach for my phone. I need to call Lily and ask her what the hell she's playing at. Tell her to take the damn video down right now, before any more damage is done. My finger hovers over her number. I'm so angry I can hear the blood rushing in my ears, like wind in a conch shell.

But something stops me from calling her. Furious as I am, I don't want to say something I'll regret. I need to talk to her calmly, explain why her video is such a bad idea. I know my niece well enough to recognise that ranting at her over the phone will get me nowhere. This is a conversation we need to have later and face to face.

I'll text instead and invite her round to mine for a coffee after school, I decide. I should be back from the wedding by half three.

The wedding.

Fuck.

19

A chill sweeps through me as I check the time on my phone. It's half past twelve and I was supposed to be at the restaurant for Marian and Bob's wedding reception fifteen minutes ago.

I tap out a quick text to Marian.

Car trouble. Be with you in five.

I have never been late to a wedding before. Never. Damn bloody Lily and her bloody video! I chuck the phone back onto the passenger seat, turn the key and slam the gear stick into first, flying out of the car park and almost taking out a man on a motorised scooter. I hold up an apologetic hand as I pass. He shakes his head and gives me a filthy look.

Luck is on my side, and I find a parking space in a residential street a two-minute walk from the high street. I grab my phone and camera bag, lock the car and head towards the restaurant at a jog.

When I arrive, I'm hot and sweaty, but Marian and Bob don't seem to notice. Marian ushers me over, her face lined with concern as she asks about my car.

'Bob's youngest is a mechanic. He'll look at it for you if you like, won't you, Den?' she calls to her stepson, who is sitting halfway down the table.

'That's so kind of you, but there's really no need. It's booked in for a service and MOT next week anyway,' I lie.

This time, when Marian offers me a glass of Prosecco, I accept, hoping the alcohol will calm me. I need to get my shit together. These photos aren't going to take themselves. I have a couple of sips, then set the glass on the table and ferret around in my camera bag for the second memory card.

Once I've swapped the cards, I spend a moment formatting the second card. It's a good habit I picked up from Ralph during my time at *The Post*.

'When you press erase, you're not really deleting the pictures on the card, you're just allowing the camera to over-write the existing files,' he explained, after my camera showed a file error one day. 'If you're not careful, errors like this'll lose you pictures. Get into the habit of formatting a card every time you put it in your camera. Formatting is like bleaching a towel instead of just rinsing it out. Your memory card will be completely clean.' He shook his head. 'Didn't they teach you this stuff at that fancy college you went to?'

Once I've checked the card is clean, I work my way around the room to a soundtrack of clinking glasses and happy chatter, capturing the guests as they tuck into the wedding breakfast. But my heart's no longer in it. I'm too busy worrying about Lily's video and the damage it'll wreak. While I go through the motions, a smile fixed on my face, I know the photos won't be a patch on the ones I took this morning. I just have to hope Marian and Bob don't notice.

When at last it's time for the speeches, I force myself to focus on the task in hand. Marian's eyeliner has smudged, and strands of hair have broken free of her neat French twist. Bob's cheeks are ruddy from the Prosecco and his stomach strains over the waistband of his trousers. Still, as they gaze into each other's eyes during the toast, I can't help but think they're the most beautiful couple I've ever photographed, and I hope I've done them proud.

The arrival of the waiting staff with trays of coffee cups is my cue to leave and I say goodbye to Marian and Bob, promising to have their contact sheet with them in the next few days.

'We couldn't be more grateful,' Marian says, hugging me.

Bob presses an envelope into my hand. 'Just a little something to show our appreciation,' he whispers with a wink. 'You've been a trouper.'

It's only once I'm back in my car, scrolling through the photos frame by frame, that I remember switching the memory cards before I left the register office. The shock of seeing Lily's TikTok video made me clean forget. So I switched them again at the restaurant and formatted the card without checking.

Beads of sweat break out across my brow as I realise my mistake. The card I thought contained the photos of Arabella and Barnaby's wedding, photos I've already safely downloaded onto my computer, actually contained the ones from this morning. All those beautiful shots of Marian getting ready, of Bob waiting for his bride, of the happy couple signing the register and being showered with confetti as they left the register office.

I formatted the wrong card. I know without checking that the photos on the second card are of Arabella and Barney. I've deleted the wrong photos because I wasn't concentrating.

It's unforgivable. The worst sin a wedding photographer can commit. The memory card that should have contained hundreds of photos of Marian and Bob's happy day is as clean as a bleached towel.

20

I drive home in a daze, worry nipping at my heels like a bad-tempered terrier. How the hell am I going to explain to Marian and Bob that, through sheer incompetence, I've deleted most of their wedding pictures?

I have professional indemnity insurance in case I'm ever sued by an unsatisfied client. But even if Marian and Bob made a claim and the insurance company settled, all the money in the world won't make up for the fact that I've failed to capture most of their wedding day.

To my surprise, Lily is sitting on the low wall outside my flat, her heels kicking the bricks as she stares at her phone.

She jumps to her feet when she sees my car and hooks her thumbs into the pockets of her school blazer.

'All right?' she says, not meeting my eye.

'Not really. What are you doing here?'

'Nice to see you too, Auntie Lara,' she says, hauling her bag over her shoulder. 'I thought I'd drop by on my way home, but perhaps I shouldn't have bothered.'

I sigh. My memory card catastrophe had pushed Lily to the back of my mind, but I still need to talk to her. 'Sorry, it's been a bitch of a day. Come up. I think there are a couple of Magnums in the freezer.'

She trails her bag behind her like a petulant child as she climbs up the narrow staircase to my front door, and I want to snap at her to pick it up or she'll scuff the bottom, but I bite my tongue. It'll only antagonise her.

I drop my camera bag on the floor in the hallway and Lily makes a beeline for the freezer. She hands me a Magnum and we sit across from each other at the tiny kitchen table.

'Why's your day been a bitch?' she asks, tearing open the wrapper with her teeth.

'I deleted most of the wedding photos of the nicest couple you're ever likely to meet.'

Her eyes widen. 'Oh, crap. How on earth did you manage that?'

I look at her levelly. 'Because I'd just seen your TikTok video.'

Her gaze drops.

'Were you going to mention you were doing this at some point, because I really would have liked some warning, Lily.'

She fidgets in her seat. 'You'd only have told me not to do it.'

'Damn right I would!' I cry. 'What were you thinking? Or did you even stop to think at all?' The Magnum is melting in my hand and I shove it back into the wrapper, my appetite gone. 'Gran's going to be livid.'

'She doesn't need to know.'

'Of course she needs to know! And anyway, she's going to find out soon enough when a load of journalists turn up on the doorstep.'

Lily crosses her arms. 'I can handle them.'

I stare at her, incredulous. 'Are you for real?'

'I'll give them what they want, and they'll be happy. I'll piggyback off the exposure to create a platform for my online content. Job done.'

I shake my head. 'You've opened Pandora's box.'

'You're overreacting,' she scoffs. 'As usual.'

'You think you're so worldly-wise, but you know nothing, Lily. You weren't there ten years ago. The press intrusion was brutal. Reporters stopped at nothing to get a new angle. They doorstepped our neighbours. They stole photos from our social media accounts. They even ran kiss-and-tell interviews with your mum's old boyfriends.'

Lily's Magnum is also melting, a trail of vanilla ice cream sliding down her wrist, but she doesn't seem to notice.

Conflicting emotions play across her face. Surprise. Guilt. Anger.

Anger wins.

'How dare you make me feel guilty I wasn't there after Mum and the twins died. I was in a coma in hospital,' she spits.

'You must have realised what it was like for us.'

'What it was like for you?' It's her turn to laugh. 'What do you think it was like for *me*? Mum, Jack and Milo all dead. Dad missing. My whole family gone in a puff of smoke. How d'you think that makes me feel? I'll tell you, shall I? It makes me feel like shit.'

'So what do you hope to achieve by dredging it all up again?' I ask, bewildered.

Her gaze drops to the Magnum, and she pulls a tissue from her blazer pocket and wraps it around the melting mess.

'I've been getting flashbacks,' she says.

At first, I'm not sure I've heard her correctly. 'Flashbacks?'

She gives a tiny nod. 'About the night it happened.'

I sit up straight. 'You need to tell the police.'

'No!'

I frown. 'Why not?'

She closes her eyes briefly, then looks up. 'Because I don't know if they're real or if I've imagined them from, you know, my nightmares.'

Lily used to have such bad dreams she'd wake up screaming some nights. Mum would sit on her bed, stroking her cheek, until she went back to sleep.

'I didn't know you were still having them.'

'I dream about Dad, too. That I've seen him in town or in the library. Only he has his back to me and when I touch his shoulder, he turns round and it's not Dad at all, just a guy who looks a bit like him.' She glances sidelong at me. 'I actually thought I saw him the other day.'

'What?' Blood drains from my face. 'Where?'

'There was this guy at the train station. He was on the other platform. He had his back to me too, but there was something about him that reminded me so much of Dad that I almost called out. You know, to see if it really was him. But then a train came, and when it left the station, he'd gone.' Her face falls. 'I must've imagined it.'

I could tell Lily she probably wasn't imagining it, that the man at the station most likely was her father, because I have photographic evidence he's back in town.

I don't know if she believes Jason killed her mum and brothers. It's not a conversation we've ever had. Which is odd in itself, I realise. But Mum's always warned me against talking to Lily about the murders, preferring to sweep things under the carpet. The head-in-the-sand approach. In stark contrast, Lily's suddenly playing her life out on social media, while I'm caught somewhere in the middle.

Lily has a right to know, a voice whispers in my head. Jason is her father, her closest living relative.

And if I do tell her? What then? She's a resourceful kid. She'd hunt him down. She might even find him before the police do, and I can't take the chance.

There's another scenario I haven't considered. Jason's already warned me off; what if he sees Lily's TikTok video and realises she's about to reveal her memories of the night of the attack? He'll want to silence her before that happens.

Fear coils around my heart, making me breathless. I spring out of my chair and throw the kitchen window wide open.

I need to do everything I can to protect what's left of my family. And if that means lying to Lily, it's a price I'm willing to pay.

I turn back to her. 'You're right. You must have imagined it. And if you are getting flashbacks, you need to tell the police, not your five followers on TikTok. I have the number of the guy in charge of the investigation. I'll call him.'

'I have over a thousand followers, actually,' Lily says, her eyes blazing.

'Even more reason not to drag all this up again.' I toe open the pedal bin and toss my uneaten Magnum into it, swearing softly as melted ice cream drips all over the floor.

'You don't understand, do you?' Lily pushes her chair back and hauls herself to her feet. Dark shadows ring her eyes and her slim shoulders droop. She looks as though she could buckle under the weight of her grief at any moment. I'm hit by a wave of compassion and reach towards her, but she jerks away.

'I want to make sense of it all, Lara. And I don't have to ask your permission. I don't have to ask anyone. This is my story and I'm going to tell it, whether you like it or not.'

21

I eat cold baked beans from the tin for dinner, washed down with a bottle of Moretti. It's all I have the energy to fix. I check Lily's TikTok account incessantly to see if she's posted any more videos. She hasn't, but her followers now number more than fifteen hundred and every time I refresh the page, the figure jumps by half a dozen.

One look at her hashtags – #truecrime #truecrimecommunity #truecrimeaddict #unsolved – reveals the kind of content she's planning to create.

I want to phone Mum to warn her what Lily's done. I want to tell her Jason's back. Instead, I call DCI Frampton.

'Lara.' His voice lacks its usual warmth and I glance at my watch, surprised to see it's almost nine o'clock. He must be sick of me phoning when he's off duty.

'I'm so sorry, I didn't realise the time. I should've called in the morning.'

'Has something happened?'

'Yes, but it can wait.'

'Are you sure?'

I nod, forgetting he can't see me, then clear my throat. 'I'm sure.'

'Look, d'you want to meet? I can give you half an hour tomorrow morning.'

I don't have a wedding and was going to spend the day editing Marian and Bob's wedding photos. Most of which I've accidentally deleted.

'That would be great,' I say. I can give him the threatening note and show him Lily's video. 'Shall I come to the police station?'

'I'm out and about on enquiries all morning. Do you know the Salty Bean?'

'That organic place on the seafront?'

'That's right. I'll see you there at ten.'

I'm about to apologise again for calling so late when the line goes dead.

* * *

The Salty Bean's popular with young mums, and I have to fight my way past four buggies and a couple of toddlers to reach the table at the back where DCI Frampton is nursing a coffee.

He stands and holds out a well-manicured hand, a signet ring glinting on his little finger. He's a big man, with broad shoulders, a square jaw and a commanding presence, and even though he must be in his mid-forties now and his dark hair is peppered with grey, a couple of the mums glance our way, checking him out.

'What can I get you?' he asks, nodding at a passing waiter.

'A latte, please.'

He orders himself another Americano and as we wait for the coffee to arrive, he leans back in his chair and studies me.

'You have Isabelle's eyes,' he says.

I stare at him, surprised.

'There were photos of her and the children on the wall of the incident room,' he explains. 'I saw them every day for almost a year. Their faces are imprinted on my memory.'

The police scaled down the investigation not long after the first anniversary of the murders. The incident room has probably been the nerve centre of a dozen different major investigations since then. I wonder what happened to those photos. Lying forgotten in a box in a dusty storage room somewhere in the bowels of the police station, I suppose.

'How are you?' he asks, fixing me with an earnest gaze.

The waiter returns with our drinks. Once he's gone, I shrug. 'OK, I guess.'

'And the wedding photography? Business good?'

'I didn't know you knew that's what I do.'

'You took the wedding photos for some friends of mine. Annie and Connor Sullivan? They sang your praises.'

I pop a sugar cube into my latte and stir in an attempt to hide the fact that his gaze is making me feel a little flustered.

'Of course. I'd forgotten they're both in the police.'

'Connor and I were in the same intake, many moons ago.'

'But you weren't at the wedding.'

'My father was in hospital. Heart attack.'

'I'm sorry.'

'Don't be. He was a bastard.' Frampton smiles to take the sting out of his words and leans forwards, resting his elbows on the table. 'What did you want to talk to me about?'

'Someone sent me this.' I reach into my bag for the plastic wallet containing the anonymous note and slide it across the table to him. His eyes widen a fraction as he reads it.

'You think it was Carello?'

'Who else would it be from?'

He dips his head in acknowledgement. 'Where's the envelope?'

'It wasn't in one. He must've posted it through my letterbox, which means he knows where I live.'

Frampton folds the wallet and slips it into the inside pocket of his jacket. 'I'll have Forensics take a look at it.'

'Thank you. And that wasn't the only thing.' I take a deep breath. 'Lily's having flashbacks.'

He frowns. 'About the murders?'

'She told me yesterday she's started to remember what happened.' It's not strictly true, but I need him to understand just how much danger she could be in. 'I'm worried Jason'll find out and try to stop her. She's posted a video on TikTok talking about that night.'

I find Lily's video and hand him my phone. 'Do you have earbuds?'

He shakes his head, so I offer him mine. He nods his thanks, puts them in and presses play. I watch for a reaction, but his face is expressionless. His composure is reassuring. He's the kind of guy who knows how to handle a crisis, and that's exactly what I need right now. What Lily needs.

'She needs to delete the account immediately and come in and update her statement,' he says once the video is over.

'That's exactly what I've told her. But she said it's her story to tell and she'll tell it whether we like it or not. She's very head-strong, just like Isabelle.' I shake my head. 'I have no idea if Jason will see this, but the press are bound to pick up on it, and when they do, it'll be everywhere anyway. Oh, and one more thing—'

'There's more?'

'Lily thinks she saw Jason at the train station the other day. She assumed she must have imagined it, but only because she doesn't know he's back.'

'You haven't told her?'

'No. D'you think I should?'

He thinks for a moment. 'Hold fire for now. We're still

following a number of leads but I'm hopeful we'll find him in the next day or so, in which case it won't be an issue. Whatever happens, she needs to update her statement. I'll do it myself if it helps.'

'You'd do that for us?'

'Of course.' He gives me a brief smile. 'Look, I need to be somewhere.' He pats his suit pocket. 'I'll be in touch about the note. And in the meantime, it's probably a good idea not to put yourself in any potentially vulnerable situations. Just until Carello's in custody.'

I nod, fear turning the insides of my stomach to liquid. He gives my shoulder a quick squeeze then sweeps through the coffee shop and onto the street. I sit staring at the door for a long time after he's gone, my hands balled around a paper napkin. It's only when I'm preparing to leave that I look down and realise I've completely shredded it, the pieces floating to the ground like petals from a blown rose.

22

LILY

Lily sits at her dressing table and brushes her lips with a final coat of lip gloss. Her hand is steady, despite the nerves that fizz in her veins like a just-opened can of Coke.

Nerves are good. She read it in a blog. The chemicals that make your palms sweaty and your throat dry are the same chemicals that keep your brain sharp and your mind focused. It's all adrenaline. You just need to reframe it. Call it excitement, not nerves.

And she is prepared. She's rehearsed what she's going to say a dozen times. She stuck to her script for her first video, but having the freedom to go off-piste is liberating. After all, no one knows her subject like she does.

She pouts at her reflection, happy enough with what she sees. She'll never be as beautiful as her mum, but she makes the best of what she has: her dad's brown eyes, full lips and thick, chestnut-brown hair.

She picks up her phone and opens TikTok, her eyes widening a fraction when she sees that her followers have now reached six thousand. Six thousand, two hundred and ninety-two, to be precise. Her first video has nearly twenty thousand views. It needs to have had more than a million to be considered viral, but it's a start. And every time she refreshes the page, the numbers jump. She just needs to be patient.

She had to wait until she had a thousand followers before she could unlock the option to livestream. She's also supposed to be sixteen, but who tells the truth about their age when they're opening a social media account? No one, that's who.

Tonight's live is due to start at eight. She picked tonight because Gran's at yoga on Fridays so she has the house to herself. The last thing she needs is for her grandmother to barge into her room in the middle of the recording.

She spends a few minutes arranging her chair, angling her desk lamp and setting up the phone tripod she ordered from Amazon. Once she's happy with the set-up she has a quick run-through. Her nerves are intensifying, the spag bol she had for tea churning unpleasantly in her stomach.

Lara hasn't helped, laying that guilt trip on her on Wednesday. She's always been so dismissive about Lily's dreams of becoming an influencer, claiming it's not a proper job. But she's a fine one to talk. Taking pictures of people's weddings is hardly career of the year.

It was Lara's scorn that forced Lily's hand. Lily knew she had to do something radical if she was going to get her TikTok account noticed. How was she supposed to stand out in all the noise?

It was obvious, really. She needed to tap into the current obsession with true crime podcasts, books and TV shows. She's the sole survivor of a triple murder, a murder that rocked the whole country. It's Lily's USP, the one thing that makes her different.

Lily checks the time. She still has a few minutes, so she sits down and tries to steady her breathing.

Why shouldn't she turn the worst thing that happened to her into something positive? It's easy for Lara to get all high and mighty, but she has no idea what it's like to be the one who's left behind.

Gran took Lily to see a grief counsellor when she was twelve. The nightmares were getting worse and she was waking almost every night, her sheets soaked in sweat and her pillow drenched in tears.

Gran decided enough was enough when she was called into school after Lily fell asleep in the middle of a biology lesson.

The grief counsellor, who was called Gillian and had a whiskery chin and a habit of clasping her hands under her enormous bosom, asked Lily if she'd ever heard of survivor's guilt.

Lily might not be the most academic, but she wasn't stupid.

'It's the guilt people like me feel when they're the only ones in their family to survive a murder.'

Gillian nodded. 'That's right. People who have survivor's guilt can't understand why they escaped death while others lost their lives.' She peered closely at Lily. 'They might also feel guilty they didn't do anything to stop the traumatic event even though there was absolutely nothing they could have done.'

Lily stared back. It was as if Gillian could read her mind. Guilt was her constant companion, her imaginary friend, whispering things she didn't want to hear.

You should have stopped it. You're worthless. You should never have been spared.

Sometimes Lily pictured her guilt as a flesh-eating bug, nibbling away at her until one day there'd be nothing left.

During that first counselling session, Gillian went through a checklist with her and, without Gran or Lara in the room, Lily was honest with her replies for the first time in her life.

Do you have obsessive thoughts about the attack? Tick. Feelings of helplessness and disconnection? Problems sleeping? Fear and confusion? Irritability and anger? Lack of motivation? Tick, tick, tick, tick and tick.

Lily's confidence in Gillian's ability to fix her was absolute, so it came as a nasty shock when she told Lily she could only help her with strategies to manage the guilt.

'Cognitive behavioural therapy and practising mindfulness have a part to play,' Gillian explained. 'But learning to accept that what happened wasn't your fault is most important of all. You were five years old, Lily. A small child. It wasn't your fault, nor was it your responsibility to protect your mum and brothers. You were as much a victim as they were that day.'

It's almost eight o'clock. Lily hits record, straightens her back and gazes at the camera with clear eyes.

'Welcome back, my true crime-loving friends. Tonight, for the first time, I am coming to you live from the pretty seaside town of Tidehaven, which sees, on average, a murder every decade.

'So you'd think it was a pretty safe place to live, right? Wrong. Because the person who killed my mum Isabelle and my brothers Jack and Milo, the person who left me with life-threatening injuries, is still at large. Yep, the Carello Killer was never caught, and tonight I'm going to talk about the prime suspect, my dad, Jason Carello.'

23

I have tried every hack I can think of, but I haven't been able to recover the photos of Marian and Bob's wedding I accidentally deleted.

I haven't told them yet. They're still on their honeymoon in the New Forest and aren't due home until Thursday. I've already decided to offer them a full refund and pay for a bespoke photo album with the pictures I took at the reception. It's the least I can do.

It's Saturday morning, and for once I don't have a wedding. I've been up since half six editing the photos I still have. As I feared, they fall well short of my usual standards, but I do what I can to make them pop.

I'm so absorbed in my work that I jump like a scalded cat when the doorbell rings, and almost knock the mug on the table flying. Cold tea sloshes over the rim and I grab a tea towel and dab frantically before it pools out towards my laptop.

I'm still in pyjamas, and I pull on my dressing gown and peer out of the living room window to the street below. A man is standing on the pavement outside my front door. He probably has Arabella and Barnaby's wedding album, which is due to be delivered this morning, although I can't see a parcel. And something about his lanky frame is familiar. But one thing's for sure: it isn't Jason, so I head downstairs and open the door.

'Hello, Lara. You probably don't remember me—' he begins.

I gape. Standing on my doorstep is the reporter who broke the story when Isabelle, Jack and Milo were killed and then left *The Post* for *The Daily Tribune*, one of the biggest tabloids in the country. Johnny Nelson. The guy who'd... But no, I can't think about that now.

I exhale. 'Of course I remember you. What are you doing here, Johnny?'

'Ah, well, it's a bit delicate. Can I come in?'

'Now's not really convenient. I'm in the middle of something.'

His eyes drop to my dressing gown and PJs and I'm surprised to see the tips of his ears turn pink.

I roll my eyes. 'I'm working, Johnny. Just tell me why you're here.'

'I've seen your niece's TikTok videos.'

Videos, plural. Shit. I've been so focused on editing Marian and Bob's photos this morning I haven't checked Lily's account. Christ knows what she's uploaded now. My grip on the door jamb tightens.

'So?' I say as coolly as I can.

'I wondered if she'd be willing to talk to me?'

'Not in a million years.' I begin to close the door, but something is stuck in it, wedging it open. When I look down, I realise it's Johnny's foot. 'Do you mind?'

'Sorry,' he says, but he doesn't move it. 'Look, Lara, you know how this goes. Lily's talking about the death of her mum and brothers for the first time, just as we're approaching the tenth anniversary of their murders. It's dynamite. I might be the first to see her videos, but I won't be the last. It's only a matter of time before you have half a dozen of us camped out on your doorstep. Give me the exclusive and I'll make the others disappear.' He clicks his fingers, as if it would be that easy to disperse a horde of news-hungry hacks.

A movement across the street catches my eye. It's Mrs Benson from number thirty-eight. She's watering a tub of scarlet geraniums and when she sees me, she waves. I automatically freeze-frame the scene and view it from her perspective. I'm on the doorstep in my pyjamas, having a heated conversation with a man with tousled blond hair wearing a crumpled suit and yesterday's stubble. If she jumped to conclusions, I wouldn't blame her.

I sigh. 'You can come up,' I tell Johnny. 'But I'm not promising anything.'

24

I leave Johnny in the living room with a coffee while I jump in the shower and fling on some clothes. I know he'll be mooching around the flat, checking out my books and photos, but they won't tell him anything. The books are mainly non-fiction photography guides and coffee table books; the photos are exclusively black-and-white landscapes I've taken on my travels around the UK. Moorland is my favourite landscape to photograph. Nothing beats a sunrise in the Peak District, or a misty winter's morning on Dartmoor.

The flat is decorated in soft greys and creamy whites. It's tasteful. Curated. Probably a bit anodyne, if I'm honest. But when you spend your days caught up in the middle of the noisy, colourful cacophony of a wedding, having a neutral, tranquil space to come home to is a balm.

Johnny is staring out of the window when I appear, and he turns and smiles. 'Nice place.'

'Thanks. Where are you living now?' When I worked for *The Post*, he shared a house with three other reporters. It was barely a step up from student digs; the type of house where the sink is always full of dirty dishes and you wipe your feet on the way out.

I went there for a party once. An alcohol-fuelled night of drinking games and pulsating indie rock. The air thick with cigarette smoke as couples who normally wouldn't have given each other the time of day copped off together. My memories of the night are hazy, thanks to the copious number of shots I'd knocked back, but I do remember waking up the next morning wondering what the hell I'd done.

'I'm still in Alma Road,' Johnny says, perching on the sofa. He pulls something from his pocket. 'Mind if I vape?'

'Actually, I do.'

His face falls, but he shoves the vape back in his pocket obediently. He smoked like a chimney in the old days. If his desk was empty, you could pretty much guarantee where you'd find him: standing outside the fire exit, puffing away on a Marlboro Red. His fingers were stained yellow with nicotine and his suits reeked of smoke.

'Never thought you'd give up the fags.'

He grins sheepishly. 'I haven't, but I am trying.' The grin disappears and he swallows. 'Before we talk about Lily, I just wanted to say how sorry I am.'

'What, for standing me up?'

He looks confused. 'No, I meant about what happened to your sister and nephews. I never had a chance to say it back then.' He stops, rubs his nose. 'That's not entirely true. I had plenty of chances. I was too fixated on getting the story for it to even occur to me.'

And there it was. An admission – if I'd needed one – that for Johnny the story *always* came first. Grabbing something to eat then seeing *Skyfall* the day after the party had been his suggestion, not mine, yet I'd waited outside Pizza Express for almost an hour without so much as a text to say he wasn't going to make it.

It was only later that I discovered he'd stood me up because he'd been door-knocking the widow of a man jailed for a £15 million-pound pyramid scheme fraud. At the time my pride was dented but, looking back, I reckon it was a lucky escape.

Now, I eye him with suspicion. Is he really sorry, or is he just trying to butter me up before he goes for the jugular? He needs me on side if he's going to talk to Lily. She's only fifteen. He can't interview her without Gran's agreement, and he knows it. Throwing caution to the wind, I decide to give him the benefit of the doubt.

'It's OK. You were only doing your job. I get it. I'd have taken pictures of the bodies being carried from the house if it was someone else's family. Speaking of which, how is life on the *Tribune*? Still chasing ambulances?'

'Oh, I'm not there any more. I left a couple of years ago.'

'Why?' I can't hide my surprise. Johnny was always so ambitious I'd have thought he'd be running the newsroom by now.

'Call it a difference of opinion. My editor didn't appreciate me turning up for work drunk. Can't think why.'

'Who are you working for now?'

He clears his throat. 'Actually, I'm trying my hand at this podcasting lark.' He laughs self-consciously. '*Johnny Nelson Investigates*. Pete's giving me a few freelance shifts on *The Post* while I wait for the money to roll in.' Another embarrassed laugh.

'Let me guess, it's a true crime podcast.' I sit on the armchair opposite him, clasping my knees. 'And that's why you're here.'

'Guilty as charged,' he says with a lopsided grin.

'You wouldn't be touting the story to the nationals?'

'Absolutely not. I know you probably find that hard to believe. But it's the truth.'

'I still haven't agreed to anything,' I remind him. 'And you said videos plural.' I wave my phone at him. 'There's only one.'

'That's because last night's was a livestream. Luckily, I have software on my laptop that lets me download it while it's being broadcast.'

He fiddles with his own phone and passes it across. Lily's face fills the screen.

'Did you know she was doing this?' Johnny asks.

I shake my head. 'Not a clue.'

I turn back to his phone. Lily is holding a photo of her dad to the camera. A photo I took during our family's annual pilgrimage to Dorset. Jason is carrying three-year-old Lily on his shoulders. Her fingers are entwined in his hair, and they are both laughing.

'Tonight,' Lily says, 'I'm going to talk about the prime suspect, my dad, Jason Carello.'

25

Lily drops the photo onto her lap and gazes into the lens.

'Jason Carello was a lot of things. A husband, a business-man, a son, a brother. To me he was just my dad. I was five the last time I saw him, so I'm not sure if the things I remember are real or if I've made them up, but I know he smelt of lemons and loved telling terrible dad jokes. You know the kind. Like, I'd ask him to put my shoes on and he'd say, "But I don't think they'll fit".'

Lily smiles, and my heart aches for her. Jason has been painted by everyone – the press, the police... me and Mum – as the villain for so long I sometimes forget Lily adored him. She was the original daddy's girl. If she fell and scuffed her knees, it was Jason she cried for to come and kiss them better. Jason was the only one who could tease her out of a tantrum. If he didn't read her bedtime story, she refused to go to sleep. Isabelle never got a look-in.

It was worse when Jack and Milo came along. Lily was three when they were born. Jason cut his hours at the showroom so he could take her to and from pre-school. When Lily was at home, Isabelle, exhausted by the never-ending grind of nursing twins, sat her in front of the TV until Jason came home from work.

Jason and Lily's closeness added weight to the police theory that Jason murdered his wife and sons. Though never stated publicly, the assumption was that he couldn't bring himself to kill his daughter and that's how she survived his frenzied attack.

'Apparently,' Lily says, 'the first words I said when I came out of the coma were, "Where's my daddy?"'

Johnny leans across me and presses pause. 'Is that true?'

'Is this off the record?'

He lays a hand on his heart. 'Until you give me the go-ahead. You have my word.'

There's a diffidence to Johnny that wasn't there in the old days, as if the trials and tribulations of the last ten years have stripped away his cocky veneer. But can I trust him? I don't know.

'It's true,' I confirm, eventually. Lily spent almost a week in intensive care in a medically induced coma to allow her body to start healing. Mum and I kept watch by her bed around the clock. On day five her consultant said they were reducing her meds. That night the nurses removed her ventilator. The next morning she opened her eyes, stared at us blearily and croaked, 'Where's my daddy?'

Johnny presses play.

'I couldn't remember what happened, you see. As for Dad, all my gran and auntie told me was that he was missing and no one knew where he was. That's it. Every time I asked about him, they shut me down, changing the subject or making an excuse and walking out of the room. I stopped asking in the end.'

She glances down, clearly embarrassed. 'Dad was a classic car dealer and for years I had this secret fantasy that he had chartered a ship and sailed to Cuba to buy cars for his show-room, only on his way home, the ship crashed and he was shipwrecked on a desert island in the middle of the Caribbean and that's why he couldn't come back for me.

'It wasn't until Year Four that a kid at school told me my dad was a murderer who had stabbed my mum and brothers to death. That took a while to process, I can tell you.' She gives a little self-deprecating laugh, then blows a strand of hair off her face.

'Some of you armchair detectives will already know about the Carello Killings and will have made up your minds about Jason Carello, but many of you will be hearing about the crime for the first time, and I hope you can be objective.

'OK, so here's what we know. All the information I'm about to give you has come either from the inquest reports, articles from trusted newspapers or a detective in CID. All credible sources.'

This time it's me who presses pause.

'I'm going to get a glass of water. Do you want one?'

'Got anything stronger?' Johnny asks.

'It's half eleven in the morning.'

'Oh, yeah, of course. Silly me. Water would be great, thanks.'

I'm not actually thirsty, but I need a break from Lily's video. Watching her open her heart like this is killing me. I thought we were close, yet she's never told me she used to pretend her dad was stranded on a desert island. It's heartbreaking to think she's carried all these emotions around for the last ten years. I run two glasses of water and head back to the living room.

Johnny hands me his phone and I press play.

'Fact one: there was no sign of a forced entry,' Lily says. 'The back door was unlocked and the patio doors were ajar. This suggests that the perpetrator either sneaked in from the back garden or was known to my mum and she willingly let them in. There was, by the way, a gate that led from our back garden to the beach.'

'Fact two: the knife used by the perp was taken from the knife block in the kitchen, which suggests that this was not a premeditated attack but a crime committed in the heat of the moment. A crime of passion. The knife has never been found.

'Fact three: house-to-house enquiries revealed that the only two vehicles to be seen driving down our road during the crucial times were Dad's Austin Healey and a mystery white Ford Transit van. The driver of the van came forward two weeks later. He was an angler who was looking for somewhere to park while he went night fishing. His story checked out.

'Fact four: nothing was stolen in the attack. Not even Mum's expensive new laptop, which was charging on the kitchen table when the paramedics arrived, right next to the euros she'd changed up for our holiday to France the next day. This disputes the theory that it was a burglary gone wrong.

'Fact five: police ruled out a number of other violent offenders from the Tidehaven area after CCTV, phone and alibi checks.'

Lily lets out a long breath. 'For all these reasons and more, Jason Carello – my dad – was the police's number one suspect from the outset. But is he still, ten years on?

'I put this to the senior investigating officer, Detective Chief Inspector Curtis Frampton, when he gave a talk at my school's careers fair just before Easter. If anyone knows who killed my mum and brothers, it's him.'

She pauses, then glances up, as if drawing strength for what she's about to say. Returning her gaze to the camera, she says, 'I hoped with all my heart that he was going to tell me he didn't think Dad did it. I hoped he was going to say he'd always suspected it was a paranoid schizophrenic on the loose, or a jealous ex-lover, or one of Dad's old business contacts. But he didn't. He told me he was one hundred per cent certain that Dad killed Mum, Jack and Milo, and almost killed me.

'When I asked him where he thought Dad was now, he said

he'd always been convinced the Carello Killings were a murder-suicide, and that Dad took his own life soon after he left the house that night.

'It's a perfectly reasonable assumption. But Dad's body has never been found. What if DCI Frampton's wrong and he went on the run? What if he's out there somewhere, living under a false name on another continent? What if he's watching this right now?'

Lily's eyes glisten with tears. 'Dad, if you are, I need to understand why you did what you did. Because I heard you and Mum arguing the night she and the twins died. Which makes it pretty bloody impossible for me to believe that you are innocent.'

26

Johnny is watching me intently. 'Did you know Isabelle and Jason argued that night?' he asks.

'I didn't.'

'It wasn't mentioned in any of the police press briefings or in the off-the-record guidance given to the media. Nothing was said at Isabelle and the boys' inquests either. I think this is new information even the police aren't aware of.'

'Lily said she's been getting flashbacks,' I say. 'I've told DCI Frampton. He wants to come round to take a new statement from her.'

'I bet he does. You should be careful with that one. He has a bit of a reputation as a ladies' man.'

I run my hand around the neck of my T-shirt, suddenly hot. Johnny has no right to inform me what I should or shouldn't do. I'm about to tell him when his phone pings. He checks the screen and swears softly.

'What is it?'

He doesn't answer, just passes me the phone again. I stare at the Sky News alert, colour leaching from my face.

Sole survivor of Carello Killings talks for the first time

I click on the link and scan the story.

'What does it say?' Johnny asks.

'That Lily's announced on TikTok she's searching for answers about the murders. There's nothing about last night's livestream. They can't have seen it, thank God.' My stomach lurches as I read the last sentence, and I thrust the phone at Johnny and jump to my feet.

'What's wrong?'

'It says they've contacted Lily's family for a comment, which means they must have spoken to Mum. What if they're at the house? I need to go there. Now.'

* * *

I pull up outside Mum's, surprised that the only car in the driveway is her Clio. I'd half been expecting a mob of reporters and a satellite truck to be parked up outside.

Next to me, Johnny releases his seat belt and straightens his tie in the sun visor mirror. I still can't work out how he talked me into letting him tag along. I guess it was his promise to act as an intermediary if the press pack had descended in force.

I could tell him to wait in the car, but it seems ungrateful, so I haul up the handbrake, unclip my seat belt and sigh.

'I suppose you should come in.'

Mum takes an age answering the door, and I'm beginning to worry Jason's holding her hostage inside when it finally swings open.

'So you are here,' I say.

'I was in the garden.' She waves a pair of gardening gloves at me. 'Weeding the veg patch.'

'Why've you taped over the doorbell camera?'

'I told you. It was driving me crazy.' Her eyes widen as she notices Johnny standing behind me. 'Who—?'

'Johnny Nelson. I'm a friend of Lara's,' he says with an easy smile. 'We worked together at *The Post*. It's lovely to meet you.'

Mum dimples, then disappears inside to stick the kettle on. I peel the strip of black gaffer tape off the camera and beckon Johnny to follow me into the living room. The red light on the answerphone is blinking and I press play.

'Hello, Mrs Beckett, this is Felix McConnell from Sky News. I wondered if you could phone me about a story we're running about your granddaughter, Lily.' He reels off a mobile number and ends the call. I press delete.

Johnny raises an eyebrow but I shake my head as Mum comes into the room with a tray laden with her best mugs, a pot of tea and a plate of shortbread biscuits.

'What time's Lily home?' I ask, taking the tray from her.

'The usual. Why?'

I'm trying to find the words to explain when Mum fixes me with a look.

'What's going on, Lara? Why are you here?'

I sigh and motion to the sofa. 'You'd better sit down.'

* * *

Mum takes the news remarkably well, considering her family is about to be dragged through the dirt. Again.

Her hands are clasped in her lap, perfectly still. 'And how many people did you say had seen these videos?'

'The first one's had over thirty thousand views, but that'll shoot up now Sky's running the story.'

Mum considers this for a minute. 'Perhaps it's no bad thing,' she says finally.

I stare at her, mouth open.

'To have it back in the spotlight, I mean. Maybe someone

will recognise that bastard and tip off the police. He's out there somewhere, I know he is.'

I blink. *That bastard?* Mum *never* swears.

'You don't believe the police theory that Jason took his own life?' Johnny asks.

She gives a bark of laughter. 'Chance'd be a fine thing.' She shakes her head. 'He wouldn't have the balls.'

I'm in a state of shock. This is the first time in the last ten years Mum has voiced an opinion about her son-in-law. Since the murders she has focused entirely on Lily, Isabelle and the boys. Lily was right when she said her gran never spoke about Jason. It's a bit odd, now I think about it. Perhaps she thought that if she never mentioned him, Lily would forget he ever existed. As plans go, it was always going to be fundamentally flawed, because everyone recognises the attraction of the forbidden. Just ask Adam and Eve.

'It must be hard,' Johnny says, 'knowing that the man who killed your daughter and grandsons has never paid for what he did.'

'Hard?' she replies, shaking her head. 'It's intolerable.'

'But what about the press, Mum?' I cry. 'You know what they were like last time. A Sky reporter's already left a message asking for an interview with Lily. You know as well as I do it won't stop there.'

'Lily's fifteen,' Mum says. 'She knows her own mind. If she wants to talk to them, I won't stand in her way.'

Beside me, Johnny coughs. 'May I make a suggestion?' he asks.

I spin round to face him. 'Does it involve your new podcast, by any chance?'

'Actually, no,' he says mildly. He addresses Mum. 'Lara's right. Very soon the media are going to be all over you like a cheap suit. It just occurred to me that if Lily gave a press conference, perhaps in conjunction with the police, it would give everyone a chance to ask her questions and then you can draw a line under it.'

I turn his suggestion over in my mind, examining it from all angles.

'Actually, that's not a bad idea,' I admit. 'Tidehaven Police can give everyone an update on the investigation and issue a fresh appeal for information. I've always thought there must be people who felt they couldn't speak out then but can now.'

'It'll tie in with the tenth anniversary,' Johnny adds.

'You think they would do it?' Mum asks.

'I can't see them wanting to pass up a chance of finally nailing Jason, can you?' he says.

Now might be a good time to tell Mum and Johnny the police could be closer to locating their prime suspect than they think. But I can't, not if it risks jeopardising their investigation. Mum'll find out soon enough, once Jason's in police custody.

'Thank you, Johnny,' she says. 'I think it's an excellent idea.'

'If Lily agrees.'

Mum raises an eyebrow. 'I hardly think she's going to say no, given she's already been on the internet talking about her mum and brothers to thousands of strangers.'

'But recording a video in her bedroom is a bit different to talking to a roomful of journalists, Mum.'

'I'm sure the police would let you stay with her during the press conference. In fact, they'd probably insist, as Lily's only fifteen,' Johnny says.

'You're right.' Mum turns to me. 'Lara, you can sit with her.'

'Why me?'

'Because you know how the media works. You can field any awkward questions.'

'That's a great idea,' Johnny says, beaming at her.

I look from him to Mum and back again, realising with a sinking feeling that I've been well and truly stitched up.

27

LILY

Lily follows the stream of girls heading towards the school gates. Hundreds of them, all dressed in black pleated skirts and blazers. From high above, they must look like starlings in a murmuration, she thinks, or a cloud of midges swarming in front of your face on a muggy summer's evening. Or those little fish she saw on a nature documentary the other day, darting and twisting in a constantly moving ball to escape a shoal of hungry predators. There's safety in numbers.

Lily says goodbye to Meena and Katy, peels off from the swarm and heads towards the cemetery. It's the first of July, Dad's birthday. He would have been forty-two if he'd still been here.

As she walks, Lily pictures what today might have been like if her mum, Jack and Milo were still alive. It's a game she likes to play now and then. Dad would have picked her up from school in his Austin Healey. Lily loved that car: the red leather seats, the sharp blast of the horn, the way her dad would sit her on his lap, wrap the seat belt around her and let her pretend she was steering.

They'd have gone out for dinner at the Italian in the high

street. It was where they always celebrated birthdays. Lily would order... actually, she's not sure what she would order. The last time she went there was for her fifth birthday and she was still having the kids' menu.

She would probably have wild mushroom risotto, something like that, because she's been vegetarian since she was twelve. Something Gran thought was a 'phase' she'd grow out of, but she never did. And when Gran realised veggie meals didn't have to consist of nut roasts and Linda McCartney sausages, she gradually stopped eating meat too, and these days is a veggie in all but name. Which, Lily likes to think, is a double win for both animal welfare and the planet.

Dad doesn't know Lily's a vegetarian. He doesn't know she loves quiz shows and hates *Love Island* (but still watches it so her friends don't think she's weird). He doesn't know that she swims in the local pool a couple of times a week but has always been too scared to swim in the sea. That her average Wordle score is 3.9. And that eating a bar of Aero in the bath is her ultimate guilty pleasure.

All these things that make her who she is, and Dad doesn't know about a single one of them.

She was five years old with chubby legs and hair in pigtails the last time he saw her. Now, she's not sure he'd recognise her if they passed each other in the street.

Lily walks through the wrought-iron gates to the cemetery. The place gave her the creeps when she was little. All those dead bodies buried just below the surface.

She was deemed too poorly to attend the funerals of her mum and brothers, and is glad she missed them. Watching their coffins – a normal-sized one for Mum and two heartbreakingly tiny ones for Jack and Milo – being lowered into the ground would have freaked her out, because what if the police and doctors had made a terrible mistake and one of them was still alive? Unlikely, but it happens. She knows this because she once made the mistake of googling 'accidentally buried alive'. Never again.

The police thought Lily was dead at first, the night her mum and the twins were killed. It was only when one of the paramedics took her pulse that they realised she was still clinging onto life. So you can see how it could happen.

Lily makes a beeline for the yew tree on the other side of the cemetery where her mum and brothers were laid to rest. It's a silly expression, she always thinks, because Mum was one of those people who never sat down, and Jack and Milo were on the go from the second they woke up to the moment their heads touched the pillow at night. But it's a nice spot to be, probably the best in the whole cemetery – shady and cool in summer and sheltered from the worst of the winter weather – and Lily is glad about that, for their sakes.

Today, she's grateful for the shade. It's a warm afternoon, verging on muggy, and a sheen of sweat dampens her forehead.

She shrugs her schoolbag off her shoulder and crouches down in front of the grave. There's no mention of her dad on the inscription. Then again, there's never any mention of him at home either. The way everyone pretends he doesn't exist is a joke.

Gran and Lara think they can press the delete button on his life, but they're wrong. He might not be a part of Lily's present, but he is a part of her past. A huge part.

Does she hate him? It's a question she often asks herself. He destroyed her family, so of course she hates him. But she loves him too. How can she not? He's her dad. Everyone knows there's a thin line between love and hate.

Perhaps if she could understand why he did what he did, she might begin to unravel the complicated knot of emotions he stirs in her.

He loved them. Lily is sure this isn't wishful thinking on her part. She might not remember much about the night of the murders, but she remembers other things. Little things, but significant, nonetheless. Like the way he let Mum lie in every single Sunday morning while he looked after Lily, Jack and Milo. He would make pancakes for breakfast, singing along tunelessly to the songs on the radio, because he was tone deaf. And then he'd take the three of them to the beach or the play park to give Mum a bit of peace.

He bought Mum flowers every week. Always sunflowers, even in the depths of winter, because they were her favourite. He massaged her feet while they watched television. He told everyone he met how proud he was of her online shop, The Vintage Vault. Anyone could see how much he loved her.

Yet he and Mum had a blazing row the night of the murders. Lily only knows because she'd woken up thirsty and had trailed downstairs in search of a drink. She'd stopped on the bottom stair when she heard shouting coming from the kitchen, only catching fragments of the argument.

Her dad, his voice loud, aggressive. *How can I believe a word you say... won't let that happen... never come near my family again.*

Her mum, her voice high-pitched, almost a wail. *I'm scared, Jason. Really scared... Oh God oh God oh God.*

Lily couldn't make head nor tail of the row then, and ten years later it's just as perplexing. She'll tell the DCI when he comes round to take a statement, because she promised Lara she would. But she doesn't think it'll help the police answer the question that's been burning inside her for as long as she can remember.

Why did he do it? Why did her dad kill her mum?

Pins and needles are setting in and Lily pushes herself to her feet with a small groan. It's the *ouff* noise Gran makes when she plonks herself down on the sofa with a cup of tea. Lily checks the time. It's gone half four. Gran'll be wondering where she is. She stoops down to grab the strap of her bag so she can text to say she's on her way but as she does, something half-hidden behind the gravestone catches her eye.

She scoots round to the other side and freezes. Sitting with his back to the gravestone, his beady eyes expressionless and his mouth fixed in a permanent grin, is Barney Bear, the teddy she hasn't seen since the night her mum and brothers died.

28

The doorbell rings five minutes before DCI Frampton is due to arrive. Mum doesn't even glance at her phone before she jumps up and flings open the front door and I wonder why I bothered with the bloody doorbell camera.

She seems a little flustered as she leads him into the living room and motions him to take a seat. Everything gleams: the glass-topped table, the ornaments on the mantelpiece, even the patio doors. She spent the morning cleaning the house from top to bottom, as if we were expecting royalty. When I pointed out the detective was unlikely to be checking under the spare bed for dust bunnies, she gave me a withering look and muttered something about standards.

I give Frampton a quick smile. 'Lily's upstairs. I'll fetch her.'

Lily's bedroom door is closed. I knock gently and, when there's no answer, push it open. She's sitting cross-legged on her bed, AirPods in, her head nodding to music and her arms wrapped around a teddy bear.

I wave in her face and she gives a start, then pulls the AirPods out.

'Jesus, don't creep up on me like that. You scared the literal shit out of me.'

'Language,' I say, waggling my finger at her. 'DCI Frampton's here.' I pause. 'Hey, is that Barney?'

Her gaze drops to the teddy in her lap. 'Yeah.'

'I thought you'd lost him years ago. Where did you find him?'

'In the, um, loft,' she says. She slithers off the bed and tucks him under her duvet, his head on the pillow.

'I remember the day you made him.'

'Build-A-Bear,' she says. 'My fifth birthday.' I'd been scratching around for ideas for a present when I'd remembered the Build-A-Bear Workshop in town. We'd gone together, just the two of us. Lily had scrutinised every single soft toy in the place before finally settling on a classic brown bear and dressing him in a pink tutu.

She loved that bear.

When Lily was in hospital Mum sent me to Sea Gem to pack a bag of her things but, despite searching high and low, I couldn't find Barney anywhere. I'd always felt terrible I couldn't offer her even this small comfort.

'Gran must have packed him away in the attic and forgotten all about him.' I lean forwards and ruffle his hair. 'Nice to see you, Barney Bear.' I expect Lily to roll her eyes and tell me how lame I am, but she doesn't. She's chewing the skin around her thumb as she stares out of her bedroom window.

'It's OK, he won't bite,' I say, joining her. A dark-coloured BMW is parked across the bottom of Mum's drive.

'Who, Barney?' she says, with the ghost of a smile.

'Very funny.' I point to the BMW. 'DCI Frampton.'

'I was hoping he'd come in a patrol car.' Lily gives the curtains a twitch and grins. 'That would have got everyone's tongues wagging.'

I tut. 'You're impossible.'

Frampton has taken a seat in the armchair by the fireplace. His frame seems too large for the chair, and when he stands and holds out a hand, he towers over Lily. She seems completely unfazed, but then I remember she's met him before, when he came to give a talk at her school.

'Hello, Lily,' he says. 'Lara told me you've started remembering the night your mum and brothers died.'

'Bits,' Lily says.

'And that you've started a vlog about what happened. Why did you decide to do that?'

'It's not a vlog, it's just content. Why, it's not a problem, is it?'

He opens his mouth to say something, then appears to think better of it. He clicks open his briefcase, takes out some papers and offers them to her. 'This is the original statement you made a couple of weeks after you left hospital. Why don't you have a read-through and remind yourself of what you remembered back then?'

Lily's hands tremble slightly as she reads. I focus on the vase of freesias on the coffee table in the faint hope it might stop my own thoughts from drifting back to that night. The sirens. The grim faces of the paramedics. The blood.

After a few minutes, Lily offers the statement back to Frampton. 'There's something I didn't tell you at the time.'

He leans forwards in the armchair, so focused on Lily that I doubt he'd notice if a bomb went off three feet away. 'What?'

She clears her throat. 'Mum and Dad had a big bust-up that night. They thought I was asleep in bed, but I went down to get a drink and heard them arguing in the kitchen. They didn't see me.'

'What were they arguing about?'

Lily shakes her head. 'That's the thing. I don't know. It sounded like Dad was having a go at Mum for something, but I don't know what. She was crying, I do remember that. She said she was scared.'

Beside me, Mum's breath catches in her throat.

Frampton laces his fingers together. 'They didn't mention anyone else?'

'Not that I can remember.'

'And is there anything else you can tell me about that night or the days leading up to it?'

'I don't think so. Sorry, it's not much use, is it?'

'Solving a crime is a bit like doing a jigsaw. You need all the pieces before you can build the complete picture. Every nugget of information, no matter how inconsequential it might seem to you, is important. Not just important, it's vital. So if you remember anything else, you need to call me before you do anything, OK?'

'He means before you stick it in a TikTok video,' I say.

'I'm not stupid. I know what he means,' Lily snaps. She turns back to Frampton. 'I'll tell you first, I promise.'

'Have there been any sightings of Jason?' Mum asks.

I can't stop myself from glancing at the detective, who gives an imperceptible shake of his head.

'No confirmed sightings, no,' he says. It's a clever answer, because even though I'm one hundred per cent sure it was Jason in my photograph, the sighting hasn't been verified.

'I assume you'll be issuing an appeal on the anniversary?' Mum checks.

'Actually, that isn't something we're looking at currently.'

'Why not?' Her eyes narrow. 'You're never going to catch him otherwise.' She nudges me. 'Tell him about our press conference idea, Lara.'

Lily frowns. 'What press conference idea?'

'It was Johnny's suggestion,' I explain. 'He was chief reporter at *The Post* when I worked there. He said we could hold a press conference in conjunction with the police to mark the tenth anniversary and give the press the opportunity to talk to Lily.'

'What if I don't want to talk to them?' Lily says.

'It's a bit late for that now, don't you think?' I point at the house phone. The answerphone light is blinking red again. 'There are messages from at least five different national newspapers on there, all desperate to talk to you. Never mind the calls Mum's had from TV and radio reporters. I warned you this would happen, didn't I? You've let the genie out of the bottle.'

'I thought I'd opened Pandora's box,' she says sulkily.

I let it go. 'At least a press conference is a controlled environment. You can give a statement and we'll make it clear you won't be doing any other media.' I turn to the DCI. 'It'll also give you a chance to update the press on the police investigation and appeal for information. Someone out there knows where Jason is.'

Frampton makes a non-committal noise as he slips Lily's statement back into his briefcase.

'Anyone would think you didn't want to catch the man,' Mum mutters.

The detective exhales through his nose. I suppose he's thinking of the extra work a new appeal would create: the false leads and hoax calls, the resulting mountain of paperwork.

'Even if there's just the tiniest glimmer of a chance that someone'll come forward with new information, it has to be worth trying, doesn't it?' I ask.

'All we want is justice for Isabelle and little Jack and Milo,' Mum says.

'And I'll do it, if you think it'll help,' Lily adds.

Frampton sighs again.

'Let me think about it,' he says finally.

29

Outnumbered by three to one, DCI Curtis Frampton relented and called the following afternoon to say that a press conference had been arranged for ten o'clock on Thursday at Tidehaven Police Station.

'I have to be honest with you, it's not my preferred course of action.' He'd sighed audibly. 'But the district commander is under the misguided belief that all publicity is good publicity, so a press conference is what we're having.'

When we are shown to the large meeting room where the conference is being held, a woman is setting chairs in a semi-circle around a top table. Beside me, Lily falters.

'What's up?' I ask.

'Shit just got real.'

'You'll be fine. And I'll be here to hold your hand.'

She pulls a face.

'Metaphorically speaking,' I say, although I don't just want to hold her hand, I want to whisk her out of here and far away from the police station. She's fifteen, for God's sake. Far too young to be exposed to this media circus. But then I remind myself that she's a bright girl who knows her own mind. If this is what she wants to do, then I will do everything I can to support her.

Frampton is on the far side of the room, locked in conversation with Josie Fletcher, our old family liaison officer. It's a relief to see a familiar face. Josie practically moved in with Mum and Lily after Isabelle and the boys were killed, steering us through the early days of the police investigation, when the media interest was insane and journalists were camped out on the doorstep 24/7.

In her late thirties, with ash-blonde hair pulled back in a no-nonsense bun and serious, steel-grey eyes, Josie is one of those people for whom the saying 'still waters run deep' could have been coined.

She may appear composed and unflappable, but I've witnessed her unleash a torrent of fury on an overzealous tabloid reporter she once caught snooping through Mum's wheelie bin. In a surprising display of strength, she grabbed his arm and forcibly ejected him from the garden, unperturbed by the fact that he towered over her.

'Small but formidable,' is how Phil Glover, Frampton's predecessor, once described Josie. And I know exactly what he meant. Despite her petite frame, when she's provoked, she's a force to be reckoned with. It's good to have someone like that in our corner.

She and Frampton break off when they see us and come over.

'How're you feeling, Lily?' the DCI asks. 'Still happy to go through with this?'

'Of course.'

Josie asks after Mum, then introduces us to the woman setting out chairs.

'Alison's our press officer. It's her job to chaperone the media.'

'Are you expecting many?' I ask, trying to ignore my writhing stomach.

'A couple of the nationals, PA, and the BBC and ITV,' Alison says. 'Plus a couple of local papers, of course. Not a bad turnout for a cold case.'

This is what our story is to the police, I think. A cold case. Dead in the water. History. Just another in a long list of unsolved crimes in which all lines of enquiry have been exhausted. Nowhere to go but dead end after dead end. Yet to us it's as fresh in our minds as the day it happened, the grief as raw.

Alison's phone rings. She answers it, nods, then says to us, 'They're downstairs. If you wait next door Josie will come and get you when they're all seated.'

Frampton beckons Lily and me to follow him into a smaller office next to the main meeting room. He motions us to take a seat before perching on the edge of the desk.

'So here's what's going to happen. You, Lily, will sit to my right, with PC Fletcher the other side of you. Lara, you will sit to my left.' He jumps up and fiddles with the venetian blind, then turns back to us. 'I'll give a recap of the case so far and then, Lily, I believe you have prepared a short statement to read?'

She nods and pats her pocket. She's teamed her favourite wide-legged khaki cargo trousers with a black cropped top and her black denim jacket, and is wearing her hair loose around her shoulders. She's pale, but poised, whereas DCI Frampton seems... nervous.

'Then we'll take questions,' he continues. 'I've told the press office ten minutes max.'

There's a rap on the door and Josie pokes her head round. 'Sir, we're ready for you.'

Frampton nods, runs a finger around his collar, then gestures towards the door. 'Shall we?' he says.

30

There's a reason I became a photographer, I think, as we take our seats at the top table facing the small knot of reporters, photographers and cameramen. I would far rather be behind the lens than in front of it.

I spot Johnny at the back of the group, and he gives me an encouraging smile and a thumbs up, and the knot in my stomach loosens a fraction.

DCI Frampton clears his throat. 'Firstly, I would like to thank everyone for coming and explain why we are holding this press conference today. As you will all be aware, we will soon be marking the tenth anniversary of the tragic murders of Isabelle Carello and her sons Jack and Milo at their home on the Sandy Lane Bay Estate, Tidehaven.

'We are using the opportunity to make a fresh appeal for information about the murders. But first, Lily Carello would like to say a few words.'

The room is so quiet I can hear the crackle of paper as Lily carefully unfolds her statement. She glances down at it, then stares into the sea of faces.

'Ten years ago, I lost my mum and brothers in the worst way

possible. One minute we were like any regular family, looking forward to going on holiday to France. The next, I was waking up in hospital, to be told my mum and brothers were dead. No one can imagine what that's like until it happens to them, and I wouldn't wish it on anyone.'

Cameras click as Lily's voice catches, and I want to give her hand a squeeze to let her know she's doing great, but I can't because DCI Frampton is a solid wall between us.

'I'm here today to ask anyone who might have information about the night my mum, Jack and Milo died to come forward. You might not think your information is important, but it could be the piece of the jigsaw the police are looking for.'

Lily looks down at her statement. The entire room seems to hold its breath. Finally, she looks up, and when she speaks her voice is steady. 'My aunt, my gran and I deserve closure, but, more important than that, my mum and brothers deserve justice. Please, please help if you can.'

'Thank you, Lily,' Frampton says. 'And now let us turn our attention to the appeal. We are asking everyone to cast their minds back to Friday, July the eighteenth, 2014. Were you in the vicinity of the Sandy Lane Bay Estate that day? Did you see anyone acting suspiciously? Maybe you know something you couldn't share with the police at the time. If you have any information, no matter how insignificant it might seem, we urge you to contact us. I will now take questions.'

Half a dozen hands shoot up, including Johnny's. The detective nods at him. 'Yes?'

'Johnny Nelson from *The Post*. Ten years is a long time. Why have you made such little progress with this case?'

Beside me, Frampton stiffens. 'I am sure you will appreciate this is an extremely complex case in which we have faced a number of challenges, including a lack of forensic evidence and reliable witnesses. But please believe me when I say that over the past decade my team and I have left no stone unturned in our quest to find the perpetrator of this horrific crime, and to seek justice for the family.'

Frampton turns to a woman holding a microphone in her outstretched hand.

'Aisha Khan, BBC. You named Jason Carello as a person of interest at the time of the murders. Is he still your prime suspect?'

Frampton brushes a piece of lint from his lapel. 'We are extremely keen to talk to Mr Carello in relation to the matter, yes.'

A man jumps to his feet. 'Tony Rogers, *Daily Mail*. Ten years ago, you said you believed Mr Carello had taken his own life. Are you saying you no longer believe this to be the case?'

'You may remember that shortly after the bodies of Isabelle Carello and her children were discovered, a framed photograph of the family was found on the cliffs at Beachy Head, which you will know is a common suicide spot. Despite extensive enquiries, we found no evidence Mr Carello ever left the country and so, yes, it was presumed that we were dealing with a murder-suicide and that he took his own life.'

'But you said you're keen to talk to him,' the *Mail* reporter says.

'That's because last week we received a credible tip from a witness who claims they have seen Jason Carello very much alive and well,' Frampton tells him.

There is an audible gasp from the room, and Lily's statement flutters from her hands onto the table.

'As you can imagine, this is now our major line of enquiry,' Frampton continues. 'We are working tirelessly to verify the sighting and, if it is genuine, to find Mr Carello so we can speak to him.'

'Where was this sighting?' Johnny calls.

'Tidehaven,' the DCI says, after a moment's hesitation.

'Where in Tidehaven?' says a reporter I recognise from the

local ITV News. A ripple of anticipation passes through the press pack and Frampton exhales quietly.

'He was seen at Tidehaven Harbour. We believe he was staying in accommodation close by.'

'The old fishermen's huts?' Johnny asks.

Frampton nods.

'Who saw him? A member of the public?' the woman from the BBC queries.

I hold my breath.

'That, I'm afraid, I'm not at liberty to disclose.'

'Come on, Detective, you need to give us a bit more than that,' a man at the back of the room says.

The press officer, Alison, looks as if she is about to step in, but Frampton gives a small shake of his head and says, 'He was seen in the background of a photo someone took of the harbour.'

'Are you releasing this photo?' the *Daily Mail* reporter asks.

'We are not—'

'Even if it might help you find Jason Carello?' he says disbelievingly.

'If you'll let me finish,' the DCI says, trying but failing to mask his irritation. 'I was going to say that we're not releasing the photograph at this stage of the investigation. If, however, things change, rest assured you'll be the first to know. Now, I have time for one more question. Yes, you,' he says, pointing to Johnny again.

'What should people do if they see him?'

'We would urge anyone who sees Jason Carello not to approach him but to call 999 immediately,' Frampton says.

'Because he may be dangerous?' Johnny asks.

The detective is silent for a moment and once again the room holds its breath.

'Because we believe Jason Carello may be dangerous,' he finally agrees.

31

'You were amazing,' I tell Lily. We're back in the office next to the meeting room while Alison shepherds the reporters and cameramen from the building. DCI Frampton left a moment ago, muttering something about a briefing on the top floor, and Josie has disappeared in search of tea.

'Dad's back.' Lily drags her hands down her face. 'Why didn't anyone tell me?'

I cross to the window and peer through the slats of the venetian blind. The office looks out over the front of the police station. A couple of reporters are still milling about in the small visitors' car park. They're both on their phones, no doubt calling their newsrooms to deliver the bombshell that the prime suspect in the notorious Carello Killings has been seen a couple of miles from the scene of his crime.

I wonder how long it'll be before Jason realises the news is out. He'll go to ground again, of course he will, and then what chance will the police have of catching him?

'Did you know someone had seen him?' Lily asks.

When I don't immediately answer, her eyes narrow. 'You've been talking to DCI Frampton, haven't you? You even have his number in your phone. Did he tell you someone had seen Dad at the harbour?'

'I, um—'

'You're fiddling with your earlobe. You always do that when you're about to lie.' Her eyes widen. 'You *did* know. God, Lara, didn't you think to tell me my dad was back? Didn't you think I had a *right to know*?'

'It wasn't as straightforward as it sounds. DCI Frampton was keeping it quiet because he didn't want your dad to disappear again.'

'If that's the case, why did he tell you?' Her expression freezes as she processes, and then she frowns. 'Oh my God, it was your photograph, wasn't it? The photo Dad was in. That's how you know. Not because you're DCI Frampton's confidante, but because you took the photo.'

Lily has backed me into a corner, and I have nowhere to go.

'Yes, it was my photo, all right? I didn't see your dad when I took it. It was only afterwards when I was editing it that I saw someone who looked like him in the background.'

She frowns. 'Someone who looked like him?'

'OK, I was ninety-nine per cent sure it was him.'

'So why didn't you tell me?' There's a desperate edge to her voice. I always assumed any love she had for her father died the day he killed her mum and brothers. I know mine did. I'd loved Jason like a brother, but he took that love and he stamped all over it. Now I feel nothing for him but hatred.

'Why do you think I didn't tell you? I wanted to protect you.'

'Dad would never hurt me.'

'You don't know that, Lily. What if he's seen your TikTok videos and knows you're having flashbacks? What would you do in his shoes? You'd want to stop anything incriminating being revealed, wouldn't you? And we both know what he's capable of.' I shudder, an image of Isabelle's bloodied form pushing its way into my head. 'All I want is to keep you safe.'

A single tear trickles down her face, and she swipes it away.

'Lily,' I say, moving towards her, but she shakes her head and holds out a hand to stop me.

I retreat to the window. 'I'm sorry you're so upset.'

Her eyes blaze. 'But not sorry you didn't tell me?'

'I did what I thought was best for you.'

'And when did you get to play God with my life? I had a right to know Dad's back, and you had no right to keep it from me.'

'I can explain, Lily.'

Her lips curl. 'Don't bother. I'm not interested in anything you have to say.'

32

My heart is heavy as I leave the police station. Lily refused point-blank to let me drive her home, instead muttering something about catching the bus.

I call Mum to warn her, and she's almost as angry as Lily.

'Did you not think we needed to know that bastard is back? And why did you let Lily catch the bus? He could be following her, for all we know.'

'I tried to give her a lift but she wouldn't get in the car. She's not speaking to me.'

That's an understatement. Lily was so angry she couldn't even look me in the eye when she shouldered past me on the stairs.

'Honestly, Lara, as if I haven't got enough to worry about.'

'I'm sorry, Mum, but DCI Frampton swore me to secrecy. I had no choice. Look, I've got to go. I'll call you later, OK?'

I yelp in surprise when a figure steps out from behind a police van into my path.

'Jesus, Johnny, don't creep up on me like that!'

'Sorry.' He grins, unrepentant. 'Well, that was a corker of a press conference, wasn't it? Who knew evil Jason Carello was back in town?'

'I'm surprised you're not at the office, polishing your splash.'

'The story's already filed. We don't hang around waiting for the print edition these days. The website comes first, second and third. And I'll edit the audio for the podcast tonight.' He peers at me. 'Are you OK? You look like you've lost a pound and found a penny.'

'Lily's not speaking to me.'

'Want to talk about it?'

'Off the record?'

He lays a hand on his heart. 'Goes without saying.'

I sigh. 'All right. I could use a coffee.'

Johnny grins. 'Actually, I was thinking of something stronger. Pub?'

'Go on, then. Which one?'

'How about the Rose and Crown for old times' sake?' It was our local when I worked at *The Post*. In fact, some of the older staffers spent more time propping up its bar than they did at their desks. Suddenly I yearn for those days, when all I had to worry about was impressing Ralph, our intractable picture editor, and my future lay before me, untarnished and full of possibilities.

Thankfully, we've beaten the lunchtime rush and the pub's still quiet when we arrive. Johnny finds us a booth at the back and disappears in the direction of the bar, returning a few minutes later with two pints of lager and a couple of packets of crisps.

My lager-drinking days ended when I left *The Post*, and these days I prefer wine. But today the once-familiar feel of a pint glass in my hand is a comfort, and I take a grateful sip, my lips smacking as the clean, crisp liquid hits my taste buds.

'Sounds like you needed that,' Johnny says. He's already a

third of the way down his pint and is working his way through his packet of crisps. 'Why's Lily not talking to you?'

'You promise this is off the record?'

He watches me keenly. 'Don't you trust me?'

If I'm honest, I don't know who to trust. Johnny might claim to be my friend but at the end of the day he's a journalist, and for journalists, the story's always king.

I consider him for a moment as he takes another long draught of beer. His messy blond hair needs a cut and there's a reddish-brown stain just above the breast pocket of his jacket.

He sees me noticing, spits on his fingers and dabs at it ineffectually. 'Last night's McDonald's,' he says sheepishly.

He's let me down before. But he needs to keep me on side if he wants the inside track on this story. He would be mad to compromise a potential scoop for his fledgling podcast. Once again, I decide to give him the benefit of the doubt.

'Lily guessed I took the photo DCI Frampton was referring to.'

'The one with Carello in it?'

'Yes.'

He gives a low whistle.

'And now she's mad at me for not telling her I'd seen her dad. It's understandable, I suppose, but I'm worried what he'd do to her if he found her.'

Johnny drains his pint and tips his glass towards mine, which I'm surprised to see is half-empty.

'Yeah, why not?' I say. 'Thanks.'

While he's at the bar, I tap out a text to Lily.

Please don't be mad at me, Lils. I was just trying to do what I thought was best. I'm sorry. Lara xx

'What now?' Johnny says, plonking himself back down.

'I need to find Jason.'

'You really think he'd harm his own daughter?'

'She's starting to remember what happened the night Isabelle and the boys died. Her testimony could lock him away for life. I know Jason. He won't let that happen.'

Johnny sucks in air. 'Leave it to the police, Lara. Half the force is out there looking for him. He won't stay under the radar for long.'

I take another sip of beer. The alcohol is blurring the edges of my anxiety, but my resolve is sharper than ever. I must find Jason before he finds Lily.

'So what are you going to do?' Johnny asks.

I smile grimly. 'I'm going to pay a visit to an old friend of his.'

33

Trev's Auto Repairs is located on a small industrial estate a couple of miles from the pub.

'Who's Trev?' Johnny asks, when I tell him where I'm heading.

'He was the mechanic at JC Classics. He worked for Jason for years. If anyone knows where Jason is, it's Trev.'

'I'm coming with you,' Johnny says, pulling himself to his feet. He flexes a bicep. 'You might need some muscle.'

'Trev must be almost sixty by now. I think I can probably handle him myself, thanks.'

'I might be useful. I can have a shufti round the place while you're talking to him.' He taps his nose. 'They don't call me Johnny the Scoop for nothing, you know.'

I roll my eyes. 'All right, if you insist. I suppose a second pair of eyes won't hurt.'

'There's just one problem.' Johnny jangles his car keys in his pocket. 'I've drunk too much to drive.'

'It's OK, the walk'll do us good. Anyway, I need to pop to the supermarket on the way to pick up a packet of chocolate digestives.'

I would never admit it to him, but I'm glad of Johnny's company as we head towards Trev's garage. Alone, I wouldn't be able to stop brooding over my argument with Lily. But Johnny's aimless chatter about the good old days at *The Post* helps keep the dark thoughts at bay.

'That's it,' I say, pointing to a prefab building ahead. I'd been surprised how easy Trevor Mason had been to track down. His garage was the first hit that showed up on Google. Trev's Auto Repairs: Your Car's Best Friend.

Two cars, an old blue Peugeot and a newer-looking silver BMW, are parked side by side on the garage forecourt. The up-and-over metal doors to the workshop are open, and inside I can see a third car hoisted high in the air on a lift.

A radio somewhere inside the workshop is playing a glam rock song. Outside, there are piles of old tyres everywhere. I glance at Johnny and he cocks an eyebrow, as if to tell me it's not too late to change my mind, but I shake my head. I need to find Jason and, right now, Trev is the only lead I have.

'Hello!' I call. 'Trev, are you there?'

'Depends who's asking,' says a voice, and Trev appears from the back of the workshop, rubbing his hands on an oily rag.

'I don't know if you remember me, but I'm Lara, Isabelle's sister. And this is Johnny.'

His face splits into a grin. 'Of course I remember you.' He turns to Johnny. 'She makes a lovely cuppa, does Lara.'

'I'll stick the kettle on now, shall I?' I hold out the biscuits. 'I brought chocolate digestives.'

'Cracking.' Trev beams. 'Kettle's in the office. Should be enough milk in the fridge.'

'Still two sugars?' I ask him.

He pats his stomach. ''Fraid so.'

'Black no sugar for me, please,' Johnny says.

Trev sweeps a pair of jump leads off an old garden bench so

Johnny can sit down, and I head past a car covered in a thick grey tarpaulin to the office at the back of the workshop.

A girlie calendar hangs on the wall behind the ancient-looking kettle. Miss July is striking a pose beside an old Jaguar E-Type, wearing a pair of denim dungarees that leave little to the imagination. In my current state of permanent anxiety, I take a crumb of comfort from the fact that some things never change.

Trev and Johnny are talking animatedly about cars when I return with the coffees. I peel open the packet of biscuits and offer them to Trev, who takes one, dunks it in his drink and takes a bite with a grunt of appreciation.

He has aged since I last saw him, which must have been at Isabelle, Jack and Milo's funeral. His hairline has receded, exposing a deeply lined forehead, and the pouches under his eyes are more pronounced than ever.

'So, to what do I owe this pleasure?' he asks through a mouthful of biscuit.

I glance at Johnny, who shrugs and says, 'He's going to find out soon enough.'

He's right. Once the press conference is on the news, everyone will know Jason's been spotted in Tidehaven. 'Have you heard Jason's back?' I ask.

Trev's eyebrows shoot up. I'm watching him carefully, looking for a sign that he knew this already. A tell, like a shift in his posture or his gaze that suggests he's lying, but he seems genuinely surprised.

'Back? What, here?'

I nod. 'The detective leading the murder enquiry has just announced it at a press conference.'

'That Frampton bloke?'

'You know him?' I ask, surprised.

'Everyone knows Curtis Frampton,' Johnny says. 'I told you, his reputation precedes him.'

'I don't understand why you have such a problem with him.'

'Because he's an arrogant tosser?'

Aware that Trev is watching our exchange keenly, I pull the conversation back to the only thing that actually matters: Jason and his current location.

'Has Jason been in contact with you?' I ask Trev.

'Me?'

'Come on, Trev. You and he go back years. You probably know him better than anyone. If he needed help, he'd come to you, right?'

Trev holds his hand to his heart. 'I haven't clapped eyes on Jase in ten years, and that's God's honest truth.'

'What do you think happened to him?' Johnny asks.

Trev dunks the last of his digestive in his coffee. I offer him another but he shakes his head.

'I never believed he topped himself, if that's what you mean. Jase was like one of them jack-in-a-boxes. No matter how many times you slam the lid, the little bugger keeps popping back up.'

I know exactly what Trev means. Jason was irrepressible, a force of nature. He had an infectious energy and zest for life that rubbed off on everyone around him. Challenges were opportunities and hurdles mere stepping stones to help him navigate setbacks.

I remember the morning of my interview at *The Post*. I'd jumped in my car, my stomach in knots, only to hear a faint clicking sound when I turned the ignition. No matter how many times I tried, the engine wouldn't turn over. Mum was at work and Isabelle had taken the kids swimming, so in a panic I phoned the one person I knew would help: Jason.

'I'll be right over,' he said. 'And don't fret, we'll get you there.'

He turned up less than fifteen minutes later in a canary-yellow Lamborghini Miura.

'It's the fastest car in the showroom,' he said, as I fixed the seat belt. 'How long have we got?'

I pulled a face. 'Ten minutes?' The journey into town normally took fifteen. Jason nodded, slammed his foot on the accelerator and the car roared out of the drive.

We made it to *The Post* with a minute to spare. It was only later that I found out Jason picked up two speeding tickets that day, risking his licence to make sure I was on time for my interview.

I'd always had trouble reconciling the Jason I knew with the man who had supposedly leapt off a cliff to his death. And what about the man who'd killed his wife and two of his children? That man wasn't the Jason I knew either.

'If he didn't kill himself, where has he been for the last ten years?' Johnny muses.

Trev rubs his chin. 'Ain't that the million-dollar question.'

34

Trev puts his mug on the workshop's grimy floor. 'Look, Jason knew a lot of people. People with boats. People with planes. People who owed him a favour or two, if you know what I mean.'

'Dodgy people?' I say.

'People who owed him a favour,' Trev repeats.

Johnny's eyes widen. 'You think some of his associates might have helped him leave the country, as a favour?'

Trev belches quietly under his breath. 'That's not for me to say.'

He doesn't have to. I can tell from his expression that's exactly what he thinks. That one or more of Jason's shady business associates put their resources at his disposal to help him vanish. Far better to fake your own death and disappear. You can't charge a dead man. Jason could have been on a helicopter or boat to France before the bodies of Isabelle and the boys were cold.

'But why come back now?' Johnny asks.

'I told you, because he's worried Lily's starting to remember what happened,' I say.

Trev's face lights up. 'Lily? Now she was a chip off the old block. A proper little daddy's girl,' he tells Johnny. 'How's she doing? She must be, what, fourteen now?'

'Fifteen,' I say. Lily always loved visiting the showroom with her dad, who let her climb all over his precious cars. Once, when she spilt a carton of orange juice over the leather seats of his beloved Austin Healey, he'd just ruffled her hair and laughed.

'Any chance I can use the toilet, mate?' Johnny asks.

Trev nods. 'First door on the left past the office.' Johnny loops all three mugs on his little finger and saunters off towards the back of the workshop.

'I'm worried about Lily, Trev. I'm worried Jason has come back for her.'

Trev sucks in a breath. 'Look, I'm not saying Jason was an angel. He wasn't, by any means. The things he used to get up to when he was young.' He chuckles, then collects himself. 'But he loved them kids, and he loved Isabelle. I don't think you should worry that pretty little head of yours.'

I bite down on my lower lip to stop myself from squealing with frustration. Trev is so, so wrong. Can't he see? Jason is a desperate man facing a ticking time bomb. Of course he's a danger to Lily.

'Nice little outfit you've got here,' Johnny says, reappearing. 'D'you still specialise in classic car repairs?'

'Not these days. Can't afford to. Talking of which, I have a pair of brake pads that need replacing, so if we're done here...?'

'We are. Thanks, Trev.' I fish about in my bag for a business card. 'If you hear from Jason, will you call me? Please?'

'Can't promise anything,' he replies, but he takes my card and slips it into the pocket of his coveralls anyway.

As we're leaving, a thought occurs to me. 'Trev, how do you know Curtis Frampton?'

He cocks his head. 'Didn't you know? He and Jason were mates.'

* * *

'Mates!' I hiss, once Johnny and I are out of earshot. 'How the hell did Frampton wind up on the investigation team if he and Jason were *mates*?'

'They played golf together,' Trev had announced, genuinely surprised I had no idea. 'Though Jase always said they spent more time at the nineteenth hole than they did on the bleedin' golf course.'

His revelation has knocked me sideways. How could Frampton even pretend to be impartial when he was friends with the police's prime suspect at the time of the murders? The investigation must have been compromised.

'I spent quite a lot of time at the showroom when I was home from uni, taking photos for Jason,' I tell Johnny. 'Trev told me once that Jason used some dodgy practices when he first started selling cars. Cut and shuts, clocking cars, that kind of thing.' I cast my mind back to the long-ago conversation Trev and I had in the cluttered workshop at JC Classics. 'Trev said Jason had cleaned up his act by the time he met Isabelle, although he still did the odd cash only sale that didn't go through the books. When I asked how Jason had never been caught, Trev said he reckoned he had a friend in the police. What if that friend was DCI Frampton?'

Johnny shakes his head. 'Jason probably played golf with half the movers and shakers in Tidehaven, and Frampton probably still does. You know what this place is like. Everyone knows everyone.'

'I know, but all the same. And another thing. Did you notice how Trev said he hadn't *seen* Jason. It doesn't mean he hasn't *heard* from him.'

'You're right, he did.' Johnny steps into the road to let a woman pushing a buggy past. 'He also out-and-out lied to us. He said he didn't repair classic cars any more, right? So what was a 1965 Austin Healey 3000 doing hiding under a tarpaulin?'

His words are like a sucker punch.

'A what?'

'An Austin Healey. It's a classic British roadster. That's a two-seat soft-top car to you.'

'I know what a bloody roadster is. What colour was it?'

'Cream and blue. What's wrong? You look like you've seen a ghost.'

'That's Jason's car,' I gasp. 'His pride and joy. I thought it'd been sold when the garage went on the market.' I shake my head in disbelief. 'Why would Trev keep Jason's car if he wasn't coming back?'

35

I decide to go and see Mum on my way home, on the off-chance Lily will agree to speak to me. We might enjoy a bit of banter, but this morning's argument feels serious, and I want to make things right.

On my way through the estate, I rehearse what I'm going to say.

'I didn't want to worry you, Lily.' Too feeble.

'I have your best interests at heart.' Too worthy.

'I have to keep you safe because I love you and you are all I have left of my sister.' Too toe-curlingly honest.

As I run through a pathetic list of justifications, it hits me how angry I'd have been if the situation had been reversed, because the truth is, I don't blame Lily for being livid. I was playing God. My intentions may have been honourable, but what does it matter when the end result backfires so spectacularly?

Mum has taped over the doorbell camera with gaffer tape again and I peel it off before ringing the bell.

Her face falls when she sees me. 'Oh, I thought you were Lily.'

'Sorry to disappoint.'

'Don't be chippy. I wasn't expecting you, that's all.'

'But she's been home since this morning, right?'

Mum runs a distracted hand through her hair. 'No, that's why I'm so worried. I keep phoning her, but it just goes straight to voicemail. I only agreed she could have the day off school to go to the press conference on the condition she came straight home and spent the afternoon doing her schoolwork.'

'But the press conference finished four hours ago.' I massage my temple. 'Maybe she went back to school after all.'

'I've already phoned them. She's not there.'

'Have you checked Find My iPhone?'

Mum shakes her head.

'There you go. We'll soon see where she is.' I take my phone from my bag and click on the Find My iPhone app. 'I don't believe it. She's stopped sharing her location.'

Mum checks her phone. 'Same here.'

Shaking my head, I call Lily. It goes straight to voicemail.

'Lily, it's Lara. I'm at Gran's. She says you've not been home since the press conference. I just want to check you're all right.' I pause, glance at Mum. She's fiddling with her phone, her face strained. 'Look, Lils, I know you're mad at me, and I get why, I really do. But Gran's worried. We're both worried. So can you call me as soon as you pick up this message, please?'

I tap out yet another text to cover all bases, then check again for missed calls. There aren't any.

'Shall I make us a cup of tea?' I don't wait for an answer, and busy myself filling the kettle and warming Mum's teapot, which is yellow and shaped like a beehive. I usually chuck teabags into mugs, but the ritual of making tea in a pot gives me something to do. 'Don't worry, she'll turn up when she's over her strop.'

'But that bastard's out there somewhere. What if he's snatched her? Perhaps we should phone the police. In fact, I think we definitely should. Give me that DCI's number. I'll call him. He'll know what to do.'

'Just wait a minute, Mum. You need to calm down. Let's give it till six o'clock, and if she's not back by then I promise I'll call him, OK?'

She sighs but gives a tiny nod.

'Why don't we find something nice on the TV to watch while we wait?' I say, carrying the two mugs of tea into the living room. I find an old rerun of *Escape to the Chateau* but I can't concentrate on it, so I pick up my phone and scroll through a few news websites to see how they've covered the press conference.

It's the lead story in most of the tabloids' online editions. Curious to see Johnny's take on the conference, I call up *The Post*'s website.

A major search has been launched following the reported sighting of a man wanted in connection with the shocking triple murder of Tidehaven mum Isabelle Carello and her sons Jack and Milo.

During a press conference at Tidehaven police station today, the detective leading the murder investigation revealed that the force's prime suspect, Mrs Carello's husband Jason, was spotted in the harbour area a week ago.

DCI Curtis Frampton has warned the public not to approach Carello as he is believed to be dangerous.

Lily Carello, the only survivor of the horrific knife attack ten years ago, attended the press conference with her aunt, Isabelle's sister, Lara Beckett.

Now fifteen, Lily urged the public to help her secure justice for her mother and brothers...

I skim-read Lily's statement, then focus on Frampton's

appeal, hoping to God Johnny hasn't disclosed I was the witness who saw Jason at the harbour.

DCI Frampton was quick to defend his team's lack of progress on the decade-old case, claiming they had 'left no stone unturned' in their quest to find the killer.

He said locating Carello was a priority and added: 'We are working tirelessly to verify the sighting and, if it was genuine, to speak to Mr Carello.'

Carello, a classic car dealer, was snapped in the background of a member of the public's photo while staying in one of the converted fishermen's huts at Tidehaven Harbour.

Police, who are currently refusing to release the photo, are appealing for anyone who may have seen him to call 999 immediately.

It's weird seeing my name in Johnny's report, and not in a good way. How many of my wedding clients will catch me on the news and make the connection? I don't want people's sympathy, however sincere. I had a gutful of it when Isabelle and the boys died. Always the focus of people's stares, wherever I went. That's the problem with small towns. Everyone knows you, and my face was plastered all over the papers, thanks to a freelance photographer who gate-crashed the funeral and took a raft of pictures of my tear-stained face.

Wanting a distraction from Jason and his crimes, I close *The Post* and open my website, hoping a scroll through some of my wedding photos will soothe me, but the page won't open. An error message appears, saying the website took too long to respond. When I hit refresh, all I get is a stark 'This site can't be reached'.

'Mum, can I use your iPad for a minute?'

She looks up, startled, as if she'd forgotten I was here.

'Mum, your iPad?'

She gives her head a slight shake. 'It's in the kitchen, next to the toaster.'

I traipse into the kitchen, stack our mugs in the dishwasher and gaze out of the window, hoping to catch sight of Lily tramping up the road towards the house, The clock on the oven says 17:43. If Lily doesn't arrive in the next seventeen minutes I'll have to call DCI Frampton. 'C'mon, Lily,' I murmur. 'Come home, please.'

'No sign of her?' Mum says when I sink back onto the sofa and key her passcode into the iPad.

'Not yet.'

'What are you looking up?'

'I was trying to load my website but the bloody thing seems to have crashed.'

Although I don't really expect Mum's iPad to yield a different result, I refresh the page anyway, only to be met with the same persistent error message.

Common sense tells me there's a simple explanation for the loading issue. But, after everything that's happened, it feels like the universe is conspiring against me.

I fling the iPad onto the sofa and burst into tears.

36

LILY

Lily thanks the bus driver and steps onto the pavement. A waft of warm air drifts past as the double decker trundles away. She's pretty sure the driver recognised her. Something about his sympathetic smile when she showed him her travel card suggested he'd seen her on the lunchtime news. She'll have to get used to it, she supposes, as she hitches her bag onto her shoulder and sets off for home. She could do without being recognised in the street, but it won't hurt her engagement rate on TikTok. Every cloud.

She checks her phone as she walks. Her WhatsApp notifications have gone crazy, her friends incessantly messaging her to tell her they've seen her on this website or that TV channel. There are four missed calls from Gran and two from Lara, but there's no point phoning them now. She'll be home in fifteen minutes.

Lily's head is all over the place. She's pleased with how the press conference went – at least, her part in it. She likes to think she did her mum, Jack and Milo proud. But she is still beyond furious with Lara. She was bang out of order not telling Lily she'd seen her dad. That's Lara all over. She pretends to have Lily's best interests at heart, but the fact is she's a bloody control freak.

Lily's stomach growls, reminding her she hasn't eaten since the single slice of toast she forced down at breakfast. She skipped lunch because her stomach was still churning after her row with Lara, and now it's a quarter to six and she's famished.

As she nears the edge of the estate, Lily hesitates. A detour across the large area of waste ground the developers are yet to build on would shave a good five minutes off her walk. Gran would have kittens – she's always drumming into Lily the need to prioritise her personal safety, to stick to busy streets and avoid shortcuts – but Gran's not here. She'll be perfectly safe. It's not like it's dark or anything.

Her stomach rumbles again, and the decision is made.

The air is still and humid, a storm threatening. Lily can almost taste the rain in the air. Pewter-grey clouds jostle for position on the horizon as if they're holding their breath and waiting for lightning to strike.

She keeps her head down, watching her feet as she navigates the uneven ground which is peppered with flints and lumps of hardcore. She pushes all thoughts of Lara to one side and instead plans her next video. She's going to livestream again tonight. It makes sense to capitalise on the coverage from this morning's press conference.

Ahead, a car door slams, jolting her, and her head jerks up in time to see a dark-coloured saloon disappearing behind the wooden hoardings the builders erected to keep the local kids out. Probably a delivery driver, lost in the estate's bewildering labyrinth of cul-de-sacs and no through roads. Even so, Lily's heart beats a little faster as she quickens her pace and heads for home.

* * *

Lily slots her key into the lock and lets herself into the house. She's barely hung her jacket on the newel post when Gran darts out of the living room and envelops her in a tight hug.

'Thank goodness you're safe. We've been going out of our minds.'

Lily disentangles herself from her grandmother's embrace. 'It's not even six.'

'But you said you'd come straight home after the press conference. Where've you been?'

'The library.'

'I called school, Lily. They said you hadn't signed in.'

'That's because I was at the library in town,' Lily says patiently. 'Why all the fuss?'

'Because you weren't answering your phone.'

'And you've kicked us off Find My iPhone,' Lara says, leaning against the doorframe with her hands folded across her chest. 'Why?'

'What's she doing here?' Lily asks her gran.

'She was worried too. We were about to phone the police.'

'The police?' Lily's incredulous. 'Why on earth would you do that? I was perfectly fine.'

'Because we didn't know you were fine,' Lara snaps. 'For all we knew, you were lying dead in a ditch, or you'd been kidnapped by people traffickers, or... or you were trussed up like a turkey in the back of some pervert's transit van.'

'Je-sus,' Lily says, sidestepping her gran and marching into the kitchen. 'You really need to get out more.'

She heads straight for the fridge and pours herself a large glass of milk, then plucks a banana from the fruit bowl. 'I'm going upstairs. I have an essay to finish.' As she walks past Lara, she notices her aunt's eyes are tinged pink, like she has a bad case of conjunctivitis. But she doesn't ask why she's been crying. Lara'll only lay on more guilt.

Instead, Lily stalks upstairs, slamming her bedroom door behind her, grateful to be on her own at last.

37

LILY

Lara leaves just after half past six and at seven, Gran calls Lily down for dinner.

'Lara's only like she is because she cares about you,' Gran says, as she serves Lily a generous helping of macaroni cheese.

'Yeah, well, she needs to wind her neck in.'

'I've said it before and I'll say it again: you two are as bad as each other. Now, you haven't forgotten it's my book club tonight? I can give it a miss if you want.'

Lily frowns. 'Why would I want you to do that?' Her face clears. 'Oh, I see. You think I'm worried Dad might come for me. I'm not, Gran. He wouldn't risk it, even if he did know where we live.'

'OK, but I can come straight home if you need me.'

'I'm nearly sixteen! You've got to stop treating me like a child.'

Gran looks at her levelly. 'Only if you stop blaming us for caring.'

Guilt prickles Lily's skin. 'All right,' she says. 'It's a deal.'

'And if you let us put you back on Find My iPhone.'

'You strike a hard bargain.' She sighs. 'Fine.'

Once her gran's left and Lily's sure she's not going to pop back to collect a cardigan or a forgotten book, she shuts herself in her room and sets up her phone and lighting.

After a couple of practice runs, she opens the TikTok app and hits the pink Go Live button.

'First of all, I would like to thank everyone who has watched, liked and subscribed to my account,' she says, as she gazes into the lens. 'I have been absolutely overwhelmed by the response.

'Next, I want to tell you about the press conference I took part in today, during which the police appealed for information about the murders of my mum and brothers. If you want to take a look at the BBC's coverage, click the link in my bio.

'And, so, here's the thing. The senior investigating officer in the case, DCI Curtis Frampton, dropped a bombshell at the press conference. He announced that there had been a sighting of Jason Carello here in Tidehaven just over a week ago. Yup, it looks like my dad's back in town.'

Lily tips her head back and stares at the ceiling. This is harder than she thought. She takes a deep breath, then returns her gaze to the camera.

'It's too early to say how I feel about the possibility that he's back. Maybe I'll be ready to talk about it next time. But tonight I'm going to tell you what I remember about Friday, July the eighteenth, 2014, the day of the murders.'

A deep rumble outside stops Lily in her tracks. 'Blimey, did you hear that?' she says, cupping her ear. 'Thunder, right over the house.' She shivers, even though it's warm in her bedroom.

'Anyway, where was I? Oh yes, the day my dad murdered my mum and brothers. Well, I hope this doesn't disappoint, but it started like any other Friday morning. Mum woke us up at half past seven, and we had cereal for breakfast. Shreddies for me. Weetabix with a chopped-up banana each for Jack and Milo.

'Mum had this thing where we had to leave the house at half past eight on the dot, and if we didn't muck about we were allowed to watch a bit of CBeebies before we went. The longer we took to get ready, the less TV we were allowed to watch. Quite clever, when you think about it. Well, that morning I was annoyed with my brothers because they were messing around when we were supposed to be cleaning our teeth, so we missed *Octonauts*.' She bites her lip. 'I told them both I hated them.'

Lily looks down at her hands, which are clasped in her lap. Her black nail polish is chipped and her left thumbnail is red and sore because she can't stop worrying at the loose skin around it.

'By the time Mum picked me up from school I'd forgotten all about the missed episode of *Octonauts*. So had Jack and Milo. That doesn't stop me feeling guilty. Every. Single. Day.

'It was the last day of the summer term and we were going to France on holiday the very next day. Mum had already packed our suitcases. I remember they were lined up in the hallway when we got in from school.' Lily closes her eyes and allows herself to be transported back to the house that hot summer afternoon. 'Mum was about to get us a drink when her phone rang, so she asked me to get them instead, and she went out into the garden. When she came back inside her eyes were red and puffy. She looked like she'd been crying.'

Lily had asked her mum what was wrong.

'Nothing for you to worry about, my darling,' she'd said. 'And tomorrow we'll be in France for two glorious weeks, and I won't have to worry either.'

Lily is about to recount this conversation, but something stops her. Instead, she describes how she, Jack and Milo had spent the lull between teatime and bath time deciding which of their toys they were going to take to France, and how her dad had arrived home from work just in time to read their stories.

'Everyone was excited, that's what I remember most. It was

the twins' first holiday abroad and Dad had told them all about this train we were catching which would take us under the sea. I think they thought we'd be able to see fish out of the car window.' Lily smiles.

'Mum and Dad both kissed me goodnight. Everything was fine. Normal. I went to sleep, but woke up thirsty maybe an hour later, so I snuck downstairs to get a drink.'

Lily's pulse is racing and she takes a couple of deep breaths to slow her heart rate.

'That's when I heard Mum and Dad arguing in the kitchen,' she recalls. 'Well, Mum was crying and Dad was shouting. It freaked me out because they never argued. Like, literally never. Dad adored Mum. Worshipped the ground she walked on. I crept back upstairs before they could see me. I had a drink from the cold tap in the bathroom and took myself back to bed.'

Lily's bottom lip trembles. 'The next time I woke up I was in hospital, and everyone else was missing or dead.'

38

The first few splatters of rain start to fall as I leave Mum's. She offered to give me a lift to the police station to pick up my car, but it's her book club night, and anyway, I could use the walk to clear my head.

So much has happened today I'm struggling to process it all. The press conference and DCI Frampton's decision to tell the world Jason's been seen here in Tidehaven. My argument with Lily, who is still not speaking to me. The visit to Trev's garage and his revelation that Jason and Frampton were friends. Johnny discovering Jason's Austin Healey hidden under a tarpaulin at the back of Trev's workshop. And now, my entire website has vanished into thin air.

Behind it all looms the shadowy figure of my brother-in-law, Jason Carello.

It's raining in earnest as I near the town centre, and before long I'm drenched, water pasting my hair to my head and running in rivulets down my back. A flash of lightning illuminates the sky as I wait for the lights on the pedestrian crossing outside the police station to turn green. Moments later, there's an answering rumble of thunder. The storm can't be far away.

My Fiesta's in the furthest corner of the small visitors' car park at the police station, and I march towards it with my head bowed, swearing as I step in a puddle that sends water splashing up the back of my leg.

It's as I'm ferreting around in my bag for my car keys that I see it: a yellow wheel clamp on the rear offside wheel.

'You have got to be kidding me.' I bend down and give the clamp a tug, as if it's going to fall away at my touch, but the steel is cold and unyielding.

'Shit.' I pace around to the front of the car, my hands on my hips. A ticket has been tucked under one of the windscreen wipers. I tear the plastic cover off and scan the contents.

This vehicle has been clamped. It is an offence to try to remove or otherwise interfere with the wheel clamp. Please read the instructions on the back of this notice to find out how to have the vehicle released.

I turn over the sheet of paper, which is already growing soggy in my hands.

In order to have the clamp removed, you have to pay a fee of £65. This includes a penalty charge of £25 and a clamp release fee of £40.

I stare at the soggy penalty notice with a growing sense of disbelief. Just when I thought today couldn't get any worse, fate deals me another blow. It's the final straw.

I give the clamp a vicious kick, yelping when pain shoots through my big toe and into my foot.

'Are you all right?' says a voice, and I spin round to see DCI Curtis Frampton staring at me in concern.

'No, I am not fucking all right,' I yell. The anger and frustration that have been simmering inside me all week reach boiling point, bursting out in a furious torrent. 'What gives your lot the right to clamp my bloody car? I was parked here perfectly legitimately, and now I'm going to have to pay sixty-five pounds I can't afford to get it back. How the fuck am I supposed to work tomorrow without my car? Well?'

'First of all, it's not the police who've clamped your car,' Frampton says mildly. 'It's the council. We share the car park with the council offices next door. Secondly, it does clearly state that you can only park here for two hours, and as the press conference was at eleven this morning, it suggests your car's been here for the last eight.'

'I couldn't drive it home then because I'd been to the pub,' I say without thinking.

He frowns. 'Would you consider yourself to be over the legal limit to drive now?'

'I had two pints seven hours ago. I'm perfectly OK to drive. Go ahead and breathalyse me if you don't believe me.'

'I don't think that's necessary.' His cheeks dimple as he smiles. 'Look, why don't I call my contact at the council and see if I can't get him to send someone out to release your car tonight? You'll still have to pay the fee, I'm afraid, but at least you'd have it for tomorrow. And be thankful they didn't impound it. That would have set you back another hundred quid.'

'Thank you,' I say, with as much grace as I can muster. 'That would be kind of you.'

'Don't mention it. Why don't you come and wait inside? You're soaked.'

I let him guide me back across the car park and up the disabled access ramp to the police station. He has a word with a blonde woman behind the counter, then comes back to me.

'Shirley's going to bring you a cup of tea while I make that call. I'll be as quick as I can. Will you be all right here?'

I nod. He smiles again and disappears through a door into the police station.

A few minutes later, Shirley arrives with a weak cup of tea in a paper cup. 'The DCI said you looked like you needed this.'

'Thank you, I do,' I say gratefully. 'Sorry about the puddle.' We both inspect the pool of water that has dripped off my clothes onto the lino floor.

Shirley chuckles. 'I'd better put the wet floor A-board out so we don't get sued if anyone slips.' She returns moments later and places the board by my feet.

'You're Isabelle Carello's sister, aren't you?'

'That's right.'

Shirley nods to herself. 'Thought I recognised you from the press conference. I saw it on the lunchtime news. You know DCI Frampton, then?'

I take a sip of tea. It's lukewarm and as weak as it looks, and I hide a grimace.

'Not really,' I tell her. 'He just saw me in the car park and offered to help.'

'That's the DCI for you. He can't say no to a damsel in distress,' she says with a wink.

I'm about to tell her I am neither a damsel nor in distress when the door opens and Frampton strides out.

'There's good news and bad news,' he announces. 'The good news is, I've fixed it with my contact at the council, and not only is he going to send someone round to release your car, he's also going to waive the parking charge and release fee. The bad news is, he can't get anyone out till first thing tomorrow morning. Is that going to be a problem?'

'No, my wedding's at two. I'll have plenty of time to pick it up. Thank you, I really appreciate it.'

He waves my thanks away. 'Why don't you let me give you a lift home?'

It's only a twenty-minute walk back to my flat, but the rain is still coming down in sheets, and although I'm already drenched, the thought of venturing back out in it isn't appealing.

'Are you sure?'

'Of course. I wouldn't offer if I wasn't.'

'Then thank you.'

He takes the paper cup, crushes it into a ball and chucks it over the counter into, I presume, a bin, then stands in front of the automatic doors so they open, giving a small bow as I step past him. As I leave, I glance back at Shirley, who is watching us with a knowing smile on her lips.

39

I slide into the passenger seat of DCI Frampton's dark blue BMW, sending droplets of rain scattering over the interior.

'I'm going to make your seat all wet,' I say.

'Don't worry, it'll soon dry.' As he releases the handbrake, I can't help noticing he doesn't wear a wedding band. 'Where do you live?' he asks.

'Elmwood Road. Second right past the sports centre.'

'I know it.' He taps the steering wheel as he waits for a lorry to pass, then pulls out of the car park, stopping almost immediately when the lights of the pedestrian crossing turn red. An old woman in an ankle-length mac shuffles across the road, dragging a protesting terrier behind her.

'Lily was great today,' Frampton says, waiting until the old woman and her dog are safely on the pavement on the opposite side of the road before he sets off again.

'She was.' My voice is flat and he must notice, because he glances at me, one eyebrow raised.

'She put two and two together and guessed that I took the photograph of Jason,' I explain. 'She's furious I didn't tell her, and now she's not speaking to me.'

'She'll get over it.'

'I'm not sure she will. She's as stubborn as her mother.' I realise I'm worrying the strap of my bag, pleating it over and over, and force my hands to still before changing the subject. 'Have you had much of a response to the appeal?'

'We have. In fact, the new incident line hasn't stopped ringing. There haven't been any credible sightings of Carello so far, but it's early days. According to the press office, a few of the papers are publishing backgrounders along with the appeal tomorrow, so it's getting plenty of exposure.'

'That's good, I guess.'

'It's what you wanted, isn't it? To stir it all up again? In a good way, I mean,' he adds quickly.

'I didn't want to stir anything up. In fact, I wish I'd never taken that bloody photo. Everything's been going wrong since.'

He looks at me again. This time his forehead is wrinkled. 'Like what?'

'Where do I start? I've messed up a wedding job, then someone – probably my brother-in-law, hell-bent on revenge – sends me a threatening note. I've fallen out with my niece and my car's been clamped. Oh, and my website's crashed. God knows how I'm going to fix that. I don't have the money to get an IT person in.' I sigh. 'It feels like the world is out to get me.'

'I can see why you're feeling a bit sorry for yourself.'

I grimace. 'Put like that, it does sound like a bit of a pity fest. Sorry, ignore me. I'm fine.'

'I can't help you mend bridges with Lily or sort out the wedding job, but I might be able to help with your website. I did a stint on the cybercrime team up at headquarters before I came back down to Tidehaven. What's the problem?'

'Every time I try to open it an error message appears, saying it took too long to respond and the site can't be reached.'

'Could be a number of things. Want me to take a look?'

I feel a glimmer of hope. 'Are you sure? It seems a terrible imposition.'

'Nonsense.' He smiles at me. 'I can have a look now, if you like?'

'Don't you have plans?'

'Not tonight. Tell you what, a Chinese has just opened at the end of your road, hasn't it?'

I nod.

'Why don't we pick up something to eat, and I'll sort out this glitch for you.'

I may be soaked from head to foot, but it doesn't stop a feeling of warmth spreading through me. 'That would be great,' I say. 'Thank you.'

* * *

I warm a couple of plates in the microwave, grab two beers from the fridge – alcoholic for me, non-alcoholic for DCI Frampton – and pour the bag of prawn crackers into a bowl. I've already laid the takeaway dishes on the coffee table in the living room, where my knight in shining armour is sitting with my laptop on his knees, tapping away, a look of deep concentration on his face.

'Looks like you've been the victim of a DDoS attack,' he says.

'A what?'

'A Distributed Denial of Service attack. It's when hackers overwhelm a website's server with a flood of traffic, overloading the server and causing the website to crash.'

My eyes widen. 'Can you fix it?'

'I can try. I came across these types of attacks occasionally when I was on the cybercrime team. But shall we eat first?'

'Of course. Sorry.'

He closes the laptop, sets it on the floor by his feet and I pass him a plate. We eat in silence for a while, then Frampton says, 'Who d'you think could be behind the cyberattack?'

I swallow my mouthful of beef in oyster sauce. 'Jason, who else?'

He looks at me in surprise.

'He's the only person I can think of who could possibly want to cause trouble for me. If he saw me taking the photograph down at the harbour – and I'm pretty sure he did – he now knows I've handed it over to you lot. Thanks to me, the whole country's looking for him. It stands to reason he'd want to lash out. Johnny says—'

'Johnny?'

'Johnny Nelson. We used to work together at *The Post*.'

'The guy making a nuisance of himself at the press conference this morning?'

'Asking awkward questions is a speciality of his. Yes, that's him.'

Frampton leans forwards and helps himself to another spoonful of egg fried rice. 'I asked our press officer about him. Seems he has a bit of a reputation.'

Funny, I think. *That's what he said about you.* 'What kind of a reputation?'

'That he'll go to any lengths to get a story. And I mean any lengths.' He pauses, as if weighing up whether I can be trusted with the information he's about to impart. 'Did you know he was arrested by the Met for handling stolen goods?'

'Johnny?'

'Seems some little scrote offered him a mobile phone he'd stolen from a member of the Cabinet. Your friend Nelson agreed to pay ten grand for a look at the messages. When he realised there was nothing on there he could use, he abandoned the story. Unfortunately for him, the disgruntled phone thief grassed him up to the Met.'

'Was he charged?' I ask.

Frampton shakes his head. 'The Crown Prosecution Service decided it wasn't in the public interest. He may have got away with it this time, but I've got his card marked, and you would do well to remember he's happy to break every rule in the book when it suits him.'

'Thank you.' Deflated, I push my knife and fork together. 'Can I get you another beer?'

'A glass of water for me, please.' He passes me his plate and picks up my laptop. When I return with our drinks, his fingers are dancing across the keyboard with practised ease.

'The first thing I need to do is to pinpoint the source of the attack and block it,' he says, his eyes not leaving the screen. 'Once I've filtered out any malicious requests and rerouted the legitimate traffic, I should be able to get the website back up and running.'

I leave him to it while I clear the coffee table and scrape the remains of our meal into the bin before loading the dishwasher.

'Coffee?' I call from the kitchen.

'Please. Decaf, if you have it.'

As the kettle boils, I replay Frampton's words. Was that the real reason Johnny left *The Daily Tribune*? Not because he'd turned up drunk, the story he'd spun me, but because he'd handled a stolen phone belonging to a politician. And not just any old MP, but a member of the Government. I feel a stab of betrayal. Of course he's only sniffing around because he's after a story for his podcast. My disappointment weighs heavy as I trudge back into the living room.

Frampton leans back with a satisfied grin. 'All sorted. Your website should be back up and running.'

He swivels the laptop round so I can see the screen, then hits refresh. My website slowly loads.

I try to dredge up some enthusiasm. 'That's amazing. I don't know how to thank you.'

He smiles modestly. 'I'm just glad I could help.' He closes

the laptop and hands it to me. 'I should go. But if you ever need any tech help, just call me. Anytime.'

It's not until the tail-lights of his car have disappeared into the gloomy night that I realise I forgot to ask why he'd never mentioned he and Jason had been friends.

40

That night my dreams are dark, nightmarish. I wake in a daze, my legs tangled in the duvet and my heart thudding. At half past seven, I haul myself out of bed.

The rain has gone, leaving a cloudless sky in its place, and I decide to take the longer route through the park to the police station to make the most of the sunshine.

On the way, I call Mum.

'How's Lily?'

'You can ask her yourself.'

Mum may think she's holding her hand over the phone, but I can still hear the hushed conversation taking place on the other end of the line.

'Lara wants to check you're OK.'

'Lara can take a hike.'

'Just talk to her, Lily, please.'

'Not a chance. Anyway, I need to go. I'm going to be late for school.'

And a long sigh from Mum, who comes back on the phone and says brightly, 'She's running a bit late, but she says hello and that she'll ring you tonight.'

'Mum,' I say, hurt making my voice flint hard. 'Don't bother pretending. I heard every word.'

'Oh.' She is silent for a moment. 'It's hard for her, knowing her dad's back. She feels conflicted. You can understand that, can't you?'

'I'm sorry?' I splutter, as though I've misheard her. 'Her dad killed her mum and brothers and left her for dead. What is there to be conflicted about?'

'Go easy on her, Lara. You may have lost your sister, but Lily lost her entire family. Her emotions are all over the place. She'll come round. Just give her a bit of time.'

'Why do you always pander to her, Mum? It's like she can do no wrong. Just because she lost Isabelle and the twins doesn't mean she has the right to act like a spoilt brat.' I've been so focused on the call that I haven't realised I've arrived outside the police station. 'Look, I've got to go. I'll call you tonight, OK?'

'I'll be back from yoga just after nine.' Her voice is tight, and a wave of guilt washes over me.

'All right. And Mum, I'm sorry. I didn't mean to have a go. It's just sometimes Lily's impossible. Why can't she see I'm just trying to help?'

'Infuriating, isn't it?' Mum agrees, and then she is gone.

* * *

My car is where I left it last night, in the far corner of the car park. The fixed penalty notice has disappeared, as has the wheel clamp. Frampton's contact at the council was as good as his word.

Knowing that at least someone is on my side lifts my spirits, and as I drive home, I banish the events of the last few days from my mind and concentrate on Brooke and Callum's wedding.

They are getting married in their local church and are

having the reception in the village hall next door. Brooke is wearing a wedding dress she's made herself; everyone is bringing food for the reception and the gardens of friends and family have been raided for the flowers.

Brooke's budget for photography was tiny, and perhaps I should have told her I usually charge four times the amount she had set aside. But she was so amenable and easy-going, that I found myself offering to take photos for a fraction of my usual fee.

And, hours later, as I'm clicking away, I'm glad I did. The village hall is an explosion of colour thanks to the abundance of flowers in painted jam jars, homemade bunting and Chinese lanterns. The wedding is intimate, relaxed and refreshingly unpretentious. Just two people, surrounded by their loved ones, vowing to spend the rest of their lives together.

Tall and slim, with wavy fair hair and cerulean-blue eyes, Brooke reminds me of Isabelle, although my sister's tastes were significantly more expensive when she and Jason tied the knot. No homemade dress for Isabelle – she wore a stunning Suzanne Neville designer dress, a sculpted vision in Italian crepe with a plunging neckline and a scooped low back. She'd glowed as Dad walked her up the aisle. No one would have guessed that just a couple of hours earlier she'd had her head in a toilet bowl, heaving up her breakfast.

'Morning sickness is the pits,' she'd groaned, as I rubbed her back and held her hair out of the danger zone, hoping my own dress wouldn't end up speckled with vomit.

Although I'd been adamant I wasn't going to be a brides-maid, Isabelle had guilt-tripped me into it, as we both knew she would. I hadn't long graduated, and getting married seemed an inordinately grown-up thing to do, but that didn't stop me enjoying the wedding preparations. Jason had been firm that no expense should be spared for his new bride, and Isabelle had taken him at his word.

Mum, Isabelle and I spent many a happy hour visiting wedding venues and bridal shops and choosing flowers and music. Summits would be held in cafes over coffee and cake. Plumping for a midweek wedding meant Isabelle could have the day she'd always dreamt of, even at such short notice. And it was the happiest of days. No one watching the beautiful bride and her handsome groom exchanging their vows could ever have guessed that tragedy was waiting in the wings.

I'm so invested in documenting Brooke and Callum's own magical day that every photograph is a little story in itself: Callum, his best man and two ushers walking over the zebra crossing from the church to the village hall in single file, like The Beatles on the *Abbey Road* album cover; Brooke's grandmother laughing as she tousles the hair of one of her great-grandchildren; the look of unadulterated delight on the face of Brooke and Callum's five-year-old son as sweets spray out of a donkey pinata; wedding guests huddling under a colourful canopy of umbrellas when the sun disappears and the heavens open.

I stay later than I'd intended because I'm enjoying myself so much, and it's gone nine o'clock when I head for home, tired but happy, a giant slab of homemade chocolate wedding cake and a jam jar of freesias on the seat beside me.

The rain has settled to a fine drizzle, and when my phone rings it takes a moment for me to hear it over the gentle swish of the windscreen wipers. I glance down to see Lily's name flashing on the screen and smile to myself. She's obviously forgiven me.

'Hey, Lils, how's it going?'

There is silence on the other end of the line. Perhaps she's dialled my number by accident.

'Lily?' I say. 'Are you there?' I hear an intake of breath, and then a sob. A feeling of panic rises in my chest. 'Lily, are you all right?'

'Something's happened to Gran.'

'Gran?' The panic solidifies like a hard lump of gristle at the back of my throat. 'What? What's happened to her?'

'The police are here. There's been an accident.' Lily's breath catches. 'Oh, Lara, you need to come quickly. Gran's in hospital.'

41

Ten minutes later I'm turning into Mum's cul-de-sac. I pull up behind the patrol car parked on the road outside her house, yank up the handbrake and hurtle through the drizzle to the front door. It takes an age for my fumbling fingers to locate the right key on my key ring but eventually I find it, slide it into the lock and let myself in.

Lily is in the living room with two police officers. She jumps up from the sofa when she sees me and flings her arms around me. Her entire body is trembling.

'She'll be OK, I promise,' I soothe. I look over her head to the two officers. 'What happened?'

'I'm afraid Mrs Beckett was hit by a car on her way home from her yoga class,' the younger of the two says. 'She was found lying in the road by a dog walker. He called an ambulance and she's been taken to hospital with a suspected fractured pelvis and concussion.'

'But she'll be OK?'

'You're best phoning the hospital for a condition check.' The officer glances at his older colleague, who gives a slight nod.

'But the paramedics told us they didn't think her injuries were life-threatening.'

'You saw her?'

He nods. 'We'd just been to a report of some nuisance youths five minutes away, so we were first on the scene. Mrs Beckett was more worried about you and Lily here than she was about herself.'

'That sounds like Mum,' I say, shaking my head. I guide Lily back to the sofa. Her eyes are slits and she is sobbing silently. I put my arm around her shoulder and give her a squeeze. 'See? The police say she'll be fine.'

Lily gulps, and nods, and I fish a tissue from my pocket and hand it to her.

'What about the driver?' I ask.

The younger officer clears his throat. 'We're yet to locate the driver.'

'They didn't stop?'

'They didn't,' he confirms. 'At this stage we're treating it as a hit-and-run.'

I shake my head as this sinks in. Mum was hit by a driver who didn't have the decency to pull over and see if she was all right, never mind alert the emergency services. What kind of person would do something like that?

'Someone must have seen what happened,' I reason. 'And what about CCTV?'

'No witnesses have come forward as yet, and there aren't any cameras in that area.'

'There are over six million CCTV cameras in the UK and you're telling me there isn't a single one in that road?'

'I'm afraid not.'

'Brilliant,' I mutter, shaking my head.

'Obviously there'll be a full investigation into the collision,' the older officer says. 'Don't worry, we'll find out who did this.'

* * *

Once the police have gone, I throw some clothes and toiletries for Mum into an overnight bag and we drive straight to the hospital.

'It's a nasty break,' the ward sister tells us when we arrive at the acute medical unit. 'They're operating tomorrow and she's going to be in hospital for at least a couple of weeks. The paramedics said it was a hit-and-run.' When I nod, she tuts. 'Whatever is the world coming to?'

Mum is sleeping when we are shown to her bay. I sit on the chair beside the bed, the bag of clothes on my lap. Lily perches on the edge of the bed, takes Mum's hand in hers and bends down and kisses it lightly. Mum looks diminished, somehow, the force of her personality muted by the stark hospital lights, the plumped-up pillows, the starched sheets.

As I watch, I'm transported back to another hospital bed, this one with the sides up and machines bleeping and flashing beside it. The quiet murmur of the intensive care nurses as they went from patient to patient, checking vitals, writing notes, exchanging a few words with grim-faced relatives.

Lily, just five at the time, looked tiny in that bed too. Her skin was so pale it was almost translucent, and her beautiful chestnut-brown hair had been plaited so it didn't get in the doctors' way. Mum and I would sit either side of her and massage her hands and stroke her face for hours at a time, as if our touch alone could pull her back to us.

And now we are sitting by Mum's bed, and Lily is smoothing the hair away from Mum's face, and tears are welling behind my eyes and I blink them back furiously. I can't break down. I need to stay strong for them both.

Mum stirs, and her eyes flutter open.

'Gran,' Lily whispers. 'We're here. Lara and me. We've been so worried. Are you OK?'

Mum looks from Lily to me and back again, then smiles.

'I'm absolutely fine.'

'Fine? Your pelvis is broken in three places,' I tell her. 'You've got to have an operation to pin and plate it in the morning.'

'I'll be home before you know it.'

'That's not what the nurse just told us, Mum. She said you're going to be here for at least a couple of weeks.'

Her brow wrinkles, and she turns to me.

'You'll look after Lily?' she asks.

'Of course.'

'I'm fifteen,' Lily says indignantly. 'I don't need looking after.'

'I know you don't,' I say. 'But we could probably both use the company, right?'

She blows her fringe out of her eyes. 'Yeah,' she admits. 'I guess it would be nice.'

'That's settled then. We'll drop by my place on the way back so I can pick up some things.'

Mum winces as she shifts in the bed, but when I jump up to adjust her pillows, she waves me away impatiently.

'Don't fuss, Lara. I'm not an invalid.'

'Er, you literally are,' Lily says, rolling her eyes.

'What happened, Mum?' I ask. 'The police said it was a hit-and-run.'

'I was on my way home. It was raining and I'd left my waterproof in the car, so I borrowed yours, Lily. I didn't think you'd mind.'

'Course not, Gran.'

'I must have nodded off in shavasana because the next thing I knew, Colette was waking me up saying we had to be out of the hall asap because salsa started at nine. So I was probably in a bit of a tizzy when I left.' She frowns. 'Colette offered me a lift but I knew she'd be going out of her way so I told her I'd be fine. It's only a ten-minute walk home.'

'You should have said yes to the lift, Gran,' Lily says. 'You wouldn't be here if you had.'

'There's no point crying over spilt milk. It is what it is.'

'What do you remember about the crash?' I ask.

'I was crossing Napleton Road when this car came out of nowhere. I'm sure I looked both ways, only the hood on Lily's coat's a bit snug and when it's zipped all the way up to your chin, you can't see very well. It was probably my fault.'

'Gran!' Lily exclaims. 'The driver drove away without even bothering to check you were OK. It was *not* your fault.'

'Lily's right,' I agree. 'Even if you didn't see the car coming, it should have given way to you the moment you started to cross the road.'

'It was raining cats and dogs. They probably didn't see me.'

'What make of car was it?'

'I don't know. I think it was black, but it could have been dark grey or blue, I suppose. It was going so fast it was hard to tell.'

'What about the driver?'

She shakes her head.

A terrible thought occurs to me. What if the driver did see Mum? What if they deliberately ran her over? I want to dismiss it out of hand. In fact, it's ludicrous to even think the collision could have been intentional. But Mum was wearing Lily's coat with the hood up. At five foot three, Mum's only an inch or so shorter than Lily and they're a pretty similar build. Visibility wasn't great. Someone could have easily mistaken her for Lily.

I can think of only one person in the world who would wish Lily harm. The only person who would stand to benefit if an accident were to befall her. I know it's preposterous, but as the theory begins to take shape, it becomes impossible to ignore.

To Jason, Lily is a threat, an obstacle between him and freedom. He has everything to gain and nothing to lose if she were to die.

What if he followed Mum to the yoga class, thinking she was Lily? What if he waited outside for her to finish and then drove straight at her as she crossed the road on her way home?

And the possibility that Jason, the man Mum once regarded as the son she never had, could have ploughed into her and then callously sped away, leaving her for dead, sits like curdled milk in the pit of my stomach.

42

'Poor Gran,' I say, as we wait for the barrier in the hospital car park to judder into life and let us out. 'But she'll be all right.'

I'm pretty sure I'm reassuring myself as much as I'm soothing Lily, who rubs her face and mutters, 'You hope.'

'She's going to need a lot of support when she comes home. I'll do what I can, but we might need to think about finding some extra help.'

'I can do it,' Lily says. 'I'll have broken up from school by then.'

I glance at her. 'I know you'll do what you can, but she'll need help with washing and stuff. Personal care.'

'I know that. I want to do it. It's my fault this happened,' she says quietly.

'Of course it's not your fault. Why would you say that?'

'Because everything's gone wrong since I started posting those videos. You were right. I should never have done it, and now it's too late to take it back.'

'You weren't to know. And I've made mistakes too. I should have told you I saw your dad in my photo. Trouble is,' I say, giving her a rueful smile, 'I still think you're five, not fifteen. I need to remember you're old enough to handle this stuff.'

'You do,' she agrees. 'You can't protect me forever.'

'I know, but you can't blame me for trying. Am I forgiven?'

'I guess.' She mock-glares at me. 'As long as you stop trying to mother me.' Her eyes widen a fraction as she says this, as if this has only just occurred to her, and she's uncomfortable with the thought. My heart gives a little flip. Have I been trying to step into Isabelle's shoes all these years?

'Thank goodness for that,' I say lightly, as if her words aren't hanging between us, awkward and heavy. 'And I get that you want answers, Lils. We all do. Justice, too. Why should the person who killed your mum and brothers get away with it?'

Lily examines her nails which, I notice, have been bitten to the quick. 'I keep remembering how much Dad loved Mum, and he did, Lara. I didn't make that up.'

'I know.' I reach out to squeeze her hand. In the weeks and months after Isabelle and the boys died, I sifted through every memory I had of Isabelle's life with Jason. I examined everything with forensic detail, looking for clues of what was to come. A short word here, an instance of controlling behaviour there. But I didn't find any. Not a single one.

No one really knows what goes on behind closed doors, of course, but from my vantage point just outside their little family unit, Jason appeared to genuinely worship my sister.

And what of Isabelle? I hardly saw her that long, hot summer ten years ago. Punishing hours at *The Post* left me with little time or energy for meeting up. I relied on Mum to be my link to her world. It was Mum who told me about Isabelle's nasty bout of bronchitis; Mum who reported back after Lily's first parents' evening; Mum who gave me regular updates on my sister's valiant attempts to potty-train the twins.

I regret it now; am stuck in a loop of remorse and self-recrimination. I should have made time for Isabelle and the children. Busy as it was, my job was no excuse. I could have been there for my sister as she juggled her own work commitments with the demands of having three kids under five. I *should* have been there for her. But on the few occasions I did text to see if she was around, she was always too busy to fit me in.

A couple of times when I turned up at the house unannounced, conscious I hadn't seen my niece and nephews in weeks, Isabelle was distracted, spending more time checking her phone than talking to me.

Could she have been cheating on Jason? It's possible, I suppose. But the last time I saw them both, the week before they were due to take the kids to France, they seemed closer than ever.

DCI Phil Glover and his team considered the possibility that Isabelle was having an affair but abandoned that line of enquiry when they couldn't find any evidence to substantiate it. So the theory that Jason killed Isabelle and the boys because she'd threatened to leave him for another man was as groundless as the hunch that the attack was a burglary gone wrong.

The fact is, no one knew then why Jason pulled a kitchen knife from its block and attacked his wife and children that terrible night, and a decade later, we're still none the wiser.

'Here we are,' I say, pulling in behind a rusty Ford Transit van. 'D'you want to stay in the car while I grab some stuff? I won't be long.'

Lily nods and reaches for her phone. I dart through the rain to my front door, scoop up the post from the mat and flick through it as I trudge up the stairs to my flat.

There are a couple of bills, a bank statement and a leaflet about a new retirement village on the outskirts of Tidehaven. But what stops me in my tracks is a hand-posted letter which simply says *Lara Beckett* on the envelope in jerky handwriting.

43

A shiver passes through me. What if it's another threatening letter? In which case, I should take it straight to the police station without opening it. But if it isn't, I'll look like a complete idiot. I compromise, pulling on rubber gloves before slicing the envelope open with a paring knife.

I shake the envelope upside down and a single sheet of folded paper drifts onto the counter by the kettle. I glance through the window to the street below, needing to reassure myself Lily is OK. My car is parked under a streetlamp about fifty metres down the road. Lily's face, lit up by the screen of her phone, is just about discernible from here. I check the pavement both sides of the road, but the street is deserted. Lily is fine. I unfold the letter.

Dear Lara,

Thank you so much for the wonderful album of wedding photographs you so kindly gave us. We are so grateful to you for making sure we will always be able to remember our special day.

Lots of love,

Marian and Bob xx

I laugh shakily and slip the note back into the envelope. Marian and Bob came home from their honeymoon yesterday. They were in the middle of unpacking when I'd turned up on the doorstep with a bunch of flowers, the album and a grovelling apology.

'I don't know what happened. I switched the memory card over twice, which meant I reformatted the card with your photos on.'

'You mustn't blame yourself, Lara. These things happen,' Marian said.

'She's right, love,' Bob agreed. 'We still have our memories of the day up here.' He tapped his temple. 'And these wonderful pictures of the reception. But we appreciate you coming round to tell us in person.'

I'd wished they'd ranted and raved at me. As it was, their kindness just amplified my guilt, and I'd left their bungalow feeling worse than I had when I'd arrived.

At least it seems they've forgiven me. I drop the letter onto the pile of post, grab a holdall from under my bed and rush round the flat, packing enough clothes to last me a few days. I'm scanning my bedroom checking for things I might have forgotten when my phone chirps. Assuming it's Lily wanting to know how much longer I'm going to be, I answer without checking the screen.

'Hey, Lara. Whassup?'

'Johnny, why are you phoning? It's almost midnight.'

'Issit?' The words flow together, their edges blunted. He's drunk, I realise. In a bar, judging by the chatter and laughter in the background.

'It is,' I say shortly.

'Ker-rist, I'm so, so sorry. Did I wake you?'

'No. I'm—' I'm about to tell him about Mum's accident when I remember DCI Frampton's words. *He's happy to break every rule in the book when it suits him.* 'I've got to go.'

'Did I do something to upset you?'

'What?'

'Because if I did,' he continues, cutting across me, 'I'm sorry. Really, really sorry. I'm a jerk.'

I clench my jaw. Outside, Lily is waiting for me. I don't have time to listen while he wallows in self-pity. But I do have a couple of questions I'd like him to answer. One-handed, I zip up the holdall and swing it over my shoulder.

'Why are you really calling?' I ask pleasantly, as I turn off my bedroom light. 'Because you have a burning desire to talk to me, or because you're looking for a bit of colour for your piece?'

'Piece? Piece of what? What're you talking about?'

'And there you go again, as disingenuous as ever. But I won't be falling for that a third time.' I walk through to the kitchen, the phone pressed to my ear.

'Lara, help me out here,' Johnny pleads. 'I know I stood you up all those years ago and I'm really, really sorry. I was a prick. What else can I say? But I don't know what I'm supposed to have done wrong this time.'

I give a short bark of laughter. 'Cut the bullshit. I know what you did when you were in London. It's despicable. I think it's best for everyone if you don't bother to contact me again, OK? Goodbye, Johnny.'

I end the call, turn off the light and press my forehead against the door as darkness envelops me like a shroud.

44

LILY

Lara throws her bag onto the back seat and slams the door so violently the whole car shakes. Lily is about to ask her what's wrong when she clocks her aunt's expression and thinks better of it. Lara's mouth is set in a grim line as she stamps on the clutch. The gears grind and the little car leaps forwards, almost hitting the bumper of the van in front.

'Shit,' Lara mutters. She throws the car into reverse and the car jerks backwards. Then she accelerates into the road, the Fiesta's engine groaning with the effort.

Sod it, Lily thinks, throwing caution to the wind. 'Are you all right?' she asks.

'I'm fine.'

'Only you seem a bit... tense.'

Lara finally looks at her. 'Sorry.'

'Want to talk about it?'

'Not really.' Lara's face softens. 'But thanks anyway.'

They drive home in silence. Lily's just glad to be out of the hospital. She hates everything about it: the lingering smell of disinfectant and wee; the squeak of the nurses' shoes on the polished vinyl floor; the unforgiving brightness of the lighting that drains even the healthiest of complexions to a corpse-like pallor. It reminds her of when she was five. And she hates anything that reminds her of when she was five.

The rain is still drumming against the windscreen and the Fiesta's wipers are struggling to clear it. The thought of Gran's crumpled body being left in the middle of the road like a sack of rubbish as the rain pounded down on her makes Lily so angry she can almost taste it.

It must be why Lara's so livid, and Lily feels a sudden affinity with her aunt. She's glad they've made up, even if it had to be under such awful circumstances. She flicks a sideways glance at Lara.

'Thanks for everything,' she says.

Lara smiles properly for the first time all night. 'You're very welcome.'

It's gone midnight when they pull up outside the house. Lara mutters something about needing a shower and Lily pours herself a glass of milk and takes it up to her bedroom. All she wants to do is curl up under her duvet and forget about this nightmare of a day. She changes into her pyjamas and sits on her bed, scrolling through her phone as she sips her milk. Her TikTok account now has over twenty-five thousand followers, a number she'd never have believed possible even a couple of weeks ago. But it gives her no pleasure. The price her family is paying isn't worth it.

And it's all pointless anyway because she's no nearer to discovering the truth.

She picks up Barney Bear and fiddles with the strap of his cherry-red satchel. It's plastic but made to look like patent leather. It clashes horribly with his pink tutu, but, aged five, Lily hadn't cared. It was fun and shiny; Barney just had to have it. Lily used to hide things from her brothers in the satchel. Things she didn't want them to find, like her favourite glittery hair slide and the pearlescent oyster shell she found on the beach. Her pretties, Dad used to call them.

She absent-mindedly opens the satchel and feels inside, curious to see if any remnants from her childhood are secreted there. Her fingers close around a folded piece of paper. She pulls it out and unfolds it. Reads it. Closes her eyes. Opens them again and reads it a second time.

Four words and a phone number. Four words that have the power to blow up her life.

Lolly, call me. Please.

45

LILY

Lily's not sure how long she sits on her bed with the note in her trembling hands. Half an hour? An hour? At some point Lara pokes her head around the door and says goodnight, and somehow she dredges up a smile and says, 'See you in the morning.'

The note is from her dad, she has absolutely no doubt. He was the only person who ever called her Lolly. Everyone else – the rest of her family, her friends – have always shortened her name to Lils.

A memory floats to the surface. They were at the beach. Mum in a pretty yellow sundress, holding the twins' hands as they paddled in the shallows, both as naked as the day they were born. Dad was helping Lily build a sandcastle when they heard it: the delicious chime of an ice-cream van approaching.

Dad had looked at Lily, pointed to the van, which was pulling into the car park further up the beach, and said, 'Lolly, Lolly?' and she had found this so funny she'd laughed until tears rolled down her cheeks and her tummy hurt.

She's not laughing now, because nothing about this is at all funny. Dad has made contact and he wants her to phone him.

He left Barney and this explosive note at the cemetery a week ago. He's probably wondering why she hasn't called him already.

She knows she should show the note to Lara. But Lara will be straight on the phone to that twat Frampton, and the net will close around her dad, ending any chance Lily has of talking to him.

She cannot under any circumstances let that happen. She is consumed by a need to speak to him. She has to know what happened the night of the murders. It's like the urge to itch a mosquito bite. Even when you know the constant scratching will make the bite bleed, you just can't stop.

She picks up her phone and calls the number. It answers after three long rings.

'Dad?' she whispers. 'It's me. Lily.'

'You rang.'

He sounds different to how she remembers. There's a heaviness to his tone, as if he's on the verge of tears. But it's definitely him. She knows with every fibre of her being.

Even so, her voice is clipped when she replies. It's the only way she can keep a lid on all the emotions buzzing around in her head.

'Why are you contacting me?' she asks.

'I had to, Lily. There's something I need to tell you.'

'About Mum and the twins?'

'That's right. But not on the phone. I want to tell you face to face. I want to see you, Lily. I have missed you so, so much, baby girl.' His voice catches. Lily says nothing, letting him fill the silence.

'Can we meet?' he says.

'I... I don't know.'

'I know what you're thinking, but you'd be safe. I never meant for you to get hurt. I never meant for any of you to get hurt. And I'll never forgive myself for what happened.'

'The police are looking for you,' she says.

He gives a hollow laugh. 'Of course they are. I'm public enemy number one.' His voice breaks into a cough, a hacking sound that grates on Lily's already shredded nerves.

'D'you remember the cottage your nan and grandad stayed in when we moved to Sea Gem?'

Lily does. It was a tiny weatherboarded holiday let tucked down a stony track half a mile beyond the western boundary of the Sandy Lane Bay Estate. Nan and Gramps had rented the place for the week so they could help with the move. There was a hammock in the garden and a pebble-lined path that led straight down to the beach. Lily had spent a night there, sleeping on the top bunk in the second bedroom. She'd drifted off to the sound of the sea and the bell-like tinkle of wind chimes blowing in the breeze.

'Yes,' she says. 'I know it.'

'I'll be there on Saturday.'

'I don't know if I—'

'I'm asking you to trust me, Lolly. Come, please, and I'll explain everything.'

46

I'm showered and dressed by eight o'clock on Saturday morning. It's the day of Sean and Bianca's wedding at a beautiful country house fifteen miles from Tidehaven. Sean is a successful property developer who is in his late forties and on his third marriage. Bianca is a former swimwear model with her own YouTube channel and over a hundred thousand followers on Instagram.

Today is a big deal for me. Bianca has already told me she'll be posting my pictures all over social media, and the exposure I'll get could bring in a slew of new bookings.

It's a glorious morning and the weather is set fair for the day. I've already been to the venue to scope out opportunities, and I'm feeling a buzz of anticipation as I check my camera bag one last time.

When I poke my head around Lily's door, she's still asleep, her body curled around Barney Bear. She's meeting her friends Meena and Katy in town this morning, and this afternoon she's offered to visit Mum in hospital, which is just as well, as I'm not likely to be home until the early hours.

Back downstairs, I phone the hospital.

'Maggie had a comfortable night,' a nurse tells me when I'm put through to the ward. 'She's a force of nature, your mum, isn't she?'

I stifle a smile. 'She is.'

'The police were here again first thing, asking her about the accident. I hope they catch whoever hit her.'

'So do I. What time d'you think she'll be out of surgery?'

'Try calling after two.'

I thank her, leave a note for Lily saying her gran's had a good night, and head out of the house. The drive to the wedding venue should take just over half an hour but I'm leaving myself an extra hour, just in case, because being late is not an option. I'm lucky Marian and Bob were so nice about the memory card cock-up, but not all couples would have been so forgiving, which is why I need to be at the top of my game today. I've been so focused on Jason and Lily these last couple of weeks that my work has suffered. Wedding photography is a notoriously competitive industry and I've spent five long years growing my client base and building my portfolio. I can't afford to stuff up again.

My head's so full of the forthcoming wedding that it's not until I've stowed my camera bag in the boot of the car and am unlocking the driver's door that I notice the flat tyre.

It's OK, I tell myself. These things happen. At least there's a spare in the boot. I've never changed a tyre before but how hard can it be? I have plenty of time. And then I notice the back tyre's flat, too. I dart around to the other side of the car. Two more flat tyres. Not just flat, I realise with shock, but slashed. I drop onto my haunches and examine the front nearside tyre. Someone has taken a knife to it, and they haven't just scored it, they've hacked at it, taking chunks of rubber with them.

I stand up and look around wildly in case whoever's done this is watching me from a vantage point further up the close. They're not, of course. They're long gone.

I check the cars parked on neighbouring driveways. Their tyres are fine. So, too, are the cars parked on the other side of the road. The realisation that my car is the only one to be targeted sends a tremor of unease through me. But I don't have time to wonder who did this and why. I have a wedding to get to.

I can't take Mum's Clio – it's in the garage waiting for a new clutch to be fitted – so I'm straight on Google, looking up the phone numbers of local taxi firms. The first number rings out, the second is answered by a bored-sounding woman who tells me she can't get a car to me before nine forty-five. I'm ringing the third when I become aware of a car slowing down and someone calling my name.

Johnny, wearing shades and a baseball cap, is sitting in a little red sports car at the bottom of the drive.

'What are you doing here?' I ask, eyeing him with suspicion.

'I've brought you breakfast.' He reaches onto the passenger seat and waves a paper bag at me. 'Pastries and fresh orange juice. It's an apology for drunk-dialling you last night.'

'How did you know I was here?'

'I'd already tried your flat, and when you didn't answer I assumed you'd be at your mum's. So,' he says with a smile, 'fancy some breakfast?'

'I don't have time. I've got a wedding in Stonecross at ten. And some moron's slashed my tyres.'

His eyes widen as he takes in the lacerated rubber.

'Bloody hell,' he says, shaking his head. He nods to the passenger seat. 'Jump in. I'll take you.'

Hope flares inside me. 'Are you sure?'

'Of course. The old girl could do with a run.' He pats the steering wheel and I yank open the passenger door.

'Might a camera be useful?' he asks.

'Christ.' I clutch my face. 'Yes, it would. I'll get it. Thank you.' I grab the camera bag from the boot of the Fiesta and chuck it onto the back seat.

'Thank you,' I say again, as I fix my seat belt. DCI Frampton's warning about Johnny is still ringing in my ears but I ignore it. The fact is, I need a lift.

'Whereabouts in Stonecross is the wedding?' Johnny asks.

'Willowbrook Hall.'

He whistles. 'Very nice. Big do, is it?'

'Big enough.' I tell him about Bianca and her thousands of Instagram followers.

'So, this is huge for you.'

'Yep.'

'And who might want to ruin it?'

'I have no idea.'

It's a lie, of course. The moment I saw the deep gouges in my poor car's tyres, I knew exactly who did this and why.

LILY

The wind ruffles Lily's hair as she cycles along the sea wall towards the Sandy Lane Bay Estate. Her heart is racing, and not just with the exertion of the cycle ride. It's been crashing in her chest since the minute she woke this morning and remembered that today is the day she's going to see her dad.

She told Lara she's meeting Meena and Katy in town, and her aunt believed her, because why wouldn't she? Lily has never been a fibber, not even when she was small. But this is more than a fib. She isn't lying by omission. It's not even a little white lie. She is telling the biggest whopper she has ever told in her life and if Lara knew where she was really going, she would lose her shit.

Which is precisely why Lily hasn't told her.

As a precaution, Lily has taken herself off Find My iPhone again. Just for today. Not that Lara will have time to check up on her, because she has a wedding. Some fancy do at a country house. The bride's a well-known influencer with, like, a hundred thousand followers on Instagram. Lily was secretly impressed when Lara told her.

Gran won't check Lily's location because she's due to have

her operation this morning. All being well, Lily's going to catch the bus in to see her during visiting hours this afternoon as Lara won't be finished with the wedding until late.

All being well.

And if it isn't?

Lily stops that train of thought right there. Her dad wants to talk. That's all. And she wants to hear what he has to say.

The sea wall is about to peter out and Lily skids down the grassy embankment to the road. It's just a couple of hundred metres from here to the little toll booth at the entrance to the estate. Cars have to pay eight quid for the privilege of parking there, but bikes and pedestrians go free and the guy manning the booth waves as she pushes her bike through.

Once in, she stops to get her bearings. She was five when she was last here, but little seems to have changed in the past ten years. There are three main residential streets, all running parallel to each other and the beach. Their house, Sea Gem, was in Chetwynd Avenue, the road nearest the beach, and on an impulse, Lily swerves right and pedals furiously towards it.

When she reaches their old house, she leans on her handlebars and gazes up at it, reacquainting herself with the huge windows and curved white walls that always reminded her of a ship when she was little.

To her surprise, four cars are parked in the driveway and a babble of male voices drifts towards her from the back garden. A burst of laughter, as staccato as a gunshot, rings out.

'Stag do,' a voice behind her says, and Lily almost drops her bike in surprise. She looks round to see an elderly woman in the front garden of the bungalow next door. Her lined face is tanned and her chalk-white hair is piled on top of her head in an untidy updo. She peels off a pair of gardening gloves and brushes a stray strand of hair away from her face with the back of her hand.

Orange ice lollies, Lily thinks. This woman used to come

round to the house with homemade orange ice lollies on hot summer afternoons. She searches her memory for a name. Mary? Marilyn? No, Maureen. That's it. Her husband had a beard like Father Christmas and played the ukulele.

'I suppose I should be grateful it isn't a hen party,' the woman – Maureen – continues. 'They're far worse.'

'I used to live there,' Lily blurts.

'You did?' Maureen's head snaps round and Lily squirms under the scrutiny of her gaze. 'Goodness, are you Lily? Lily Carello?'

Lily nods. Maureen's hand flutters to her chest and for one awful moment Lily is worried she might be about to have a heart attack, but she quickly composes herself and her face breaks into a smile.

'Well, I never. I used to make you and your brothers ice lollies. Do you remember?'

Lily smiles back. 'Orange ones,' she says, and Maureen claps her hands in delight.

'That's right! How lovely to see you.' A shadow crosses her face. 'I'm so sorry about what happened.'

'It's not your fault.'

'I know. But, still.' She dips her head towards Sea Gem. 'What brings you back here?'

Lily can hardly tell the old woman she's about to meet up with her dad, who also happens to be the most wanted man in the county right now, so she improvises. 'I was on a bike ride and thought I'd come and see if it looked the same.'

'And does it?'

'Actually, it looks bigger. Grander. Like the house of a stranger. Who lives there now?'

'No one.' Maureen tuts. 'No families would touch it after... well, you know. It's an Airbnb now. They've put a pool in the back garden and advertise it as a venue for stag and hen dos. Just as well I'm as deaf as a post when I take my hearing aids out, otherwise I'd have to move.'

'Is your husband...?'

Her face falls. 'Dave died a couple of years after you lost your mum and brothers. It's just me now.' She brightens. 'I don't suppose you have time for a cup of tea?'

'I'm really sorry, I can't today. My gran's in hospital and I'm visiting her later. But I'd like to come another day, if that's all right with you?'

'It would be lovely,' Maureen says, snapping her gardening gloves back on. 'Just call in. I'm always here.'

Lily waves goodbye and sets off past Sea Gem. Maureen will assume she's doing a loop of the estate before returning to town along the sea wall, not that she's heading out to the isolated cottage half a mile past its western fringes.

Before Lily set off this morning, she checked the location on Google Street View, but the Google car with the 360-degree camera on top can't have ventured beyond the last house on the estate, because the pictures stop short of the track that leads to the cottage. It's as if the place doesn't exist.

Has her dad been staying there since he left the old fishermen's huts at the harbour? It's risky, sticking so close to home when the whole world is looking for him. Maybe he thinks his best bet is to hide in plain sight. Perhaps he plans to hand himself in once he's spoken to Lily. Who knows what's going on in his head. Lily sure as hell can't second-guess him.

She pedals past the last two houses, but before she turns right down the track to the cottage, she stops her bike and pulls out her phone to see if she still has a signal. There's one bar. Whether it stretches the half-mile to the cottage is another matter.

The track is rougher than Lily remembers and is pitted with deep potholes and sharp-edged flints. She swings a leg over the crossbar and begins to push. Not because she doesn't think her bike would cope with the rocks and craters – it's a mountain bike, of course it would – but because it grants her a little extra time to get her head round the fact that in a few minutes she will see her father.

That's if he's even here. It hadn't occurred to Lily until this morning, as she'd thrown her uneaten toast in the bin, that her dad never actually specified a time to come. What if he meant this afternoon? She can't come back later because she'll be at the hospital with Gran, and she can't leave him a note because she didn't think to bring a pen and piece of paper with her. What if he thinks she's a no-show and he vanishes again?

A feeling of helplessness rises inside Lily like seasickness. She is at the mercy of forces that are out of her control, the truth dangling tantalisingly beyond her grasp. The possibility that it could slip through her fingers is unbearable. She cannot – she *will* not – miss this chance to fill in the blanks in her past.

48

Johnny, it transpires, has his own theories about my slashed tyres.

'Maybe it's a climate change activist,' he says.

'My car's a six-year-old Ford Fiesta with a 1.1 engine, not a diesel-guzzling four-by-four,' I point out.

'Or a rival wedding photographer.'

I snort. 'Of course it's not a rival photographer. It'll be some random kid with nothing better to do.'

'Have you pissed anyone off recently?'

I tell him about stuffing up Marian and Bob's wedding photos. 'But they were so nice about it when I went round to their house to tell them. They even hand-delivered a thank-you note for the album I gave them.'

'So, they know where you live?'

'Yes, but they don't know where Mum lives. It can't have been them. Look, can you please drop the subject?'

'Sure.' Johnny's hands rest lightly on the steering wheel. The car has black leather seats and an array of chrome-ringed dials on the dashboard. I like the way the wind ruffles my hair as it bombs along the country lanes towards Stonecross.

'Nice car,' I say. 'Triumph Spitfire, is it?'

He looks affronted. 'It certainly is not. It's a 1972 MG Midget in blaze red. The best roadster to come out of Britain, in my humble opinion.'

'How long have you had it?'

It's a while before he answers, and I'm beginning to wonder if he heard me over the engine's throaty roar when he finally says, 'Just over ten years.'

'But you had a Golf when you were at *The Post*.' Occasionally Johnny had given me lifts to jobs. His beaten-up VW was a rats' nest of old cigarette packets, chewing gum wrappers, tatty notebooks, festering sandwich packaging and empty cans of Red Bull. This car, by contrast, is immaculate.

'I use the Golf for work. This little beauty only comes out on high days and holidays. And then only if it's not raining. Actually,' he says, his eyes on the road ahead, 'I bought it from JC Classics.'

'You bought this car from Jason?' I check, not sure I've heard him correctly.

'Uh-huh.'

I stare at him. 'You never thought to mention this to me?'

'What, that I owned a classic car?'

'No,' I growl with frustration. 'That you knew my brother-in-law!'

'That's because I didn't "know" him. I was passing the showroom on the way to a job about ten years ago and had a bit of time to kill so I popped in and had a mooch around. Twenty minutes later I walked out the proud owner of a classic sports car.' He chuckles. 'That guy could sell coals to Newcastle.'

I know Jason had a knack for parting people from their money. It's what made him such a successful businessman. What I didn't know is that he and Johnny had met. And it strikes me as strange that Johnny kept this quiet.

Questions buzz around my head, but I don't have a chance

to quiz him further as we've reached the turning for Willow-brook Hall. I decide to park my misgivings for now. I can't afford to waste energy worrying about Jason today. I need to focus on Sean and Bianca's wedding.

The MG crunches up the sweeping gravel drive towards the Queen Anne-style mansion. To our right is the famous line of weeping willows that gives the house its name, beyond which are acres of beautifully landscaped formal gardens.

'How much does it cost to hold a wedding in a place like this?' Johnny wonders as he pulls into a gravel lay-by to let a white van go past.

'If you have to ask, you can't afford it. You can drop me here, thanks.'

'Can't I come in and have a look round? You can pretend I'm your assistant. In fact, if you let me stay all day I can give you a lift home later.'

'I don't need a lift home. I'll call a cab.'

Johnny slides the gear stick into first and pulls back onto the drive. 'Go on, you'd be doing me a favour. I'll only end up spending the day in the pub, else. And that's never pretty.'

'But I won't be finished until gone midnight.'

'Fine by me.' He gives me a disarming smile. 'I'll carry your camera bag.'

I sigh. 'All right, I suppose you can stay. On two conditions: that you don't get under my feet and you do exactly what I say.'

'Deal,' he says, and he parks the MG and rushes round to the passenger door and opens it for me with a bow.

And in that instant, his effortless charm and easy manner remind me so much of my brother-in-law that I am momentarily blindsided.

49

Johnny hefts my camera bag onto his shoulder and looks up at the house. 'Who are we looking for?'

'Marta, the wedding planner. She'll be inside putting last-minute touches to the tables, I expect.'

'They have a wedding planner?' he says, impressed. 'What's she like?'

'The most organised person you're ever likely to meet.' I glance at him, at his fraying shirt and creased chinos, his mussed-up hair. 'She'd soon sort you out.'

'She sounds utterly terrifying.'

'She is, but her bark's worse than her bite.' Marta's wedding planning business was already well-established when I reached out to her three years ago and asked if she might be interested in working together. She summoned me to her office and scrutinised my portfolio before firing questions at me. What were my values? My photographic style? Was I happy to do boudoir shoots? How would I handle a complaint from a bride and groom? It felt like a job interview. I suppose it was.

Luckily, Marta decided I met her exacting standards and I have been one of her recommended photographers ever since.

The work she's sent my way has helped transform my fledgling career into a respected, successful photography business. I owe her a great deal.

Johnny follows me through the vast oak double doors and into the main hall, which is a sea of beautifully laid tables gleaming with silver-plated cutlery and sparkling glasses.

Marta is prowling around the room inspecting the table settings, with her hands clasped behind her back and a couple of nervous-looking teenage waitresses in her wake.

'That glass is smeary, and this setting is missing a butter knife. And can you please check every guest has a wedding favour and a packet of seeds.'

'Seeds?' Johnny whispers to me.

'Seeds,' I agree. 'Usually love-in-a-mist or forget-me-nots. They're a wedding staple these days.'

'Blimey. Who knew?'

'Mmm. Marta!' I call.

She turns round and when she sees me her face breaks into a scowl, which throws me, because we've always got on well. I check my watch, worried I'm late, but it's still only twenty to ten. Perhaps she's having a bad morning. One of those days when everything goes wrong. It happens.

'What are you doing here?' she asks.

I falter, confused. 'I'm taking the photos.'

'You told me you weren't coming. I don't like being let down at the last minute, Lara. It is not cool.'

'What do you mean, let down?'

'You should have given me more notice. It's been a nightmare trying to find someone to step in at the eleventh hour.'

'Marta, I don't know what you're talking about. I'm here, aren't I?'

She looks over my shoulder at Johnny, who is hovering awkwardly a step behind me.

'Who is he?' she asks suspiciously.

'Just someone shadowing me for the day. He's thinking of a career change.'

She isn't interested. 'You emailed me on Thursday saying you no longer wanted to work with me. No apology, no explanation. Nothing.'

'I *what*?'

Marta mutters something in Polish under her breath and pulls out her phone. She taps angrily at it, then hands it to me.

With a sense of foreboding, I skim-read the email.

Subject: The future

Marta,

It has become apparent to me that our working styles are no longer compatible, and I feel it is in the best interest of us both to part ways.

Therefore, I am terminating our association, effective immediately.

I am confident you will be able to find a suitable replacement.

As for me, I will be focusing on clients who value and respect my work.

Please do not contact me. My decision has been made.

Lara

Colour leaches from my face.

'But I didn't write this!'

Marta huffs. 'It's from your email account.'

'I swear I didn't, Marta. Why else would I be here? I must have been hacked.' I look desperately at Johnny, who takes the phone, lines scoring his forehead as he scrutinises the screen.

'Seems legit,' he says. 'Your email address is Lara Beckett ninety-one at Email Domain dot com?'

'Yes. No, wait a minute. There's a dot. It's Lara dot Beckett ninety-one. Let me see.' I grab the phone back. The account the email has come from has no full stop after Lara. 'This isn't mine. Look,' I say, waving the phone under Marta's nose. 'See?'

She regards me, her arms folded across her chest. 'Even if that is true, it's too late. I'm sorry, I had no choice but to make alternative arrangements. Luckily, Millie Ford had a slot in her diary.'

Millie Ford is a young, ambitious photographer with a huge following on Instagram and an inflated opinion of her own abilities. She won't do this wedding justice, I know she won't.

'What about next weekend?' I ask. I'm supposed to be taking the photos at another big wedding at a former priory on the outskirts of Tidehaven.

'Millie is covering your weddings until the end of October.' Marta sees my dismay and shrugs. 'I had to ask her, Lara. I have a business to run.'

'And after that?'

She sighs. 'After that, they're yours. But I don't understand. Who would do this to you?'

I'm about to tell her I have a pretty good idea who might want to wreck my career when I spot Johnny in my peripheral vision, watching me intently. I remember Frampton's warning.

I shrug, feigning bafflement. 'I have absolutely no idea.'

50

LILY

The cottage is smaller than Lily remembers. Smaller, and shabbier. It looks like the house made of wood in *The Three Little Pigs* – like it could blow down in a puff of wind.

When she stayed here with Nan and Gramps all those years ago, the cottage had been newly painted in a beautiful blue the colour of the Mediterranean, and the small garden was a riot of colour. Now the paint on the weatherboarding is peeling, and the flowers are losing the battle against an army of nettles and bindweed.

Lily leans her bike against the rickety picket fence at the front of the cottage and walks down the path on shaky legs. She steps inside the small porch and knocks twice on the door, her heart in her mouth.

Her nerves are so shredded that she startles when a shadow falls across the frosted glass panel and the door creaks open slowly.

And there he is. Her father. How can someone be both so familiar and yet a complete stranger? She doesn't recognise the khaki cargo shorts he is wearing, nor the faded navy T-shirt or the dusty Converse. She doesn't recognise his salt-and-pepper beard, nor the deep grooves in his forehead. But most of all she doesn't recognise the intense sadness in his eyes. Her father's eyes used to sparkle with life, with mischief. This man's gaze is a deep pool of sorrow.

'Lily.' His voice is gruffer than it used to be. 'You came.' Stepping aside, he gestures for her to come in. She falters on the threshold, torn between the desire to throw herself into his arms and never let go, and the impulse to jump on her bike and get the hell out of there.

She compromises by giving a curt nod and stalking past him into the hallway. The cottage smells musty, as if it's been shut up all summer, and she has to rub her nose to stop herself from sneezing.

'Would you like a cup of tea? Coffee?' her dad asks.

Lily frowns. What does he think this is – a social visit? He'll be producing a plate of fondant fancies at this rate. She shakes her head. 'You're all right, thanks.'

'Shall we sit in the garden?'

She stuffs her hands in her pockets and shrugs. 'Whatever.'

He leads her through the cottage to the kitchen and out of the back door. Lily is surprised to see the hammock is still there, flapping gently in the breeze. The wind chime too. And the pebble-lined path that leads down to the beach. For some inexplicable reason, knowing the sea is a short sprint away makes her feel safe.

They sit either end of a wooden bench that has been bleached silver by the sun.

Her dad clears his throat. 'I wasn't sure you'd come.'

'Neither was I,' Lily says. It's a lie – wild horses wouldn't have kept her away – but it wouldn't do to let him think he has some kind of hold over her, because he so doesn't. 'Although it was pretty stupid to hide your note in Barney's satchel. I almost didn't find it.'

'It's where you used to keep your pretties.' He smiles, and in that moment, Lily sees a glimmer of the man he used to be, the man she remembers. Her dad.

'I'm glad you're here. Believe me when I say I've wanted to contact you so many times over the last ten years.'

'Then why didn't you?' Lily knows how aggressive she sounds, but she can't help herself.

'Because it wasn't safe.'

'Safe for who? You, I suppose.' There are so many questions burning like acid inside her, she doesn't know where to start. So she tackles the easiest one she can think of. 'Where have you been for the last ten years?'

'Spain, mainly. A little village on the Portuguese border.'

'On your own?' Lily asks, because a horrific thought has just occurred to her. What if he'd settled down with a Spanish woman and replaced Lily, Jack and Milo with a brood of olive-skinned, black-haired, doe-eyed children? The thought makes her want to vomit.

'On my own,' he confirms. 'Apart from Valentina—'

Lily stiffens.

'My cat,' he continues. 'She was part of the fixtures and fittings when I moved into the finca.' He must see Lily's expression, because he adds, 'It's OK, my landlady's feeding her for me while I'm away.'

'And how long exactly are you planning to be away?'

'That depends,' her dad says levelly.

'On what?'

'On you. And on... other stuff.'

Lily jumps to her feet. Even though they're outside, she feels a squeeze of claustrophobia. 'I'm going to get a glass of water, if that's all right?'

'Of course it is. You know where everything is.'

She disappears through the back door into the kitchen and, after a couple of false starts, finds a set of six cloudy tumblers in the cupboard over the toaster. She takes one, filling it to the brim from the old-fashioned tap, and sips it while she watches her father through the window.

He is sitting on the bench where she left him, his face buried in his hands. His shoulders are shaking. He is crying, she realises. Great shuddering sobs, by the look of it. The sight makes her feel awkward. Discombobulated. Because what's she supposed to do, comfort him? Tell him everything is going to be OK when it so clearly isn't?

And surely he should be the one comforting her?

After a moment's hesitation, Lily grabs a second glass from the cupboard, fills it with water and retraces her steps back outside. Hearing her approach, her dad visibly collects himself, and when she offers him the glass, he somehow musters a smile.

'Why were you crying?'

'Because everything is so fucked up.' He shakes his head. 'Sorry, I didn't mean to swear.'

'Don't apologise. You should hear Lara when she's on one.'

He wipes his nose on the back of his hand. 'Lara? God, how is she?'

'She's a successful wedding photographer now.' Lily can't hide the pride in her voice. 'Though she'd rather take pictures of landscapes. In fact, she took the photo the police talked about in the press conference.' Too late, Lily realises her mistake, and closes her mouth abruptly.

'What photo?' her dad says.

'Doesn't matter.'

'And your gran?'

Lily's head drops to her chest. 'She's in hospital.'

'Hospital?'

'She was hit by a car on her way home from yoga last night.'

Her dad's reaction catches Lily by surprise. It's like someone's flipped a switch, and he jumps to his feet in an explosion of energy. 'Who? Who hit her?'

'The police don't know.' Lily's eyes widen as her dad paces

up and down the garden, his hands laced behind his head. 'It was a hit-and-run.'

'Is she all right?'

'She's having an operation on her hip this morning. I'm seeing her later.'

'Jesus,' he mutters. He drops to his knees in front of her and takes her hands in his. 'You need to be careful, sweetheart.'

His hands are rough and callused, but his grip is warm. These hands washed her, fed her and cradled her. They soothed away fevers and rubbed her hurts better. But they also stole Lily's entire family from her. She blurts, 'Why did you do it, Dad? Why did you kill them?'

When his eyes meet hers she sees her own grief mirrored back at her. She holds her breath.

'I didn't,' he says finally.

'Then who did?'

He looks away. 'I can't tell you that.'

'Why not?'

'Because it would put you in danger, and I can't bear to lose you too.'

She snatches her hands away from his and rears up out of her seat. 'You can't bear to lose me? Don't make me laugh.' She glares at him, her hands on her hips, anger coursing through her. 'Even if I did give you the benefit of the doubt and accept that someone else killed Mum, Jack and Milo – and that's a big "if", by the way – then why the hell did you fuck off and leave me? You were all I had left in the world, and you walked out on me.'

'You had your gran and Lara.'

A lump has lodged itself in Lily's throat and it's a struggle to speak, but she forces the words out. She needs to get this off her chest. 'But I wanted *you!*'

He sighs heavily. 'For right or wrong, I made a choice, and once it was made there was no turning back. But please believe me when I say that I have regretted my decision every hour of every day since.'

Lily shakes her head. 'It's all a bit convenient, isn't it? You claim it wasn't you but you won't tell me who it was. I'm sorry, *Jason*, but I don't believe you.'

'Lily!' he pleads. 'Let me explain.'

She holds up a hand. '*No!* I've heard enough. I'm going now. And don't bother trying to contact me because I never want to see you again. You are not my father. You're a... a *monster*.'

51

Marta strides off, muttering something about the flowers on the top table, leaving Johnny and me staring at each other uncertainly.

Johnny tweaks his earlobe, then pulls a face. 'What do you want to do?'

I shrug. 'Go home, I suppose. It's clear I'm not needed here.'

'Are you sure you don't want to fight your corner?'

'What's the point?' I tramp towards the door. 'Anyway, I need to check that whoever emailed Marta hasn't contacted anyone else.'

'Shit,' Johnny says, following me. 'You think they might have?' He stops. 'Hey, you don't think this has anything to do with your tyres being slashed?'

'I don't know.' I step out of the front door, almost colliding with a statuesque woman with poker-straight blonde hair and a look of lofty superiority. Millie Ford.

'Lara Beckett,' she says, doing an almost comedic double-take. 'I thought you bailed.' Her eyes narrow. 'What are you doing here?'

'There was a misunderstanding, but don't worry, I'm just going.'

'Marta's asked me to cover another four of your weddings in the next couple of months. Not ill, are you?'

'Not ill, no.' I keep my expression neutral. The last thing I need is to give Millie even a hint that my photography business is in trouble, because if she smells blood, she'll move in quicker than a pack of hyenas.

Her gaze drifts from me to Johnny and back again, and her eyes widen. 'Do you perhaps have some news of your own?' she says with a smirk.

Johnny puts his arm around my shoulder and grins. 'We couldn't possibly comment.' He drops a kiss on my cheek and I catch a whiff of tobacco. 'Come on, babe, we're going to be late for your dress fitting.' And he gently steers me towards the MG.

Once I'm sure we're out of sight, I extricate myself from his grip and hiss, 'What the hell did you say that for?'

'Better for her to think you're getting hitched than to suspect someone's playing fast and loose with your business.' He opens the passenger door for me and I slump into the seat.

Soon we're back on the road, but this time everything about Johnny's car grates on my nerves: the way the breeze messes up my hair; the slippery leather seats; the whine of the engine.

'I was joking when I said it might have been a rival photographer who has it in for you, but now I've seen Ms Ford I'm not sure I was too far off the mark,' he says, glancing at me.

'It wasn't Millie,' I say tiredly.

'Then who was it?'

I'm grateful when Johnny's phone chooses that moment to ring. He snatches it from its holder on the dashboard, but not before I see 'Unknown Caller' on the screen.

'Hello,' he mutters. 'Yes, just hold on for a sec while I pull over.' He checks his mirror, pulls onto the verge and kills the engine. 'Sorry,' he mouths to me, then climbs out of the car and starts walking up the lane, the phone pressed to his ear.

I scrabble about in my bag for my phone. I should go through my diary and call all my clients to check they haven't received similar emails to the one sent to Marta, but I don't have the energy. Instead, I scroll half-heartedly through my Instagram feed, as snippets of Johnny's one-sided conversation drift towards me on the breeze.

'You have my absolute word... Yes, I understand, but I would never reveal my source... In that case, we need to move quickly...'

I slip my phone into my pocket, wondering which poor soul is on the receiving end of Johnny's desperate cajoling.

After a few minutes it looks as if the conversation is winding up. I flip open the sun visor to check there's nothing stuck in my teeth. A piece of card floats to the floor. With a grunt I lean forwards to pick it up. It's a business card for Trev's garage in Tidehaven.

Trev's Auto Repairs: Your Car's Best Friend

I'm about to stick it back in the flap in the sun visor when something occurs to me. Johnny probably met Trev when he bought his MG from Jason, but Trev worked for JC Classics then, not at his own garage in Tidehaven. And Johnny was with me when I paid a visit to Trev's garage the day of the press conference. Why would he have needed a business card?

Of course, there could be a perfectly innocent explanation. Perhaps he wanted to book the MG in for a service and MOT and chose Trev's workshop because he's experienced in fixing classic cars.

But what if there isn't? What if Johnny's digging around in my family's business for his true crime podcast?

I want to give him the benefit of the doubt again, but I can't, because I know for a fact that nothing comes between Johnny and a story. Anger floods through me, hot and urgent. I will not let him take me for a fool. And I will *not* let him hang what's left of my family out to dry.

'Who was that?' I ask, the moment he slides back behind the wheel.

He looks at me warily. 'Just a contact for a podcast idea I'm working on.'

'What podcast idea?'

He shifts in his seat. 'I can't talk about it yet. You know, in case it doesn't check out. Sorry.' He turns the key in the ignition and the MG growls into life. 'Back to your mum's?' he asks.

I picture Mum's place: the breakfast dishes piled high in the sink; the thick silence of an empty house; my poor car with its four slashed tyres parked outside like a warning. I shake my head, a sinking feeling settling in my chest. 'Can you drop me at the hospital instead?'

Mum's still in the recovery room when I arrive on the ward, so I nurse a coffee in the cafe in the foyer while I brood over everything that's happened in the last two weeks.

I pull a notebook and pen out of my bag, hoping that if I write everything down, I might make sense of it all.

- My photo – proof Jason's back in Tidehaven.
- Lily's videos, telling the world she's starting to remember what happened – the catalyst for everything?
- Tenth anniversary of the murders – relevant, or a coincidence?
- Flowers on Isabelle's grave – Jason?

- Trev is looking after Jason's Austin Healey – does he know where Jason is?
- Johnny has Trev's business card. What story is Johnny working on? What can Trev tell him?
- DCI Frampton – Jason's golf buddy and in charge of the murder investigation. Is he protecting Jason? If so, why?
- Why did Jason slash my tyres and send me a threatening note? As revenge for me telling the police he's back in Tidehaven?

I reread what I've written several times, as if the words are going to magically rearrange themselves into something that makes sense. But the more I stare, the more jumbled it all becomes and I throw the pen down in frustration.

Keen for a distraction, I pick up my phone and check my emails. There are twelve new items in my inbox and most of them are junk. But one catches my eye. It's from someone calling themselves UnknownWatcher. Frowning, I click on it. There's no text in the body of the email, just a photograph. The hospital Wi-Fi must be slow because it takes an age for it to load and when it finally does, it's a moment before I realise what I'm looking at.

It's Lily, walking across a patch of waste ground. She's wearing the cropped top and cargo trousers she wore the day of the press conference, her denim jacket tied around her hips. Her head is angled slightly away from the camera and there's an AirPod in her ear. She is frowning, lost in her own thoughts. Behind her, the sky is granite grey. I know where this was taken, I realise suddenly. It's the waste ground at the back of Mum's estate. Mum will have kittens if she finds out Lily walked home that way. She's always drilling into her how important it is that she walks through the estate if she's on her own.

Only she isn't on her own, is she? Because whoever took this photo, whoever sent it to me, was there with her, whether Lily realised it or not.

52

I flinch like I've been slapped when my phone breaks into life, buzzing in my hand. I check the screen. Unknown caller.

'Who is this?' I snarl. 'And what the fuck do you think you're doing, taking photographs of my niece, you pervert!'

'Is that Lara?' a woman says hesitantly. 'Lara Beckett? It's Justine, the staff nurse on Rotary ward?' She says it with an upward inflection, as if she's not sure of herself. 'I just wanted to let you know that your mum's out of recovery.'

Shit. I take a deep breath and exhale slowly. 'I'm so sorry. I thought you were someone else.'

'Right. Well, she's back on the ward if you want to pop up and say hello.'

'Thank you. I'll be right up.'

I drain the last dregs of my coffee and am about to shove the notebook and pen back in my bag when I pause, then add a final line to my page of notes.

- Photo of Lily alone – another warning? Who knew where she would be?

If Jason took this photograph, what is he trying to tell me? That he can pick Lily off like a sniper whenever he chooses? And how did he know where she'd be that night? It can't have been a lucky guess. He must have been following her, and if that's the case he could be following her now.

I dial her number, my heart thudding in my ribcage as I wait for the call to connect. I won't tell her about the photo – I don't want to scare the life out of her – I'll just tell her that her gran's out of surgery and is asking to see her. She should be safe enough coming straight to the hospital from town. The phone rings and rings, then switches to voicemail.

I leave a message asking her to call me straight back, then open the Find My iPhone app but see with a flash of annoyance that she's taken herself off it again. Mum's phone is showing as being at Tidehaven Police Station. One of the police officers who found her after the accident must have taken it back with him. I sigh. I'll have to pop in to collect it, I suppose.

I take the lift to Rotary ward and make a beeline for the nurses' station where I ask for Justine. One of the other nurses points to Mum's bay, and I head over.

Justine is keeping up a steady stream of chatter as she takes Mum's blood pressure. I clear my throat and they both look up.

'Hello, love,' Mum croaks. Her hair's all over the place and her cheeks are almost as pale as her pillow. 'Where's Lily?'

'She's on her way.' *I hope*, I add silently as I perch on the chair beside her bed. 'How are you doing?'

'I feel like I've been run over by a bus, although that nice man from the police tells me it was definitely a car.'

'Your mum's a bit groggy, but she's doing great, aren't you, Maggie?' Justine says.

I catch the nurse's eye. 'I'm so sorry about before.' I grimace. 'Bad day.'

She smiles. 'No apology necessary. I was just telling Maggie here that she's to press the buzzer if she's uncomfortable and I'll be right over.' She undoes the cuff of the blood pressure monitor and scribbles something on the chart at the end of Mum's bed. 'I'll leave you to it.'

'What nice man from the police, Mum?' I ask once Justine's gone.

'You know, the one who came to the house to see Lily.'

'DCI Frampton?'

'That's him.' Mum waves her hand at the jug on her bedside cabinet. 'Be a love and pour me a glass of water, will you?'

As I busy myself pouring water into her glass and adjusting her pillows, I wonder why a detective chief inspector is visiting a sixty-four-year-old victim of a hit-and-run. It might make more sense if I had phoned to tell him about the accident and asked him to pull rank to make sure it was investigated properly. But with Sean and Bianca's wedding on my mind, I'd clean forgotten. So how did he know she was here?

'What did DCI Frampton want?' I say, handing Mum the glass. She takes a couple of small sips and dabs at her chin with a tissue.

'He said he was on duty this weekend and the accident was mentioned at a meeting. When he heard it was me, he wanted to come and check I was all right.'

I feel myself relax. Of course. It makes sense. Hit-and-runs are hardly common in Tidehaven. No doubt it's the talk of the police station.

'That's good of him,' I say.

'He's very thoughtful. He brought me those.' Mum nods at a pot of bilious salmon-pink begonias on the bedside cabinet. The housewife's pot plant of choice, available at every supermarket in the land. But Mum is clearly touched. I realise she's still speaking.

'Sorry, Mum, what did you say?'

'I said that policeman of yours was certainly a hit with the nurses. I've never seen so many in one place at the same time.'

Her giggle turns into a coughing fit, and I jump up and rub her back until it stops, glad of the distraction. I don't want her noticing my flushed cheeks.

'Firstly, he's not a policeman. No one calls them that these days. He's a police *officer*,' I say. 'And secondly, he's not "mine". Why ever would you think he was?'

'Because he spent most of his visit talking about you. And Lily, of course,' she adds. 'He's very concerned about the pair of you.'

'Concerned?'

'He's worried about Lily's videos and the rumpus they're causing, and he's afraid Johnny's taking advantage of you.'

'Never mind us. You're the one who ended up in hospital. Did he say whether they were any closer to finding the driver?'

Mum winces in pain as she slumps back on her pillow. 'No. It's a complete mystery apparently. It's as if the driver vanished into thin air.'

'People don't just "vanish into thin air",' I tell her, even though bitter experience has taught me exactly the opposite is true.

53

LILY

You are not my father. You're a monster. The words buzz round and round Lily's head on the bike ride home like a wasp trapped in a jam jar.

Jason – she refuses to think of him as Dad any more – had pleaded with her not to leave, but she couldn't bear to breathe the same air as him a moment longer. Her desire to run even overshadowed her need to know what happened the night of the murders.

'Let me explain, Lily, please?' he'd said, his voice low and urgent. 'All this,' he'd lifted his arms then dropped them again in a gesture of defeat. 'It's not what you think.'

'Not interested,' she'd said, pushing past him. She had to get away, and so she ran through the cottage and down the front path with wings on her heels. She jumped on her bike and pedalled harder than she'd ever pedalled in her life, sending gravel spraying in her wake.

Only when she reached the end of the lane did she look back.

Jason was standing in the open gateway, his shoulders slumped, watching her.

Lily slows down once she reaches the Sandy Lane Bay Estate, but even when her heart rate has returned to normal, she can't stop her racing thoughts.

Jason said he didn't kill her mum and the twins, but he point-blank refused to tell her who did, claiming it was 'for her own safety'. Lily doesn't buy it. If he was innocent, why had he run? It makes no sense.

She stops by the little toll booth at the entrance to the estate and checks her phone. There's a voicemail from Lara, left just over half an hour ago.

'Hey, Lily. I've just heard from the hospital. Gran's out of surgery. Can you call me?'

Lily phones Lara straight back.

'It's me. How is she?'

'You can ask her yourself if you like.' Lily hears a muffled exchange before Gran comes to the phone.

'Hello, love. Did you have a nice time in town?'

Lily bites her bottom lip. 'Yeah, good thanks. How are you feeling?'

'Oh, I'm fine. Well, I will be once Lara stops fussing.'

'Why isn't she at her wedding?'

'There's been a change of plan, apparently. I'll pass you back to her.'

Lara comes back on the phone. 'Where are you now?'

'Town,' Lily lies. 'I just need to pop my bike back home and then I'll catch the bus over.'

'No, don't do that,' Lara says quickly. 'Drop it at mine and you can catch the fifty-eight from the end of the road.'

Lily's about to protest when she realises it makes sense. Cycling all the way home will add at least another half an hour to the journey and she has an overpowering urge to be with her family.

'OK,' she says. 'I'll see you in a bit.'

* * *

Lily finds a seat on the top deck of the double decker, plugs in her earbuds and stares out of the window as the bus trundles through town.

After a couple of stops, two Year Seven girls from her school clamber up the steps clutching Accessorize carrier bags. When they see Lily, their mouths fall open, as if they've just come across Taylor Swift on board the number fifty-eight. Lily can hear their whispers as they shuffle into a seat a couple of rows behind her. Only when she turns round and shoots them a filthy look do they shut up.

She regrets opening up her heart on TikTok. She thought sharing her deepest thoughts would be empowering when in actual fact it has made her feel slightly grubby, as if she has been exploiting her mum, Jack and Milo for her own gain.

Which, if she's brutally honest with herself, isn't so very far from the truth.

She doesn't want to be an influencer any more, because being one is a bit like riding a roller coaster. The highs and lows. The permanent swooping sensation in the pit of your belly. The unnerving feeling that you can't step off until the end of the ride.

When Lily recorded her first video she'd felt in control of her own destiny for the first time in her life, and that was liberating. She watched her followers grow from a few dozen to over fifty thousand with a mixture of incredulity and excitement. And for a while it was great. Really great. Not only was she rocking her content and building a platform to be proud of, but everyone was so sympathetic and caring every time she posted a new video...

...until they weren't.

Over the last couple of days some of the comments have been toxic.

Here she goes again, the whiny little bitch.

Dontcha wish the silly cow would just SHUT THE FUCK UP???!!!

Nice tits, shame about the face.

Pity her dad didn't finish what he started.

Lily has tried to scroll on by, but it's almost impossible to ignore the bile. Even the nice comments, the virtual hugs and entreaties to 'stay strong, you've got this, hun', rankle.

Worse still are the sympathetic smiles people flash her when they recognise her in the street, as if they know her. They don't. How can they, when Lily barely knows herself?

Influencing is not a dream job. She doesn't want to be pressurised into posting increasingly personal content just to keep the algorithms happy. She doesn't want the online abuse or the lack of privacy. In short, she doesn't want fame. She wants to be a regular fifteen-year-old. Ordinary and unremarkable.

The two Year Seven girls have started whispering again. It's enough to make Lily's mind up. Tonight, she will delete her TikTok account. She will make one last video explaining why. She will thank her followers for watching and she will tell them that if she remembers more about the night her mum and brothers died, she will do what she should have done in the first place and tell the police, not the internet.

When Lara inevitably says, 'I told you so,' Lily will take it on the chin, and agree that trying to establish her own platform was a stupid thing to do. And maybe, if she's really lucky, her flash-in-the-pan fame will fade away.

Because Lily is very happy to be a nobody again.

54

I watch through the kitchen window as Trev fastens the last of the four ratchet straps securing my car to his flatbed trailer.

It was Johnny's idea to call him.

'He'll be glad to help,' he said as he dropped me off at the hospital. 'And you'll knacker the wheels if you drive anywhere with four flat tyres.'

Annoyingly, he was right. Trev offered to come straight over when I rang and explained what had happened, and he was pulling up outside Mum's when Lily and I arrived home from the hospital.

He jumped out of his truck, his eyes widening when he saw the slash marks in the rubber. 'To paraphrase the great Oscar Wilde, to lose one tyre may be regarded as a misfortune; to lose four looks like carelessness. Have you reported this to the rozzers?'

'I didn't have you down as a literary aficionado, Trev. And yes, I have. They've given me a crime number and told me to notify my insurance company.'

'And that's it? No forensics, no nothing?' He shook his head.

'Little wonder the country's going to the dogs. Be a love and stick the kettle on while I'll get 'er on the trailer, will you?'

Lily was uncharacteristically quiet as she followed me into the house. She kicked off her trainers, pulled out a chair at the kitchen table and sat down heavily.

'Everything OK, Lils?' I asked.

'Just peachy,' she said. 'Gran's in hospital after being mown down by a hit-and-run driver, your tyres have been slashed by a madman with a knife, and as for Jason, well, where do I start?'

I glanced at her sharply. 'What about Jason?'

'Nothing,' she said, springing up from her seat and heading for the door. 'I'm going to my room. I've got a ton of homework.'

'Want a cup?' I asked, waving a mug at her.

She shook her head and, shoulders slumped, trudged through the hallway and up the stairs. Clump, clump, clump.

Bloody Jason, I thought. The bastard still had the power to turn our lives upside down from whichever rock he was hiding under.

Now, I put two mugs and a packet of biscuits on a tray and carry them outside. Trev is fixing wheel chocks in place but stops when I appear and we both perch on the end of the trailer and drink our tea.

'One of my mates has a tyre place. Says he'll pop four new tyres round first thing Monday. You can pick her up Monday lunchtime,' he says.

'Thanks so much. You're a lifesaver.'

'Don't mention it. Jason would want me to help.'

'Jason?' It comes out more sharply than I intend and Trev's eyes widen a fraction before he downs his tea and sets his mug on the tray.

'Time I made a move.'

My inner alarm bells are ringing. Trev hasn't even taken a biscuit and he's already patting his trousers, searching for his keys. But before I have a chance to quiz him, a police patrol car pulls up at the bottom of the drive.

'Looks like they took your call more seriously than you thought,' Trev says. Is it my imagination, or does he seem grateful for the interruption? Not that he can leave – the patrol car's blocking his way.

I peer at the driver. 'Oh, it's Josie.'

'Who's Josie?'

'She was our family liaison officer when Isabelle and the twins died.' A terrible thought occurs to me. What if something's happened to Mum? Although it was a routine operation, there's always a small risk of complications. A pulmonary embolism, for instance. But the hospital would ring if Mum had taken a turn for the worse, surely? They wouldn't send the police.

Josie jumps out of the car and ambles up the drive, smiling a welcome. Not the body language of someone delivering bad news, and I relax a little.

The smile fades when she sees the slashed tyres and her jaw drops. 'What on earth happened to your car?'

'That's not why you're here?'

She shakes her head. 'I heard about Maggie and wanted to check you and Lily were all right. When did this happen?'

'Last night. I've reported it and Trev's going to get me some new tyres.' I look around but Trev has disappeared into the house, taking the tray with him.

'Trev?' Josie asks. 'The guy who used to work for Jason?' She frowns. 'I thought you'd lost touch.'

'We had.' I'm about to tell her that Jason's Austin Healey is hidden under a tarpaulin in Trev's garage when he reappears, wiping his hands on his T-shirt.

'Sorry, call of nature,' he says. He jangles his keys at Josie. 'Don't suppose you could... Wait a minute, don't I know you?'

'I just told you, Josie was our FLO.'

She nods rapidly. 'You probably recognise me from the funeral.'

His eyes narrow as he scrutinises her, then he shrugs. 'Yeah, probably.' He touches my arm. 'I'll be off then. You take care of yourself, and I'll see you Monday lunchtime.'

Josie moves the patrol car, and Trev toots a farewell as he drives away. I feel a rush of gratitude towards him. Not many people would have dropped everything to come to my rescue. I was on the cusp of telling Josie about the Austin Healey and my suspicions that Trev is protecting Jason, but I change my mind. I can't work out whether this is out of misguided loyalty or an instinctive belief that he is a good man. Whatever the reason, I will keep the information to myself, for the moment at least.

'Penny for them,' Josie says, joining me on the drive. Tendrils of her ash-blonde hair have come loose from her bun and frame her heart-shaped face. Her grey eyes are kind. Sympathetic.

'Oh, they're not worth it.' I smile. 'C'mon, I'll make you a cuppa.'

Inside, Josie takes a seat at the kitchen table.

'How's Maggie doing?' she asks.

'The operation went well, but it's going to be a while before she's back to normal. DCI Frampton went to see her this morning.'

'He went to the hospital?' Josie says, surprised.

'Apparently. He bought Mum flowers.' I pull a face. 'I thought it was odd, if I'm honest.'

Josie is silent.

'The thing is,' I continue, 'Mum was wearing Lily's coat when she was hit. And that's not all. Someone sent me this earlier.' I find the photo of Lily walking through the waste ground and show it to Josie. Her eyes bulge for the briefest of moments before she rearranges her features into her usual unruffled expression. 'What d'you think it means? Is it a threat?' I ask her.

'Possibly,' she admits. 'Has Lily seen it?'

I shake my head. 'I think she's got enough on her plate, don't you?'

55

LILY

Lily unpacks her schoolbag, setting her maths textbook, exercise book, calculator and a couple of pens on her desk. They are doing probability at the moment, which seems more useful than, say, algebra or prime numbers.

'Probability is measuring how likely something is to happen,' Mr Evans, their maths teacher, had explained in class. 'It's used in everything from economics and finance to genetics and physics. The probability of something happening lies between nought and one, where nought means impossible, and one means certain. The higher the probability, the more chance of that event happening.'

What's the probability Jason is guilty, Lily thinks, as she picks up a pen and twirls it between her fingers. He fled after the murders, abandoning his sole remaining child. If that wasn't an admission of guilt, she didn't know what was. Based on what Mr Evans said, the probability is one.

But even as she thinks this, doubts creep into her head. Why would he come back to Tidehaven if he was guilty? What was it he wanted to explain? Of course, she'll never know because she never gave him a chance.

Lily flings the pen on her desk, folds her arms over her books and buries her head in them, like a burrowing animal. Right now, she would like nothing more than to disappear down a hole and never come out. She stays like that until there's a knock at the door and Lara lets herself in.

'Hey,' Lara says, sitting on the end of her bed. She's holding her phone. With a dart of panic, Lily hopes she hasn't had a call from the hospital.

'Is Gran OK?' she asks.

'She's fine. But I do need to show you something.' Lara passes the phone over. On the screen is a photo of Lily taking a shortcut through the waste ground on the day of the press conference. She eyes her aunt with suspicion.

'If you took this to prove a point, you needn't have bothered. I won't go that way again. It's not worth the flippin' fuss,' she adds under her breath.

'I didn't take it,' Lara says. 'It was sent to me in an email. See?'

Lily glances down to where Lara is pointing. 'Who the hell is "Unknown Watcher"?' she asks.

'I don't know, but if I was going to hazard a guess, I'd say it was someone trying to warn you off posting more videos. I wasn't going to show you because I didn't want you freaking out, but Josie told me I should. This is why I've been nagging you to be careful.'

'What's the probability of someone actually doing something to me?' Lily says. 'Closer to zero than one, I'd say.'

Lara looks at her blankly. 'What?'

'Doesn't matter.' Lily hands the phone back to her aunt. 'Doesn't mean anything. Don't worry about it. I'm not going to.' She looks meaningfully at her textbooks. 'If that's all, I really need to get this done.'

'Sorry. I'll leave you to it.' Lara hauls herself to her feet, then gives Lily's shoulder a squeeze. For some weird reason the gesture makes Lily want to bawl, but she stares at the numbers in her textbook with ferocious concentration until the door clicks shut and she is alone.

Only then does she sob. Silent, juddering tears that leave her hollowed out like the coconut Dad once won for her when the fair came to town. He punched out the eye and drained the coconut's milky water before attacking it with a meat cleaver and prising the flesh away from the hairy shell with a paring knife.

If she closes her eyes Lily can almost taste the sweet, nutty flesh. Like a Bounty bar, only a hundred times better.

A memory slips, unbidden, into her head. Milk chocolate melting on her tongue on a hot summer's afternoon. Next, the tropical taste of shredded coconut. She is outside in the garden, splashing about in the paddling pool with Jack and Milo. Her mum's just had to refill it because Milo peed in the water, turning it yellow. Lily had thrown a hissy fit, and Mum had brought out a bag of fun-size Bounty bars to placate her.

Mum gave Lily and the twins two bars each and told them to be good because her friend was here and she needed to talk in peace. Lily hadn't realised there was anyone else in the house, but when she looked through the kitchen window, she could see Mum with a man. Not Daddy, this man was too tall and had really dark, almost black hair and Daddy's hair was brown and curly like hers.

Lily let the sugary sweetness dissolve in her mouth as she watched her mum and the man talking.

'Don't like it,' Jack said, spitting a mouthful of his Bounty bar into the paddling pool where it floated, white and brown, like an enormous bird poo, right by Lily's foot.

She shrieked and jumped out of the pool, sending a shower of droplets over her brothers, who made her even crosser when they fell about laughing.

'Mum!' she roared, legging it across the lawn to the back door. 'Jack's sicked in the paddling pool!'

She skidded to a halt on the doorstep. Her mum and the man weren't talking any more, they were hugging really tightly, and the man was making a funny groaning noise, like he'd stubbed his toe or something. As Lily watched, the man lifted her mum onto the kitchen island and started kissing her all over her face. And although Lily was only five, she knew that while mummies were allowed to kiss daddies and their sons and their grandads, they weren't supposed to kiss other men. It was against the law or something. And so, Lily coughed, and both her mum and the man jumped about a foot in the air, and the man said a rude word and Mummy looked so white it was as if Lily was a ghost and had just haunted her. And she stared at the man to see if she recognised him. He had a square face, thin lips and cold blue eyes.

Lily didn't recognise him then. But she does now. She clamps her hands to her face as the memory sharpens in her mind. The man in the kitchen at Sea Gem that summer afternoon ten years ago, the man who was eating her mum's face off, was DCI Curtis Frampton.

56

I spend Monday morning editing the photos from Brooke and Callum's wedding and at half eleven set off on the forty-minute walk to Trev's garage. It's a beautiful day and the sun is high in a cloudless blue sky. I try to stick to the shady side of the street but it's not long before beads of sweat have broken out across my forehead and my T-shirt is stuck to my back.

On Josie's advice I showed Lily the photo of her crossing the waste ground the night of the press conference.

'Imagine how you'd feel if something happened and you hadn't warned her,' Josie had said. And even though I hadn't wanted to worry Lily, I knew she was right.

Lily had stared at the photo for a moment, her frown deepening, then she'd shrugged. 'Doesn't mean anything,' she'd said. 'Don't worry about it. I'm not going to.'

Easy for her to say. But I made her promise to meet Meena and walk with her to the bus stop this morning, and I told her I would be outside school at three-thirty on the dot to give her a lift to the hospital to see Mum. Her objection was half-hearted, which is when I knew how rattled she really was.

I arrive at Trev's workshop just after twelve, dripping with perspiration. The radio is still playing glam rock, but the Peugeot and BMW have been replaced by a Citroën Picasso and a Nissan Micra. My Fiesta, sporting four new high-performance Goodyear tyres, is parked in front of the workshop doors. I wince, wondering how much they're going to set me back. Given the choice, I'd have gone for budget tyres. But I can't complain. Trev was only trying to help.

My eyes are drawn to the Austin Healey concealed under the grey tarpaulin at the back of the workshop. I itch to yank the tarpaulin off, like a magician doing the pulling-off-the-tablecloth trick. *So, Trev, how exactly did you come to have Jason's car in your garage?* But Trev's already spotted me and is beckoning me into his office. I head over. The questions can wait.

He pushes a half-eaten Cornish pasty to one side and plucks my car keys from a hook on the wall to his right.

'I gave her a service while she was here. Just as well, because you were running low on oil and your brake pads were as thin as a bleedin' wafer.'

'Thanks so much.' I reach in my bag for my purse, while mentally calculating how much it's going to cost me. 'What do I owe you?'

'Put that away,' he says with a wave of his hand. 'This one's on the house.'

'That's very kind, but I can't let you do that, Trev. Those tyres look really expensive.'

'Lara, love, let me do this one thing for you, please? You can make me a nice cup of tea as a thank you. You're not rushing off, are you?'

All that's waiting for me at Mum's is more editing, and I can tackle that tonight while Lily's doing her homework.

'I'm not. But are you absolutely sure?'

He nods, picks up his pasty and takes a large bite. 'You know that police bird who turned up at yours on Saturday?' he says as he chews.

'Josie?'

'That's the one. Thought I recognised her, but it wasn't from the funeral. It was bugging me all weekend, and then last night I remembered. Hackney.'

'Hackney, London?'

'Yup. My old stomping ground.'

'That's where you're from?' I stare at Trev as if he has just announced he's been selected by NASA for the next moon mission. 'But Jason's from Hackney.'

'Small world, innit? We lived on the same estate. That's how we met.'

'I knew you and he went way back. But you're much...' I break off, embarrassed.

'Older than him?' Trev laughs. 'I know, I'm almost old enough to be his dad. His parents were mates with my brother, Bill.'

'You know Frank and Viv?'

'I've known them most of my life. That's why I never minded Jase hanging around the garage. He was virtually family.'

'You had a garage in Hackney?'

'Just a small workshop round the corner from our estate. Jase and his mate Rex were permanent fixtures. Complete petrol-heads, the pair of 'em. I used to set them to work changing oil and filters, valeting the cars, changing tyres, that kind of thing. Lord knows what kind of mischief they'd have got themselves into otherwise. They were good kids. I did my bit keeping them out of trouble, and they repaid me by doing this and that around the garage. Then when Jason started buying and selling cars, I helped him fix them up.'

'And he ended up giving you a job.'

Trev chuckles, but there's a sadness behind his eyes. He might not be quite old enough to be Jason's dad, but it's obvious my brother-in-law was like a son to him.

'You said you recognised Josie from Hackney,' I remind him.

'That's right. She was Rex's little sister, always trailing around after him. Like his shadow, she was.' Trev rubs his chin. 'I'm surprised she didn't recognise me – she spent that much time sitting on an oil drum watching the boys tinkering under car bonnets.'

It's taking time for this latest revelation to sink in. 'Wait, are you saying Josie knew Jason?'

'Back in the day, yes. But we're talking nearly thirty years ago. I doubt she even remembers him now. Frank and Viv moved to Bexley when Jase was sixteen and Rex stopped coming to the workshop after that. Jojo was about three years younger than her brother, so she'd only have been about thirteen when Jase last saw her.'

'Jojo?'

'That's what she called herself in them days.'

'Are you *sure* it was her?'

'I wasn't,' Trev admits, 'until I found this.' He pulls a photograph out from under his diary and slides it across the desk to me. The five-by-seven-inch print shows the interior of a car workshop. A dusty shaft of sunlight filtering through a high window on the back wall illuminates the open bonnet of a black Ford Escort. Two boys aged about fifteen are leaning on the bonnet, grinning. I recognise Jason immediately. He had an unmistakable swagger about him even then; you can see it in the breezy tilt of his head and his confident smile. The other boy, who is holding a wrench in one hand and a can of Coke in the other, is taller than Jason by half a head. His hair is sculpted in a rigid flat top that must have taken him an age to style. His gaze is clear and challenging.

I scan the photo, taking in the oil-stained concrete floor and the line of worn workbenches on one side which are covered in tools, spare parts and cans of oil. The piles of old tyres and the grimy coveralls hanging from a row of hooks on the wall next to the obligatory girlie calendar. And then I see a girl curled up on top of an old oil drum like a cat, just as Trev described. And while the boys are grinning cockily at the camera, the girl's gaze is fixed on Rex and Jason.

But is it Josie? Her head is in profile, so it's hard to be one hundred per cent sure, but the harder I stare, the easier it is to convince myself that there is a familiarity to the determined jut of her chin and her slim frame.

'See what I mean? It's her, isn't it?' Trev says, popping the last of his pasty into his mouth, then tipping the packet up to catch the crumbs.

'I think so,' I agree.

'Rex joined the old bill when he left school. Looks like she did too, but then she always did idolise him, so it stands to reason, I suppose.'

'Is he still in the police?' I ask, wondering if Rex was one of the mates who turned a blind eye when Jason bent the rules in the old days; one of the mates who might have been there when Jason needed him ten years ago.

Trev scratches his armpit. 'Search me, love,' he says with a shrug.

57

It's half twelve when I leave Trev's garage. I have three long, empty hours to fill before I pick Lily up from school. On a whim, I decide to call Johnny, hoping to glean more about his podcast and the role my family is likely to play in it.

'I'm at a loose end,' I tell him. 'Fancy a drink?'

'You must be psychic. I was literally about to call you. Rose and Crown in half an hour?'

I'm the first to arrive and I order an orange juice and lemonade for me and a pint of lager for Johnny and take them to the same booth we sat in last time. He rocks up ten minutes later, his face breaking into a grin when he sees me. He's had a haircut, and his trademark crumpled suit looks as though it's had a trip to the dry cleaner's. He looks... good.

He slides into the seat opposite me and takes a long draught of his pint.

'Reckon I've earned that this morning,' he says. I wait for him to elaborate, but he just smiles at me over his glass, waiting for me to ask.

I give in. 'Why, what've you been up to?'

'Just a bit of what I'm best at.'

Although I'm not really in the mood for games, I am curious. 'And what would that be?'

He pretends to look affronted. 'Investigative journalism, of course.'

Warning bells ring in my ears. I take a deep breath, about to tell him he needs to keep his sodding nose out of my family's business, when he leans forwards in his seat and says conspiratorially, 'I know who the phantom tyre slasher is.'

This is not what I expected, and my hands fall to my lap. 'What? How? Who is it?'

He waggles a finger at me. 'Patience, dear heart. I'll get to it, don't you worry. But first, in true podcasting style, I want to tell you a story. A story that began with raspberry sauce and ended in murder. Are you sitting comfortably?'

I roll my eyes and he grins. 'Then I'll begin.'

I don't know what yarn I was expecting him to spin me, but I'm left stupefied when he starts blathering about rival gangs in 1980s Glasgow vying for control of the ice-cream van routes through the city's sprawling post-war housing estates.

'Some drivers sold drugs and stolen goods from their vans, which sparked a turf war between feuding gangs. It started innocuously enough, with territorial drivers squirting raspberry sauce on the windscreens of rival vans, but the intimidation tactics escalated and soon they were using bricks, baseball bats, knives and even sawn-off shotguns to control the ice-cream routes,' Johnny says. 'The feud ended in an arson attack in which six members of one family died. It was horrific.'

'It sounds it,' I agree. 'But I'm not sure what the relevance is.'

'I just wanted to illustrate how far some people will go to stamp on the competition. How much do you know about Millie Ford?'

'Not this again,' I groan. 'I thought you were joking the

other day. You don't seriously think Millie has anything to do with my tyres, do you?'

'How much do you know about her?' he repeats.

I try to think. I've only met her a handful of times, usually at wedding fairs where we've both had stalls. 'She's only been in Tidehaven about a year. I think she was in the Midlands before that. She's very good at marketing, not so good at taking photos.' I glance at Johnny. 'I don't mean to bitch, but you did ask.' I take a sip of my drink and cast my mind back. 'One of the first things she did when she moved here was to undercut the price I charge for engagement sessions.'

Johnny is watching me keenly. 'How much by?'

I pull a face. 'Fifty per cent. I charge two hundred, and she started doing them for a hundred. I wasn't about to start a price war, so I left mine as they were. Anyway, she was cutting off her nose to spite her face as there's no way she can make money on those margins.'

'I disagree. She probably sees engagement sessions as a loss leader or lead magnet. How much do you both charge for weddings?'

'I charge fifteen hundred and I would imagine she's in the same ballpark. Why?'

Johnny grabs a pen from his inside pocket and a beer mat from the table. 'Let's say you sell four engagement sessions at two hundred pounds each, and two out of the four couples book you for their wedding photos. You've made £3,800, right?'

I nod.

'But if Millie sells eight engagement sessions at a hundred pounds each and half those couples book her for their weddings, she's made £6,800. By aggressively undercutting you she's profiting big time.'

'But that doesn't make her some sort of twisted tyre slasher.'

Johnny ignores me. 'Other than the tyres and the email

Marta received, has anything else happened to you recently that has affected your business?'

'My website crashed last week. I had a shitty review on Trustpilot. And, um, someone sent me an anonymous note which was sort of threatening. But I know Millie wouldn't have done that,' I add quickly.

Johnny's forehead concertinas. 'You didn't tell me you'd had a threatening note.'

'I don't tell you everything.' I exhale loudly. 'I reported it to the police and DCI Frampton sent it off to Forensics.'

'What did it say, this note?'

I picture the sheet of lined paper and the untidy scrawl in black marker pen. 'Quit while you still have a choice.'

Johnny nods and smiles to himself, as if he already knows this. He's beginning to seriously piss me off.

'Who do you think it's from?' he asks.

'Jason, of course. Trying to warn me and Lily off. He blames me for telling the police he's back, and he's worried Lily's about to remember what happened the night he killed Isabelle and the twins.'

Johnny slips his pen back into his pocket. 'You're wrong in more ways than you can possibly imagine.'

Anger is bubbling inside me. I let it vent. 'If it's not from him, who the hell is it from? Come on, let's hear your hare-brained theories. I'm all ears.'

'Ice-cream wars,' Johnny says again, and I have to sit on my hands, literally sit on them, to stop myself picking up his pint and throwing it over him. 'If there's one thing the ice-cream wars have taught us it's that some people will stop at nothing to bury a competitor. I told you, Millie Ford slashed your tyres. She wrote that shitty review, she crashed your website and she sent that anonymous note. And before you accuse me of making this stuff up, I have evidence. She's done it before.'

'What?'

'You're right, she did use to work in the Midlands, but not as Millie Ford. I did a bit of digging and she was known as Amelia Ford-Taylor up there. She dropped the Taylor and used her nickname when she moved down south, presumably to give herself a clean slate.'

Johnny is still talking in riddles. 'A clean slate from what?'

'I spoke to a friend who works on the *Birmingham Mail* and asked if she'd heard of Amelia Ford-Taylor. I lucked out. One of her colleagues worked on a story about our favourite wedding snapper a while back. He'd been tipped off by a mate in the police who'd investigated her but hadn't found enough evidence to charge her. The copper thought there might still be enough dirt on her for the *Mail* to run a story, but the paper's lawyers got twitchy and they pulled it.'

'What was Millie... Amelia... supposed to have done?'

'She was accused of malicious communications and criminal damage, but according to the woman she targeted, she was only getting warmed up.'

'You spoke to her victim?'

Johnny nods. 'I drove up there yesterday. She didn't want to talk at first, but when I told her what's been happening to you, she agreed. Her name is Rachel Davies.' He scrabbles about in his pocket for his mobile. 'I recorded the interview in case you didn't believe me.'

He hands me the phone. A woman is frozen on-screen. I study her for a moment. She's a few years older than me, maybe late thirties, and has a blonde bob, clear blue eyes and a generous mouth. I press play. Rachel clears her throat, glances off camera as though she's checking it's OK to start, then begins to speak.

58

'My name is Rachel Davies and I am a wedding photographer, based in Edgbaston, Birmingham.'

Johnny's voice, off-screen, asks, 'When did you first meet Amelia Ford-Taylor?'

'At a wedding fair four years ago. Our stands were opposite each other, which wasn't great.' She grimaces. 'Actually, that's the understatement of the year. It was a disaster. For me, at any rate.'

'Did she introduce herself to you?'

'Oh yes, she came over and had a chat while I was setting up. She seemed nice. Charming, even. She'd only recently started out and it was her first wedding fair. She seemed a little out of her depth, if I'm honest. Her stand was a bit amateurish and her display photos weren't great either. But she was keen to learn, that's for sure.' Rachel gives a bitter laugh.

'What do you mean by that?' Johnny asks.

'Oh, she quizzed me about the business, from my price list to my advertising spend and everything in between. It would have felt like an interrogation if it wasn't for the compliments she showered on me. I was flattered.'

Rachel breaks off, as if she's embarrassed to admit this. Off camera, Johnny says, 'You mentioned earlier that she took a copy of your price list.'

'That's right. I always offer on-the-day discounts at wedding fairs for people who book me there and then. She seemed very interested in that. She studied my sample wedding albums and picked up copies of my brochure and a handful of business cards. I didn't think anything of it at the time.'

Rachel recrosses her legs. 'The wedding fair went really well for me. Three couples signed contracts and paid their deposits on the day and I had half a dozen other really positive leads, plus a couple of bookings for engagement shoots. Amelia didn't have such a great day. Every time I looked over, she was standing there twiddling her thumbs. A couple of times she sidled over and just sort of hovered while I was chatting to couples, which was irritating. Later, I found out both couples booked her for their weddings, which wasn't just irritating, it was downright out of order.'

'Are you saying she poached these clients from you?' Johnny asks.

'If you asked me to prove it, I couldn't, but yes, I believe she did.'

'And is that the last you saw of Amelia Ford-Taylor?'

'I wish it was. But after that wedding fair she set me in her sights. I'd worked in Edgbaston for over ten years and had built up a solid reputation and a strong client base. And then Amelia came along and decided she wanted my business and proceeded to take it from me.'

'What did she do?'

A hollow laugh. 'You name it, she did it. She posted a load of one-star reviews on Google and Trustpilot pretending to be my clients, saying I was unreliable, that my shots were out of focus, and that I was rude and unhelpful. She slashed her engagement package prices, charging half what I was asking.

She cloned my email account and sent a load of emails to clients saying I could no longer photograph their weddings. I only found out when I turned up to a wedding and she was already there taking photos of the bride having her make-up done. My car windscreen was smashed and my photography studio was vandalised. She even sent me threatening letters.'

'What did the letters say?' Johnny asks.

'They were all along the same lines: stop what you're doing while you still have a choice.'

'And you reported all this to the police?'

Rachel nods. She twirls a silver ring around her right thumb, round and round. 'They were very sympathetic and did look into it, but they couldn't link anything back to Amelia. She had covered her tracks too well.'

'Why are you so sure it was her? It could have been any number of your competitors – a disgruntled client, a jealous ex, anyone.'

'Because it all started the day after the wedding fair and it stopped a year ago, the week she moved down south to be closer to her parents. It's no coincidence. She resented my success and she set out to sabotage my business. And she nearly did. I was so close to jacking it all in. I was worried she'd stop at nothing to put me out of business.'

'I don't want to put words into your mouth, but are you saying you thought she might harm you?'

A shadow passes over Rachel's face. She nods slowly. 'Yes, there were times I thought she might resort to that. Please tell your friend to be careful. Amelia projects this perfect image to the world, but inside she's rotten to the core.'

The video ends. Wordlessly, I give Johnny back his phone. My head is spinning, assumptions and beliefs reordering themselves into facts and truths. The threatening note, the one-star review, the cyberattack on my website, the email to Marta, my slashed tyres.

I was wrong. It wasn't Jason at all. The only person to gain from my business going under is Millie Ford. I picture her face when we bumped into her at Willowbrook Hall. Supercilious. Contemptuous. Triumphant.

I'd always known she was ambitious, but I could never have imagined she would stoop so low. Johnny saw it. He was a better judge of character than me. I was too busy obsessing about my brother-in-law to even consider it could be someone else. How stupid I've been.

Johnny reaches across the table and touches my hand.

'Did you hear what I said? We should contact the police. Even if all the evidence is circumstantial, we can now prove a pattern of behaviour.'

'I've got a better idea,' I say, draining the last of my drink and sliding out of the booth. 'Let's pay her a visit and see what she has to say for herself.'

59

Millie Ford's photographic studio is down a small side street off the main high street. It's a fifteen-minute walk from the pub, but just five minutes in the car. I tell Johnny we're taking the car.

'I'm not sure this is a good idea,' he says as he fixes his seat belt. 'We'd be better off going to the police.'

'The police have been about as much use as a chocolate teapot when it's come to finding Jason,' I counter. 'Besides, I want to look her in the eye when I confront her. Watch her squirm.' I glance at him. 'What did you mean when you said I was wrong about him, by the way?'

He doesn't answer, and when I steal another look at him, he's examining a loose thread on the sleeve of his jacket. He gives it a tentative pull and the thread unravels.

'Johnny?'

He drops the thread and sighs audibly. 'I wish I could tell you, but I promised them I wouldn't say anything until everything was in place. I'm sorry.'

'Promised who?'

He looks as if he's about to speak, then closes his mouth abruptly.

'Please, Johnny. You owe it to me and Lily to tell us if some-thing's going on.'

He picks up the cotton thread again, winds the end around his index finger and jerks sharply, snapping it. Then he sighs. 'All I can say is that Millie Ford isn't the only person I've been looking into these last few days. I've also been following up a lead about potential police corruption. I have a source who has made some pretty damning allegations about a senior officer. Allegations that, if true, would prove that your sister's murder is not as clear-cut as everyone thinks.'

'What's that supposed to mean?'

'I told you, that's all I can say at the moment. But you'll be the first to know when I can tell you, I promise. Look, there's a parking space,' he says, clearly glad to change the subject.

I pull up outside a dry cleaner's and switch off the ignition. The anger I felt towards Millie Ford only moments ago is slip-ping like sand through my fingers. I try to hold onto it, clench my fists against the steering wheel to stop it trickling away, but it's too late. My grievance with her is insignificant compared to the loss of my sister and nephews. I turn to Johnny. 'Maybe you're right. Maybe I should go straight to the police.'

But it seems he too has changed his mind. 'No, we should call her out. Leave the talking to me. I think we can have some fun. D'you have your camera?'

'I *always* have my camera,' I scoff. I have no idea what he's planning but decide for once to go with the flow. I ping open the boot, take the Nikon from my camera bag and join him on the pavement. He has a battered reporter's notebook in one hand and a well-chewed Biro in the other.

He grins at me. 'Ready?'

'As I'll ever be.'

He opens the door and I follow him inside. It's no surprise that Millie's studio is a bit like her: all show and no substance. The walls are covered in huge canvases of her work, but the pictures are two-dimensional and unoriginal. There's no creativity, no technical flair. The shots are average, workman-like, when wedding photos should be mesmerising, unforget-table. Beautiful.

She appears from a door at the back, her smile fading when she sees me.

'What are you doing here?' she asks with ill-concealed animosity. She frowns at Johnny. 'I remember you. You were at Willowbrook Hall the other day.'

'I'm a journalist,' Johnny says. 'I have my own true crime podcast, *Johnny Nelson Investigates*. Lara's helping me out with my latest project.'

I play along. 'Yes. I've had enough of wedding photography. It's just too dog eat dog for me. You wouldn't *believe* the lengths some people go to to poach clients.'

Millie's gaze darts between Johnny and me, and she licks her lips. I smile to myself. It's clear she's rattled.

'Which leads me to why we're here,' Johnny says cheerfully. 'I've been speaking to an old friend of yours, Millie.'

'Friend might be pushing it,' I say, snapping the lens cap off my camera and slipping it in my pocket. 'Rachel despises Millie.'

'Rachel?' Millie blusters. 'I don't know any Rachels.'

'Oh, but you do,' Johnny tells her. 'Rachel Davies from Edgbaston. Ring any bells? She remembers you, at any rate. Says you tried to sabotage her business so you could steal her clients. Not the kind of thing you make up. Apparently, you employed a whole range of underhand tactics to bring her down, from crashing her website to vandalising her photog-raphy studio. The police didn't have enough evidence to charge you, but my podcast isn't bound by the same rules. That's why I'm here. I want to give you an opportunity to respond to Rachel's claims.'

Millie's face is white. 'You're recording a podcast about me?'

'I certainly am. I think I'm going to call it "Wedding Wars: Inside the Cut-throat World of Wedding Photography". Should shift a few downloads.' Johnny takes his mobile from the inside pocket of his jacket, finds the Voice Memos app and very deliberately presses the record button. 'So, would you care to comment?'

'No, I bloody well wouldn't! I know my rights. You're on private property. Get out of my studio now or I'll call the police.'

'Be my guest,' Johnny says. 'We were on our way to see them anyway. It'll save us a visit, won't it, Lara?'

'It will,' I agree. 'Because the thing is, I've been having the same problems as Rachel. Weird, eh?' I shake my head to demonstrate just how flummoxed I am.

Johnny makes a show of checking his watch. 'Our appointment at the police station is in ten minutes, so if you could respond to the allegations that would be marvellous, otherwise I'll have to say you declined to comment.'

Millie's shoulders slump. 'It'll ruin me,' she mutters.

'Probably,' Johnny agrees equably. 'Which is no more than you deserve. I suppose there is another way we can handle this. You apologise, in writing, to both Rachel and Lara for everything you've put them through, and we'll forget all about it. But we will be watching you, and if you ever try your dirty tricks again, we'll be on to the police in a heartbeat. Which is it to be?'

She looks from Johnny to me and back again. 'How do I know I can trust you?'

'You don't,' I tell her. 'But do you really have a choice?'

The studio falls silent as Millie weighs up her options. Finally, she holds out her hands for Johnny's notebook and pen, imperious to the last. 'Fine. I'll write you both an apology. And then I want you to leave.'

'Suits me,' I say. I'll be happy if I never clap eyes on Millie Ford again.

60

LILY

Lily sits in double maths and wonders how her life has managed to spin so spectacularly out of control.

Three weeks ago she was just an ordinary teenager. As ordinary as you can be when your dad (missing, presumed dead) killed your mum and brothers, anyway. She was going to school, hanging out with her mates, looking forward to the end of term. Normal stuff.

Then, Lara takes a photo of her dad, the infamous Jason Carello, just as Lily tells the world she is having flashbacks, and all hell breaks loose.

Someone runs Gran over, Lara's tyres are slashed and Lily's dad reaches out for the first time in ten years – *ten years*!

It's so left-field that if she read it in a book, she'd never believe it.

Lily can't shift the feeling that her TikTok videos were the catalyst for everything going pear-shaped. The irony is, she wasn't telling the whole truth when she revealed she was recalling details of that night. It's all still such a blur. When she closes her eyes and tries to remember, it's like navigating a foggy street when the visibility's so bad that even when you're shuffling forwards with your arms outstretched you still walk slap bang into a lamp post.

The worst of it is that if her dad had crawled out of the woodwork because he wanted to silence her, he needn't have bothered. She can remember precisely zilch about that night after her parents' argument in the kitchen. Even her recollection of the argument is hazy, to be honest. The harder she tries to grasp the memory, the more indistinct it becomes. Yet the memory of DCI Frampton slobbering over her mum like a lovesick puppy is as clear as bloody crystal.

Isn't that just typical?

Mr Evans, their maths teacher, is walking up and down the classroom collecting homework sheets. Lily bends down and ferrets about in her schoolbag for hers. As she does, the screen of her phone lights up with a message. They're supposed to leave their phones on airplane mode during lessons but no one ever does. As long as they're on mute it's fine. Lily hands Mr Evans her homework and, once he's moved on to the next desk, ducks down again to read the message. When she sees it's from an unknown caller her pulse beats a little faster.

Lily, can you spare me five minutes of your time this afternoon? I need to update you regarding the police search for your father. Please call when you pick up this message and we can arrange a quick meet. Best, DCI Frampton.

Lily exhales quietly. She knows what this is about. Yesterday afternoon, while Lara was visiting Gran in hospital, she recorded her last ever TikTok video. He must have seen it.

Totally unscripted and just a couple of minutes long, the video was her final foray into the murky world of influencing and she was glad to get it over and done with.

'Hey, guys, I wanted to jump on here one last time to let you know what's happening with my account,' she'd said. 'I won't be back on TikTok after this video. I began this journey to uncover the truth about my family, but I have come to understand that this is not the right place to do it.

'If – *when* – I remember what happened the night my mum and brothers died, I will tell the police before I tell you, because that is the right and proper thing to do. It's taken me until now to realise that.

'I want to thank you all for your support and love. It's been amazing hanging out with you and sharing my life, but it's best for me and what's left of my family to keep some stuff private, you know?

'So I'm going to say goodbye and focus on healing. Take care. And remember to find beauty in the little things, to dance like no one's watching and to surround yourself with the people you love. All that good stuff!' She'd laughed self-consciously at this, because it was all bullshit, but it was the kind of bullshit her followers loved.

Lily doesn't know how many views the video's had. She couldn't care less. She'll leave it up for a week or so, and then she'll close her account and never go near TikTok again.

Mr Evans lets them off five minutes before the bell, and Lily falls into step with Meena as they head towards the canteen. She should probably call Frampton but her stomach's growling with hunger. She'll do it after lunch.

'Coming into town after school?' Meena asks.

'Can't today. I'm going to see Gran.'

'I love your gran, she's so cool. How's she doing?'

'Not too bad.' Inside her bag, Lily's phone vibrates. Probably that creep Frampton again. 'Better get this,' she says, pulling it out and waving it at her friend. 'I'll catch you up.'

She answers without checking the screen, a dumbass mistake.

'Lily,' says her dad. 'Please don't hang up, sweetheart. I really need to talk to you. Come to the cottage. I'll be there.'

61

I park as close to Lily's school as I can without incurring the wrath of the fearsome-looking lollipop lady, and watch the tidal wave of kids surge through the gates and into the street. The wave has become a trickle when I spot Meena and Katy and I lower my window and call out to them.

'Have you seen Lily?' I ask, when they drift over to the car, bags slung over their shoulders, their eyeliner smudged and their ties askew.

'She said she was going to see her gran in hospital,' Meena says.

'She is.' I tap the steering wheel. 'I was supposed to be giving her a lift.'

'Maybe she forgot and she's gone straight there.' Katy shrugs. 'You could try phoning her.'

'I will.' I summon a smile. 'If you see her, ask her to call me, will you?'

'Sure,' Meena says.

I thank the girls and watch them stroll down the street. Once they're out of sight I call my niece. It goes straight to voicemail.

'Lils, it's me. Remember I'm picking you up from school today? I'm outside the gates now. Don't be long, yeah?'

I wait. Five minutes stretch to ten, fifteen. At ten past four I jump out of the car, wander up to the school gates and peer through, hoping to see Lily trailing out, dragging her bag behind her, but the playground is deserted. I pinch the bridge of my nose. Visiting hours end at five. We'll be lucky to get ten minutes with Mum at this rate.

I try phoning Lily again. Again, it goes to voicemail.

'I guess we've got our wires crossed and you've gone straight to the hospital. I'll meet you there, OK?'

The hospital's on the other side of town and it takes almost half an hour to fight my way through the late afternoon traffic and find a parking space. I stop at the Costa in the foyer to buy a latte each for me and Mum and a hot chocolate for Lily. By the time I arrive on Mum's ward, it's a quarter to five. Mum's sitting up, chatting to the white-haired woman in the next bed. She breaks off when she sees me and beckons me over.

'Would you believe it, Daphne's in for the same thing as me,' she says as I join them.

'Only I tripped on a garden step.' Daphne laughs. 'You must be Lara. I've heard so much about you.'

I really don't have time for this. I give Daphne a tight smile, then ask Mum, 'Where's Lily?'

She frowns. 'I thought she was coming with you.'

'She was supposed to be, but she didn't meet me at school. I assumed she must have come straight here.'

'We haven't seen her, have we, Maggie?' Daphne calls from her bed. I clench my jaw.

'Have you tried phoning her?' Mum asks.

'Of course I have. It goes straight to voicemail. And before you ask, I have left a message.'

'Have you tried the home number?'

I'm about to tell her that no one under twenty ever uses

home numbers, then pause. It has to be worth a try. The phone rings six times before the answerphone kicks in. I inject a lightness into my tone that I don't feel. 'Hey, Lils. It's Lara. Can you call me? Nothing urgent, but I'm with Gran at the hospital and I got you a hot chocolate and you're not here to drink it, which means I'll have to, and it's probably about five hundred calories or something. Anyway, call me. Please.'

I can feel Mum's eyes on me as I end the call and slip my phone into my back pocket.

'D'you think we should phone the police?' she says.

I shake my head. 'There's no point. She'll have forgotten our arrangement and is probably in town with her mates. You know how ditzy she can be.' I omit to tell Mum I know for a fact that Lily's not with her two best friends. It seems unlikely she'd have met anyone else in town. 'Or she'll walk in two minutes before the end of visiting hours moaning that the bus took ages.'

But Lily doesn't appear. By ten past five her hot chocolate's stone cold and I'm the only visitor left on the ward.

'Listen, Mum, I'd better go. They'll be bringing your tea round in a minute.'

She grabs my hand. 'Make sure you find her, won't you?'

'Of course.' I drop a kiss on her forehead. 'Don't get worked up. She's probably at home. I'll see you tomorrow.' I look pointedly at Daphne, who is still eavesdropping from her bed. 'And try to get some rest.'

62

Lily is not at home.

Images spool through my head, each one worse than the last. Lily bound and gagged in a filthy cellar; locked in the boot of a car; drugged; dead.

I hope I'm overreacting, but I know in my gut that I'm not. She is usually so good at keeping in touch, if not with me, with Mum. She knows how much we worry.

I leave yet another voicemail, beseeching her to call me to let me know she's all right. My voice sounds both shrill and quavery, if that's even possible.

I stare at the screen, about to phone the police when I change my mind. I run up the stairs two at a time and throw open her bedroom door. I should have checked in here earlier, I think, as I sift through the detritus on her desk. She could have left a note, an unwitting clue as to where she's gone, among the textbooks, notepads, pens and old phone leads. But if she has, I can't find it.

The room smells faintly of her perfume and I breathe it in deeply as I peer into her wardrobe. I search like a suspicious wife who suspects her husband of conducting an illicit affair, rummaging through the pockets of coats and jeans, fossicking through the chest of drawers and flicking through the notebooks on her bedside table.

It takes almost an hour to comb the room from top to bottom and once I've finished, I collapse onto Lily's bed, exhausted. I have found nothing, not a single thing that tells me where she might be.

Barney Bear is sitting on the pillow, a beatific smile in place. I pick him up and hold him close, memories of the day Lily made him flooding my mind. I finger his tutu, rubbing the tulle between my thumb and forefinger like a toddler with a comfort blanket.

He's wearing his little red satchel across his chest, messenger bag-style. Lily used to keep her treasures in it, I remember. Her pretties, she used to call them. The things she wanted to keep hidden from her brothers. The corner of a piece of paper is sticking out of the satchel. Curious, I peel open the Velcro fastening and tip it upside down. The paper flutters onto the duvet. I pick it up with trembling fingers.

Lolly, call me. Please.

And a phone number. It takes a moment for my over-wrought brain to grasp what this means. When I do, the contents of my stomach turn to liquid.

Jason was the only one who ever used that nickname. Somehow, he has managed to get a note to her. A note asking – no, *imploring* – her to phone him. And there's no way she would have been able to refuse. Which means... which means Lily is with Jason.

Fuck. *Fuck.*

63

Before I can talk myself out of it, I stab the number into my phone, my heart crashing in my chest as I wait for someone to answer.

The phone rings: once, twice, three times, and then there is a click, and a low voice says, 'Who is this?'

Jason. Sounding older and gruffer than I remember, but it's definitely him. My grip on the phone tightens.

'Where's Lily, Jason? What have you done with her?'

'Lara, is that you?'

'Who else would it be?'

'How did you get my number?'

I exhale loudly. 'I found the note you sent her. Where is she, Jason?'

A pause. 'With me.'

My stomach flips. 'Where are you?'

'I'm sorry, but I can't tell you that.'

'Don't be ridiculous. I'm her aunt. I need to know she's safe.' My voice is rising, an edge of hysteria creeping in.

'And I'm her father and I'm telling you she is.'

'I swear to God that if you harm a hair on her head, I'll... I'll—'

'You'll what, Lara?' Jason says mildly. 'Use your very particular set of skills to find me and kill me, like Liam Neeson in that film Isabelle used to love?'

I stare at the ceiling, trying to ignore the blood pounding in my ears. How dare he drop Isabelle's name into the conversation so casually, as if she's sitting in the next room with a bowl of popcorn on her lap and Netflix on the telly?

'You gave up any right to call yourself a father the day you killed my sister and nephews,' I hiss. 'Let me speak to Lily now or I'm calling the police.'

There's a muffled silence on the other end of the line. I pick Barney up and crush him to my chest.

'Lara?' Lily says.

'Oh, thank God. Are you all right?'

'I am.' But her voice is thick, as if she's been crying.

'Lily,' I say urgently. 'Where has he taken you?'

'He hasn't taken me anywhere. I went to him.'

'Only because he tricked you. Tell me where you are and I'll call the police.'

'Not the police!' she says vehemently.

I shake my head in frustration. 'Why are you protecting him after everything that's happened? Jesus, Lily, the man murdered your mum and brothers.'

'Not the police,' Lily repeats.

'Are you OK?'

'I'm fine, I promise. But Dad says I've got to stay here with him for the moment, so he can keep me safe.'

Keep her safe? This is worse than I thought. Jason doesn't need to keep her under lock and key; he's convinced her he's the good guy and everyone else is the enemy.

'Are you still in Tidehaven?' I whisper into the phone. 'Just answer yes or no.'

An empty, yawning silence.

'Lily, where is he keeping you?'

I hear a muffled, 'I'm coming,' and then Lily's back on the phone. 'I've got to go. The others are going to be here soon. Try not to worry, Lara. Everything's going to be all right, I promise.'

And the line goes dead.

64

Lily's words ring in my head as I stare at my phone, my finger hovering over the keypad.

Try not to worry, Lara. Everything's going to be all right. Try not to worry? Lily's with the man who killed her mum and brothers and she's telling me not to worry? And who the hell are 'the others', anyway? Jason's shady business associates who, according to Trev, 'owed him a favour' and helped him disappear the night of the murders? Are they going to help him disappear again, this time with Lily in tow?

Panic grips my heart and squeezes it tightly. A helicopter could be circling above them right now, the sound of the rotor blades growing louder as it prepares to land. Or maybe they're planning to leave by boat, a nippy little speedboat or a sleek motor cruiser, moored somewhere off Tidehaven beach.

I groan, my head buried in my hands. I can't let that happen. I need to phone the police. I'm about to dial when I hesitate. If I phone 999, there's a chance my plea for help will be lost in the barrage of calls the police must receive every day. Worse, the call handler might write me off as a crank. Why go through a busy call centre when I can phone the man at the very heart of the investigation?

I find DCI Frampton's number. To my relief, he answers on the second ring.

'Lara,' he says, his voice as calm and unruffled as ever, and I almost sob with relief. 'Is everything all right?'

'Jason's got Lily,' I blurt.

'*What?*' Even the static crackling on the line can't mask the detective's sharp intake of breath. 'How do you know this?'

'Because she's just told me. She was supposed to meet me after school but she never turned up. She wasn't at the hospital with Mum and she wasn't at home. I found a note from Jason while I was searching her room. It had his number on and I rang it and he answered. When I demanded to speak to Lily he handed her the phone, but she wouldn't tell me where they were.'

'What's his number?' Frampton asks urgently.

I grab Jason's note and reel it off. 'You think you can use it to find him?'

'That's the aim,' he says. 'Where are you now?'

'At Mum's.'

'Stay there. I'll call you as soon as I find them, all right?'

'All right,' I agree, even though the thought of sitting here doing nothing while Jason has Lily is unbearable.

'Promise you'll phone?'

But he's already gone.

* * *

I pace the living room, too anxious to settle to anything. I wonder how long it takes to track someone's location using mobile data. Do the police have to contact the network providers to see which phone mast the phone and SIM card are connected to? Do they need the phone to ping a second mast so they can narrow down the location? What if Jason has been using a burner phone that he's already discarded?

I crumple onto the sofa. If only Lily hadn't switched off Find My iPhone. I pick up my mobile, stare at it for a moment, then tap on the familiar green and blue app, more for something to do than in the hope that it's going to help me find her. Mum's phone is now showing as being on the other side of Tidehaven to the police station, which is weird, but I don't have a chance to wonder why because Lily's name is back on my list of people. I sit bolt upright, staring at the screen in growing disbelief. If the app is to be believed, she is on the Sandy Lane Bay Estate. No, not on the estate itself, I correct myself. About half a mile west.

A memory stirs. There's a holiday cottage, I remember suddenly. Half-hidden by the sand dunes. Jason's parents stayed there the weekend he and Isabelle moved to Sea Gem so they could be on hand to look after the kids. I went there to pick up Lily and the boys and take them to their new home. I zoom in closer. Yes, that's where Lily is, I'm sure of it. Did she switch Find My iPhone back on because she wanted me to find her?

I call DCI Frampton, closing my eyes briefly when it goes to voicemail. 'It's Lara. I know where they are. There's a holiday cottage west of the Sandy Lane Bay Estate.' I rack my brain, trying to picture the jauntily painted house sign on the gate. 'Cockle Cottage. I'm heading there now.'

I grab my car keys and hurry from the house.

65

A man steps out of the toll booth at the entrance to the Sandy Lane Bay Estate and announces there's an eight-pound parking charge.

I fix a smile on my face. 'Would you believe it, I've come out without my bag.'

'Then I can't let you in, I'm afraid.'

I force my smile to widen, even though I'm seething inside. 'I won't tell if you don't,' I try.

'I'm sorry, miss, but them's the rules. There's a lay-by up the road that usually has spaces.' He pats the roof of my car, a signal that I've been summarily dismissed. I hold my head high as I execute a ragged seven-point turn on the narrow lane, and stamp my foot on the accelerator, leaving a cloud of sand in my wake.

'Bloody jobsworth,' I mutter, pulling onto the main road. I know the lay-by he meant. It's popular with dog walkers who refuse to pay the estate's extortionate parking charges. It's about a mile up the road, but by my reckoning I should be able to cut straight through the sand dunes to the cottage.

I'm in luck, and there are only a couple of cars already

parked in the lay-by. I pull up behind them, check Lily's location again and set off.

Maybe the toll booth man did me a favour, I think, as I trudge through the dunes. If Jason saw my car arriving outside the cottage he might run, taking Lily with him. At least this way I'll approach the cottage from the rear, keeping an element of surprise. I try not to think about what I'm going to find. I'll have to deal with it when I get there.

The going is hard, the soft sand sucking my feet like quicksand with every step I take, and before long I'm panting with the exertion. But I press on, three words on repeat in my mind.

Must find Lily.

Must find Lily.

Must find Lily.

Before it's too late.

* * *

Eventually, the sand dunes grow smaller and when I stop to catch my breath, I can hear the gentle lapping of the sea and taste the salt in the air. Ahead lies an area of scrub. Small bush-like trees with stiff, thorny branches that are bent at the waist like curved spines. The sandy ground is a carpet of creamy sea campion and sea holly, the blue teasel-like heads nodding gently in the breeze.

I shield my eyes from the sun and peer through the scrub, hoping for a glimpse of the cottage. It can't be far from here. And then I spot a chimney poking out from the blackthorn like the middle finger of a disgruntled driver who's just been cut up on the motorway.

My pulse quickens. I am so close. But there's a problem. The blackthorn looks impenetrable; a wall of vicious spikes that would rip your skin to shreds the moment you started forcing your way through. I try to picture the layout of the cottage and garden. Lily, I remember, gave me a guided tour. 'Look, there's a hammock. I can climb in it all by myself. And a bird table and a wind chime and a path that leads all the way to the sea.' And Lily had beckoned me to follow her down the narrow, pebble-lined path that led to the beach and we'd spent a happy half an hour paddling in the shallows.

The scrub thins out to my left, and I pick my way through it. Soon, I'm standing on the beach with my back to the sea, looking for the path Lily led me down all those years ago. I see it, rub my sweaty palms on my jeans and head over.

I flit through the scrub, following the path towards the cottage. When I reach the garden, I stop and turn my phone to silent. The back door, which has been propped open with a wellington boot, is directly ahead of me. I scan the windows looking for movement. Only when I'm satisfied the coast is clear do I steal across the grass and slip inside.

The back door opens straight into the cream Shaker-style kitchen. The beech-effect worktops are empty bar a kettle, toaster and mug tree. There's a phone in a hot-pink case on the kitchen table. Lily's phone. Why doesn't she have it with her? Lily *always* has her phone with her. She's surgically attached to the bloody thing.

The door to the hallway is closed. I stand behind it, my hand resting on the doorknob. Silence fills my ears, and I am about to turn the handle when I freeze. A low, dragging sound makes the hairs on the back of my neck stiffen. It's the slow, deliberate scrape of something heavy being hauled across the wooden floorboards. A body? *Lily's* body?

And then, just as abruptly as it started, the sound disappears and silence returns. A heavy, all-encompassing silence that is more terrifying than the dragging sound from moments before.

Every nerve in my body is on edge as I press my ear against the door and listen. If I can catch a whisper, a breath, I might understand who's on the other side of this door and what they are doing.

I wait. Two minutes turn into four... five. And then there's a loud click and I have to bite the inside of my cheek to stop myself from screaming, because it sounds exactly like a gun being cocked.

66

No shots are fired. Instead, a car door slams outside and an engine roars into life. Gingerly, I ease open the door and peer around. The hallway's empty. I shuffle out of the kitchen to the front door and try the Yale lock. The latch makes the same clicking noise I'd thought was a gun. I let out a long breath.

There are four doors off the long, narrow hallway, all of them closed. I start with the door to the main bedroom. It's at the front of the cottage and has white walls, blue-painted furniture and a cheerful blue and white quilt on the bed. Apart from a large rucksack propped against a wicker chair in the corner, the room is empty. I sidle over to the rucksack and unzip the small compartment on the top. There's money in there – a wad of euros – and a European passport in the name of Austin Healey. My gaze drifts across to the passport photo. It is of Jason. Older and thinner with a thick beard and impressive sideburns, but still recognisably my brother-in-law.

If only travelling under a false passport was the worst of his crimes.

I pick the rucksack up by the nearest strap and feel its weight in my hands. Perhaps this was the body I thought I'd heard being manhandled through the house. I let the strap slip through my fingers and the rucksack drops onto the floor with a thud. If it's here, it means Jason's here too. Perhaps he's taken Lily to one of his dodgy mates to source a fake passport for her. That's fine. They'll be back eventually. I can wait.

I cross the room to the window. Lily's mountain bike is propped against the picket fence. She must have gone straight home to fetch it while I was waiting for her at school, and then cycled here to meet her dad.

I head back into the hallway. I'm so convinced the cottage is empty that I fling open the door to the living room and step inside without a second's thought.

A figure is sprawled awkwardly on the stripped wooden floor, her hands and ankles bound and a bloody graze on her temple.

Lily.

I sprint over, drop to the floor and cradle her head in my lap. Fear spikes through my veins as her eyes roll back in her head.

'Lily!' I cry, feeling for a pulse. 'Lily, it's me, Lara. Wake up!'

Lily doesn't wake up.

Pushing down the panic rising in my chest, I feel her neck for a pulse. Her skin is warm and baby soft. Of course it is – she may think she's on the cusp of adulthood, but when all's said and done Lily's still a child.

I feel a flicker of a pulse, faint but steady, but my relief is soon overshadowed by a fury that bubbles like lava inside me.

Jason, that conniving, murderous *bastard*, lied to me. He promised me Lily was safe when nothing could have been further from the truth. Was she trussed up like a turkey when she spoke to me? I picture him holding the phone to her ear, a knife glinting in his other hand, her eyes wide with terror.

It's why she told me not to call the police. She realised her life was hanging by the flimsiest of threads, and if she'd given me even a hint that she was in danger, he probably would have killed her.

Just like he killed her mum and brothers.

Thank God I ignored her pleas and called DCI Frampton. It's been over an hour since I left the voicemail. Surely he's picked it up by now. Perhaps the police are already on their way, a cavalcade of patrol cars hurtling through Tidehaven, sirens wailing and blue lights pulsing. I cock my head, listening hard, but can't hear anything.

In my arms, Lily shifts and her eyelids flutter open. Her eyes are glassy and she's clearly struggling to focus. I smile, tucking a wayward strand of hair behind her ear.

'Hey,' I say, my chest expanding.

'W... where am I?' she whispers.

'In the cottage by the sea Nan and Gramps stayed in when you were little. You... you came here to meet your dad, but it's OK, he's gone and the police are on their way. They'll catch him, Lily. Everything's going to be all right, I promise.'

I'm mirroring her words to me, I realise. I don't blame her for trusting Jason, but it was so nearly her downfall. What if I hadn't found his note? It doesn't bear thinking about.

I'm so lost in my thoughts that I almost miss the emotions chasing each other across her face. Confusion. Dismay. Panic. She struggles to sit up, but her wrists and ankles are still bound by cable ties. I berate myself for not thinking to cut her free.

'Lily, wait. You'll hurt yourself. Let me help.' I lift her shoulders as gently as I can until she's sitting on the floor with her back against the sofa.

'Not... the... police,' she croaks.

I do a double-take; I can't help myself. 'Seriously?'

'You don't... understand.'

'Damn right I don't.' It staggers me how Jason has brainwashed Lily so comprehensively in such a short space of time. But I suppose I shouldn't be surprised. When he was on form, he could charm the birds from the trees, and she always was a daddy's girl. I climb stiffly to my feet. 'I'm going to find some scissors so I can cut those ties.'

'Please don't leave me,' Lily whimpers.

I give her a reassuring smile. 'It's OK. I'll be right back.'

I'm working my way through the kitchen drawers looking for a pair of scissors when I hear the low thrum of a car engine at the front of the house. It throws me for a second, as I'd expected blaring sirens. Which means it might not be the police at all...

My fears are confirmed when the front door clicks open. Heavy footsteps thud across the hallway and into the living room. I look around wildly, my gaze falling on the set of kitchen knives on a rack on the wall by the toaster. I grab a paring knife because it's the only one small enough to fit into the pocket of my jeans, and creep out of the kitchen.

The door to the living room is ajar. From within I hear a dull thud and a groan of pain. My fingers tighten around the knife in my pocket as I push the door open.

A man is standing over Lily, his back to me. I yelp in surprise, and he spins around.

67

'Thank God you're here,' I say, stepping into the room. Sunlight floods through the window, leaving DCI Frampton's face in shadow. 'Look what he's done to her.' I point at Lily, who's crouched in a ball, her face white with terror. 'She's been hit on the head. You need to radio for an ambulance, but first we need to untie her.'

I'm about to pull the knife from my pocket when he takes a step towards me.

'There's really no need.' His voice is dispassionate, his face expressionless. And, for a reason I can't fathom, my stomach lurches. Something isn't right.

I hold my ground. 'DCI Frampton, Curtis, you need to do something. Lily's hit her head.' I touch my temple to demonstrate. 'She needs an ambulance,' I repeat.

Still he stares at me, his face as blank as a mask.

'*Please,*' I plead. 'Jason's going to be back any minute to finish what he started.'

Lily begins to rock, her soft keening filling the room. I'm by her side in a flash, wrapping my arm around her shoulder and pulling her close to me. She is saying something, her voice choked with tears.

'What, Lily? What is it?'

'I tried to tell you, but you wouldn't listen,' she sobs. 'It wasn't Dad.' She dips her head towards the detective. 'He killed Mum and the twins, and he did this to me.' She holds out her bound wrists.

Frampton throws his head back and barks with laughter. I stare at Lily in disbelief. She's got it all wrong. Jason killed Isabelle, Jack and Milo and then he fled. Everyone knows that: the police, the media, us. If he didn't kill them, why disappear?

It's as if Lily's read my mind. 'That bastard set Dad up.' Her gaze jerks up to Frampton. She sounds so sure of herself that I almost believe her, and then I remember she's only just regained consciousness after being knocked out cold.

'You hit your head, Lily. You're confused. It's hardly surprising. That's why we need to get you to hospital. To get you checked out.' I scowl at Frampton, who still wears the trace of a smirk on his face.

'I'm not confused. He killed them, Lara.'

What a ridiculous thing to say. Frampton never knew Isabelle. But the more I think about it, the more I realise their paths *could* have crossed. Frampton and Jason were golf buddies. It's possible he'd been introduced to Isabelle at some golf club do.

The day I met Frampton in the Salty Bean he told me I had my sister's eyes. He'd been quick to explain that the walls of the incident room were plastered with photos of Isabelle, Jack and Milo and their faces were imprinted on his memory. And it made sense. I certainly hadn't questioned it at the time. But now, in hindsight, it seems a strange thing for him to say. And if he knew Isabelle, how the hell did he end up leading the investigation into her murder?

'Is this true?' I ask him.

The smirk has disappeared from his face and he is watching us both with contempt.

'What do *you* think, Lara?'

'I... I... I don't know.' I think back to that summer and how distracted Isabelle had been, always too busy to see me. Constantly checking her phone when I did pop over. The police ruled out the possibility she was having an affair, but that doesn't mean they were right. Hell, Frampton was on the murder team from day one. He could have buried the evidence.

Curtis Frampton is an attractive man. The young mums in the coffee shop obviously thought so. Mum had been positively simpering when he turned up at the house to take Lily's statement. A flush creeps up my neck as I remember that even I'd been flattered by his charms.

And my sister, my elegant, beautiful sister, had a track record of falling for charmers.

'Did you know Isabelle?' I ask.

His face twists. 'Know her? I *loved* her. And she loved me.'

For a moment I'm speechless, my mind a blank, but then the questions tumble in, fast and furious.

'You were having an affair? Did Jason know?'

He snorts. 'Of course not. He was too busy making money to have any time for Isabelle. He didn't appreciate what he had, so I took it from him. I *worshipped* her. I was going to give everything up for her – my career, my home, my friends – so we could start afresh somewhere new. I was even prepared to take on her brats. We were going to leave the day before they were supposed to go to France. I'd rented a place in Cornwall while we decided where we would live. Isabelle's and the kids' bags were already packed so we could leave without a scene. And then she chose him, the bitch. She chose that jerk over *me*.' He prods himself in the chest as he says this, a muscle pulsing in his jaw.

'So you killed her because she chose Jason, not you. And the boys. You stabbed two little boys in their beds while they slept. How could you? How *could* you?'

I am crying now, tears coursing down my cheeks as I remember arriving at Sea Gem that night. The young police officer vomiting in the garden; the eerie quietness of a house that usually rang with the sound of children's voices; the blood. *So much blood.*

I charge at Frampton, pummelling his chest with my fists. 'You bastard, you bastard, you bastard!'

He swats me away like I'm an irritating fly, then shoves me onto the sofa. 'Sit,' he orders. He bends down to take something out of a bag by the side of the sofa. Cable ties, I realise with horror. On the floor by my feet, Lily lets out another whimper. I want to comfort her, but the words won't come. What can I possibly say that's going to make this any better?

Frampton squats beside me. 'Phone,' he says, holding out a hand. I give it to him because what choice do I have? He slips it in his pocket and then secures a cable tie around my wrists so tightly I can feel the plastic biting into my skin, before tying another around my ankles.

'There,' he says, standing up and admiring his handiwork as if he's just finished putting up a shelf. 'Stay here.' He smirks, knowing we're hardly in a position to leave. 'I'll be right next door. I have a score to settle.'

68

LILY

Grief presses down on Lily's chest. The weight of it is suffocating, unbearable. Until now, she thought the worst day of her life would always be the day Gran and Lara told her Mum, Jack and Milo were dead. Now she knows that was just a dress rehearsal for today: the day she realised she was completely alone.

She knows her dad's been as good as dead for the last ten years. Everyone else thought so from the beginning, and the courts made it official three years ago. But Lily had always harboured a hope that he was out there somewhere, biding his time, waiting for the right moment to come back to her.

She'd also hoped there'd been a terrible misunderstanding and the police were hunting the wrong man, because she still couldn't believe that her dad, her funny, loving, devoted dad, could have done what they said he'd done.

This afternoon her hopes were fulfilled.

Her dad had seemed slightly manic when she arrived at the cottage just before five. There was a pent-up energy about him, as if he'd just found out he'd won the jackpot on the lottery.

Lily had followed him into the living room and watched

warily as he stood by the window, his back to her and his hands deep in his pockets.

Finally, he turned to face her, and as he talked, a calmness settled over him that Lily found mesmerising. 'I don't really know where to start, so I suppose I should start with the truth. I didn't do it, Lily. I didn't kill your mum and brothers, and I didn't hurt you. It wasn't me.'

'Then who did kill them?'

He hesitated, and Lily thought she saw a flicker of concern cross his face.

'What is it you're worried about, Dad?'

'That telling you will put you in danger. And that you'll think badly of your mum.' He held Lily's gaze. 'What happened wasn't her fault. All marriages have their ups and downs, and ours was no different. Isabelle was a beautiful person, inside and out, and I want you to remember that. Promise?'

Lily had stared at him with trepidation, wondering what was coming next. Was he going to claim her mum had killed Jack and Milo, then killed herself? She wasn't naive; she knew it happened. Women gripped by postpartum psychosis, their sense of reality turned inside out. But her mum? She was always so graceful, so serene. She used to say she'd found her vocation when she'd become a mum.

'Lily?' her dad pressed.

'OK, I promise. But Mum would never have done it.' Lily's voice wobbled. 'She loved us.'

'God, Lily, I didn't mean...' He tugged his beard. 'It wasn't your mum.'

'Then *who*?'

His eyes locked onto hers. 'Curtis Frampton.'

Of course. Her mum's lover. Lily had known about the affair since she was five but had locked the memory away so deeply it had only just resurfaced.

Her dad watched her closely. 'You don't seem surprised.'

'I saw them together when I was little. He came to our house.' She was about to tell him how she'd caught them kissing but thought better of it. 'I've only just remembered,' she added.

'Frampton and I were friends. Used to play golf together. Did each other favours, if you know what I mean?' When Lily shook her head, her dad cleared his throat. 'I'd give him deals on cars if he turned a blind eye to... erm... certain practices at the garage.'

She narrowed her eyes. 'What kind of practices?'

'Clocking cars, cash only sales, that kind of thing. Frampton did very nicely out of our arrangement,' he said bitterly. 'Course, he was a lowly detective sergeant when we first met, but he was ambitious even then. I suppose that's something we had in common. As well as golf, and—' He looked sidelong at Lily. 'Your mother.'

A dark cloud crossed his face. 'Your mum stopped by the garage once when Frampton was picking up the keys to a new car. I was working such long hours at the time that I suppose it was inevitable her head was turned when he showered her with attention.'

Lily was still finding it hard to stomach the thought of her mum and the smarmy detective getting it on. He was ancient, for a start. And so bloody pleased with himself. She was trying to chase the image of them together away when she became aware her dad was still talking.

'Frampton became increasingly possessive, wanting to know where she was all hours of the day, quizzing her about the time we spent together as a family. He gave her an ultimatum – me or him – and couldn't accept it when she chose me.'

'How d'you know all this?' Lily asked.

Her dad rubbed the back of his neck. 'Someone sent me a note claiming she was having an affair—'

'Who?' Lily demanded.

He shook his head. 'I don't know, and it doesn't really

matter. I didn't believe it, not at first, but then your mum told me the night before we were supposed to leave for France. It all came out in one huge torrent; how she'd felt flattered by his attention at first, then found herself in too deep. How he'd become more and more controlling, threatening to expose their affair if she refused to leave me, how she was scared of what he might do if she didn't.

'I told her not to worry, that she was safe, but she became hysterical. She was convinced Frampton was about to turn up on the doorstep with a sawn-off shotgun, so I said I would go to his place, try to talk some sense into him, man to man.'

Lily thought back to the argument she'd overheard the night her mum and brothers died. She hadn't understood it then, but it made sense now.

Her dad, yelling.

How can I believe a word you say?

Won't let that happen.

Never come near my family again.

Her mum, pleading.

I'm scared, Jason. Really scared. Oh God oh God oh God.

'I should never have left you all.' Her dad's face was stricken. 'I had no idea he was already on his way over. I have regretted that decision every minute of every day for the last ten years. And when I came back and saw what he'd done...' He buried his head in his hands.

A sob rose in the back of Lily's throat. 'I was still alive and you left me. How could you do that?'

He sat down heavily and buried his face in his hands. 'I thought you were all dead, and I knew Frampton would frame me for the murders. I had means and I had motive, I knew he would make sure of that. Who would believe me? No one, that's who. I was a coward, so I ran, and I will never forgive myself for that.'

69

I listen with growing disbelief as Lily recounts her conversation with her father. I'm finding it hard to get my head around it all. If what she says is true, Frampton killed Isabelle, not Jason. We've been wrong all along.

'What was Isabelle *thinking*?' I cry. 'And why did your dad run away? He must have known he'd look as guilty as hell.'

'He went to one of his old friends, asking for help,' Lily says. 'Dad meant help with finding a barrister and clearing his name. But his friend said no one would ever believe him and talked him into disappearing so he could prove his innocence from abroad.'

'So he staged his own suicide and then fled?'

Lily shakes her head. 'That's not what happened.'

I stare at her in surprise.

'Frampton left the photograph on the cliffs at Beachy Head. He faked Dad's death and now he's going to kill him.' Her eyes fill with tears and I lean over and rest my head on her shoulder. It's a silent offering of love, the only gesture I can make while my hands are tied. Her shoulders start to shake and a fresh wave of anger washes over me. We can't just sit here while Frampton rewrites history for the second time. We have to do something. I wriggle away from Lily and struggle to my knees. As I do, something sharp digs into my hip. The knife! How the hell did I forget the knife?

Double-handed, I reach into my pocket.

'What are you doing?' Lily hisses.

'I've got a knife!' I whisper back, producing it with a grin. Lily's surprise turns to understanding and she holds out her arms so I can begin sawing at the plastic tie. The knife's blunt, the handle slippery, and it's almost impossible to cut through the tie with my own hands bound.

'Ow,' Lily says, drawing her hands back as I nick her skin.

'Sorry,' I say, appalled.

'It's OK.' She extends her arms. 'Just hurry up.' I try again, using smaller movements this time. Eventually the tie falls away. Lily winces as she rubs the circulation back into her wrists, then takes the knife and efficiently cuts through the ties binding my hands and ankles before freeing her own feet.

'Now what?' she says.

I gawp at her for a moment because the truth is, I don't know. Even though there are two of us, Frampton's easily strong enough to overpower us both, and I don't suppose he'd stop at tying us up next time.

'Call the police?' Lily prompts. 'The *real* police.'

I nod. Of course, that's what we should do. But Frampton has my phone and Lily's is on the kitchen table. I scour the room, looking for a landline, but there isn't one. I haul myself to my feet. My legs are pipe-cleaner weak, and my hands are trembling.

Lily looks up anxiously. 'Where are you going?'

'To get your phone. It's in the kitchen.'

'There's no signal in the cottage. I checked.'

I paste on a reassuring smile. 'Then I'll run to somewhere that has one.'

'Don't leave me.' Her face is pale, her eyes red-rimmed. 'Please, Lara. Don't leave me here on my own.'

'I have to, Lily,' I say, dropping a kiss onto her forehead. 'I'll be right back. I promise.'

She clutches my hands, then releases me.

I creep across the room to the door and turn the handle. It rattles but doesn't open. The bastard's locked us in. I glance back at Lily, who points to the big picture window.

The latch is stiff, but I jiggle it till it opens, then climb onto the sill and jump down, landing in a patch of faded pink achillea. I creep around the side of the cottage, passing the weathered front door and stopping by the window to the main bedroom. I peer in. Everything is as it was earlier. The blue-painted furniture, the blue and white quilt, Jason's rucksack propped against the chair in the corner. I exhale slowly and make my way round to the next window. This one must be the bathroom because it's made of frosted glass. I press my face against it but I can't see anything.

I scurry round to the back door. Lily's phone is still on the kitchen table, and I scoop it up and check the signal. Lily was right, there isn't one. But I know I had one when I parked my car, so if I climb onto the nearest sand dune I'm sure I'll pick up at least one bar.

Not wanting to risk Frampton glimpsing me through a window, I head down the path to the sea. Any hope I might've had of spotting a dog walker or angler on the beach is dashed – it's deserted, not a soul in sight.

I turn west, jogging awkwardly along the shingle, the small stones shifting beneath my feet, my arms flailing for balance. I stop at the first sand dune and clamber up it, my eyes on the phone. One bar! Before I can hit the emergency button on Lily's lock screen, a text flashes up. Johnny. I can only see a couple of lines of the text, but they halt me in my tracks.

Tell your dad I have our smoking gun. Be with you in thirty mins.

I check the time it was sent. Twenty-eight minutes ago. Why is Johnny texting Lily, and what does he mean, he has their smoking gun? But I don't have time to wonder about that now. I need to call the police.

The call handler is telling me he'll have a patrol with us as soon as he can, but demand is exceptionally high right now, when I hear it: the low rumble of an engine. I recognise the sound at once. Johnny's MG.

'Please hurry,' I say, ending the call and sprinting back to the cottage. I know I have to intercept Johnny before he storms in and a panicked Frampton hurts Lily, but as I round the corner to the potholed driveway, my chest burning from the effort, the front door is wide open and I realise I'm too late.

70

I burst through the front door and into the living room. The sight that greets me chills me to the bone. Curtis Frampton is by the fireplace, one arm wrapped around Lily's neck, the other holding a knife to her throat. The same knife I used to cut our ties and left on the coffee table when I went in search of Lily's phone.

Johnny is standing stock-still, his back to me, telling Frampton to put the knife down, that hurting Lily will only make matters worse, that he can't claim another life. Frampton's expression is hard and unflinching. He knows he holds all the cards.

Lily notices me and whimpers, the sound cutting me to the quick. I step forwards and Frampton's gaze tracks from Johnny to me.

'Stay where you are or I will kill her,' he says tonelessly.

I stay where I am.

'Look,' Johnny says pleasantly. 'You of all people should know how this goes. You've killed three people, you've lied and you've manipulated evidence over and over again. You're finished, so you might as well hand yourself in.'

Frampton's eyes are as cold as steel. 'I haven't killed anyone.'

'Sir, you don't have to do this,' a voice says, and I spin round to see PC Josie Fletcher, our family liaison officer, standing behind me.

'Josie, what are you doing here?' I gasp, but it's as if I'm invisible. Her focus is on Frampton.

He cackles, the sound reverberating around the room. 'Fuck me, if it isn't the intrepid PC Fletcher, dragged here on a fool's errand.' His face hardens. 'What the fuck are you doing here, Fletcher?'

'You should know I made a statement before I left the nick, sir. Detailing everything I know about the murders of Isabelle, Jack and Milo Carello.'

'Statement? What statement?' Frampton blusters.

'That you have spent the last ten years framing the wrong man for the murders. Jason didn't kill them.' She looks at him levelly. 'You did.'

'You're out of your tiny mind,' Frampton says, his tone bitingly cold.

'D'you know, I always worried we were looking for the wrong man,' Josie says. 'Then one day when I was visiting Sea Gem to pick up some of Lily's clothes for the hospital, I bumped into Jason and Isabelle's neighbour, Maureen. She said something that didn't make sense then, but as the months went by it niggled me. A red flag that I should have taken more notice of, but I couldn't believe – didn't *want* to believe – it was significant.' She shakes her head almost dolefully.

'Maureen saw your car the night of the murders, sir. Not in Chetwynd Avenue, oh no, you weren't stupid. No, she saw you drive it onto the beach behind the two houses. She described it as a blue and cream Austin Healey, and everyone reasonably assumed it was Jason's car, the one that used to have pride of place in his showroom. But that day I was at the house picking up Lily's clothes, Maureen talked about a Frogeye Sprite. When I asked if she was sure she laughed and said her father once owned one. She used to love the frog-like headlights.'

'Jason's car was an Austin Healey 3000,' I say.

Josie nods. 'You're right. It was an easy detail to miss. But it was obvious we were dealing with two different cars.' She turns to Frampton. 'I mentioned it to you at the time, do you remember?'

He doesn't react.

'Memory failing you, is it, sir? Just as well I can remember then, isn't it?'

If looks could kill, Josie would be ten feet under, but she seems unperturbed by Frampton's icy glare.

'You said Maureen's husband told you she'd recently been diagnosed with dementia and to disregard anything she said. So I did. Because I trusted you.' She laughs bitterly. 'It's a shame you didn't think to mention that you bought a blue and cream Frogeye Sprite from Jason's garage the previous year, isn't it?'

Josie, I realise, is Johnny's smoking gun.

Johnny takes up the reins. 'Josie wasn't on the murder squad, but she started noticing little inconsistencies in the investigation that when taken in isolation weren't significant, but when put together looked deeply suspicious.'

'It felt to me as though evidence was being found to fit the case against Jason,' Josie said. 'Anything that went against the team's working theory that Jason killed his wife and children wasn't just discounted, it was buried. But what concerned me was why.'

'Tell them about the photo, Josie,' Johnny prompts.

'What photo?' Frampton snaps.

'The one taken the night Jason was presented with a trophy at Tidehaven Golf Club,' he says.

'You were in it,' Josie tells Frampton. 'And so was Isabelle. And there was no mistaking the look you were giving her.

Desire, longing, call it what you will.' She shrugs her shoulders dismissively. 'And you know what they say about the camera.'

'It never lies,' Johnny finishes.

'You were having an affair with Isabelle, weren't you, sir?' Josie says. 'I'm not sure exactly what happened that night, but I can hazard a guess. You asked her to leave Jason, and she refused. You went to her house to talk her into changing her mind and when you couldn't, you killed her, because you had already decided that if you couldn't have her, no one else could. And then you killed her boys and attacked Lily in a fit of jealous rage.'

'If you were so certain, why didn't you say something then?' Frampton says smoothly.

'Because I didn't think anyone would believe me. Everyone thought Jason was guilty. Why else would he have fled the scene?'

'Why are you coming forward now?' I ask her.

She turns to me. 'When Jason came back, I knew I couldn't risk him being convicted for three murders he didn't commit. And then Johnny called me, wanting to talk about the case. I decided it was time the truth came out.'

She takes another step towards Frampton. 'Curtis Frampton, I am arresting you on suspicion of the murders of Isabelle, Jack and Milo Carello, and the attempted murders of Lily and Jason Carello. You do not have to say anything...'

As Josie reels off the caution, I blink. *Attempted murder.* Does that mean Jason's not dead? I glance at Lily, but she's staring at the floor, her face hidden by a curtain of hair. Frampton is clutching the knife so tightly his knuckles are almost translucent.

'You and that bastard Carello are setting me up,' he spits. 'I would never have killed Isabelle. I loved her and she loved me!'

Suddenly there is an almighty roar from behind us and I whirl around to see Jason hurtling through the door, his face contorted with rage. He charges at Frampton with the ferocity of a bull tearing into a matador. Frampton, caught unawares, drops the knife. Josie is across the room in a second and kicks it out of his reach. Jason rugby tackles Frampton to the ground. Lily runs into my arms. And in the distance, I hear the wail of sirens.

71

ONE MONTH LATER

I pull into Mum's drive, kill the engine and grab my bag from the passenger seat. Lily and Mum pounce on me the moment I let myself into the house, as I knew they would.

'Well?' Mum says.

'He's still denying everything,' I say, shrugging off my jacket and hanging it on the back of a chair. 'They've set a date for the trial. January the eighth.'

'And his bail application?' Mum asks.

'Turned down.'

'That means he's still in prison?'

'He is.'

'That's good.'

It's an understatement. We've all been on edge for the last few days, worried a lenient judge might decide to grant Curtis Frampton bail at his first Crown Court hearing. I tagged along with Johnny, who was covering the hearing for *The Post*, because I wanted to face the man who ripped my family apart. I wanted to see if he was full of remorse or unrepentant. But I should have known it would be the latter. I have a feeling he'll go to his grave denying the fact that he killed my sister and nephews.

'Tea?' Mum asks.

'Please.' I follow her into the kitchen. 'His barrister's claiming all the evidence against him is circumstantial.'

'Which it is,' Lily says bitterly. 'But only because he destroyed all the forensics that linked him to the scene.'

Josie dropped this bombshell when she popped round to tell us Frampton wasn't just denying killing Isabelle, Jack and Milo, he was also pleading not guilty to Lily's false imprisonment and to being behind the wheel of the car that hit Mum.

An internal police inquiry is underway after Frampton's former colleagues in CID discovered critical forensic evidence went missing during the original investigation. But even without the forensics, the evidence against him is piling up. Maureen, Isabelle's next-door neighbour, has gone on record to say it was Frampton's Frogeye Sprite she saw parked behind Sea Gem on the night of the murders, not Jason's Austin Healey 3000. Despite Frampton's claims to the contrary, Josie says she's a credible witness.

Frampton's dark blue BMW was caught on the doorbell camera of a house in Napleton Road moments before Mum's hit and run. The guy who lived there had been away on a business trip when officers carried out their house-to-house enquiries, but came forward with the footage when he arrived back in the country and saw the witness appeal on a local news website.

When police executed a search warrant following Frampton's arrest they found Mum's mobile in the glove compartment of his car, which explains the strange journeys I saw on Find My iPhone. And when Frampton's own phone was sent off for analysis, a deleted photo of Lily walking across the waste ground was recovered.

Josie says the investigation team's working theory is that

Frampton sent the photo to me hoping I would show Lily, and that she would assume it was taken by some weirdo who'd been watching her TikTok videos and, totally creeped out, she would stop making them. Frampton couldn't risk her remembering seeing him at the house the night of the murders.

'And to think I brought out my best china when he came round to take Lily's statement.' Mum tuts. 'What a waste.'

Even if there isn't enough evidence to convict him of killing Isabelle and the twins, Frampton should do time for the false imprisonment and driving offences. And everyone knows what kind of reception police officers get in prison, so I reckon he'll get what he deserves, one way or another.

Mum hands me a mug of tea. She's getting stronger every day. The first couple of weeks after she came out of hospital were tough, but we muddled through, and now she's talking about signing up for the Tidehaven 5k fun run next Easter. I *think* she's joking, but with Mum you never know.

Lily has started a summer job as a waitress in the Italian restaurant in town and loves it so much she's dreaming about opening her own restaurant one day. She's definitely inherited her parents' ambition and entrepreneurial spirit. Mum and I are just relieved she's abandoned her plans to become an influencer.

That's not to say she's come out of this ordeal unscathed. The deaths of her mum and brothers seemed to hit her anew after Frampton's arrest, and her nightmares returned with a vengeance.

Mum was straight on the phone to Gillian, the grief counsellor Lily saw when she was twelve. When I asked Lily about her first session, she just said, 'Gillian's chin is more whiskery than ever, if that's even possible.'

I got the message: it's none of my business. I haven't asked since. But four sessions in, she seems more at peace with herself than she has in a long time.

I think I'm finally coming to terms with Isabelle's death, too, not least because this time Mum isn't sweeping everything under the carpet, and we're all getting better at talking about our feelings. It helps that Jason reminisces about Iz and the boys all the time.

'D'you remember when Jack stuffed a pea up Milo's nostril and we had to take him to Minor Injuries? And that time we found them in our bedroom, and they'd drawn all over their faces with Isabelle's Yves Saint Laurent lipstick and Touche Éclat?'

In fact, he talks about them so much I can almost pretend they are still here with us, in another room, just out of sight. Which, I think, is as much as you can ask for.

Like Lily, Jason is a damaged soul. I don't think he'll ever forgive himself for fleeing after he came back from Curtis Frampton's place and discovered the bloodied bodies of his wife and children. Perhaps if he'd realised Lily was still alive he would have stayed. Perhaps not. He says he always intended to prove his innocence from Spain, but with Frampton on the investigation team he knew it was futile. Weeks turned into months, months into years. Jason convinced himself Lily was better off without him, but the pull of the tenth anniversary was too much for him to ignore and so he returned, just like the swifts in Mum's garden.

Back in Tidehaven, he set about clearing his name, contacting the one reporter who knew more about the case than anyone else: Johnny.

Johnny started digging, and one of the first people he spoke to was PC Josie Fletcher, our family liaison officer. Suddenly he and Jason had their smoking gun.

I've been wrong about so much these past two months, but I was right about one thing: it was Jason who left the sunflowers for Isabelle, Jack and Milo. But it wasn't to freak us out, it was because he loved them.

We're all glad he came back. Our little family feels more balanced, more *solid*, with Jason home. He might have his demons but Trev was right – he is a human jack-in-a-box and it's impossible to keep him down for long. He is arranging for his cat, Valentina, to be flown over from Spain with the rest of his belongings, and he's already talked Trev into letting him use his forecourt to sell cars. Jason's going to sell the Austin Healey to fund his fledgling business. I have absolutely no doubt he'll make a success of it.

The doorbell peals. Mum picks up her phone and checks the screen.

'It's Josie,' she says. 'Let her in, will you, Lily?'

'Yes, Gran.' Lily doffs an imaginary cap and slopes off to open the door. It's funny how Mum changed her tune about the video doorbell after Curtis Frampton was arrested.

'If you can't trust the police, who can you trust?' she said, then asked me to tear the tape off the camera.

Josie appears and Mum ushers us all into the living room.

'Where's Jase?' Josie asks.

'The garage,' I tell her. 'Trev's got him doing something to a carburettor.'

Her face falls. Johnny reckons she has a thing for Jason. I laughed my head off when he told me this a couple of weeks ago, but as I take in her newly blow-dried hair and her carefully made-up face, I wonder if he's right. She certainly spends enough time round here. She's always popping in on her way home from the police station under the pretext of checking on Mum and Lily.

Trev was right: Josie and Jason did grow up on the same Hackney estate in the nineties. Sometimes I wonder why she never mentioned the connection, but it was so long ago, and it's not like she was on the investigation team or anything, so I suppose it doesn't matter. We have so many reasons to be grateful to Josie. She risked her career when she blew the whistle on Frampton, and that takes guts. If she hadn't, my brother-in-law would be behind bars.

My phone pings with a text from Johnny.

Pick u up in ten.

He's had a tip-off that a local fruit farmer is forcing migrants to live in squalid metal shipping containers while he's living the life of luxury in a £2 million pound Georgian farmhouse down the lane.

'He's cramming eight people into every tin box,' Johnny told me over a pint at the Rose and Crown last night. 'And if the cramped conditions, disgusting portable loos and primitive shower facilities weren't bad enough, he's creaming forty quid each off their weekly pay packets for their accommodation. He's going to be the first immoral bastard I expose on my podcast. Want to come with me?'

I'd been about to remind him I'd vowed never to cover a news story again. The words were on the tip of my tongue but I took a sip of my beer, considered how I felt and found myself saying, 'Yes, of course. Tell me where and when and I'll be there.'

I don't know who was more surprised, me or Johnny.

Wedding photography pays the bills, but it's never been my vocation. My heart is in news, always has been, and with Frampton behind bars I finally feel ready to return.

'You will be careful, won't you?' Mum says, as I hitch my camera bag over my shoulder and prepare to leave.

'You need to stop worrying, Mum,' I say with a reassuring smile. I peck her on the cheek. 'The bad guy's behind bars. We're safe now.'

72

JOSIE

Josie pretends to listen as Maggie witters on. Something to do with a pair of trousers from Marks & Spencer that she thought were black, but Lara said were navy, which is what Maggie wanted, so that was all right, but now she's decided black would be better because they would go with that nice sequined top she picked up half-price in Sainsbury's, and she's worried she's left it too late to exchange them. *Jesus.* Josie tuned out a while ago, although she keeps half an ear open in case she catches any interesting snippets about Jason.

This ability to zone in on snatched information, subtext, body language and the nuances of family life is what makes her such a great family liaison officer. Yes, FLOs are there to support families who have been the victims of crime, but they are police officers first and foremost. Their job is to act as a conduit through which information can flow from the police to the families, but it goes both ways. She's on the ground, in the circle of trust, and she hears – sometimes is even handed on a plate – information that can have a case sewn up in hours.

Because it's always the husband, isn't it? And if not the

husband, someone in the family. Families are a hotbed of resentment, petty jealousies, secrets and lies, and the Carellos are no different.

Look at Isabelle. Beautiful, elegant Isabelle, with her kooky vintage clothing company, her stunning beachside home and her three model-perfect kids. Who'd think she was dropping her knickers for an idiot like Curtis Frampton?

And Jason. Well, Josie knows for a fact that Jason also played away.

So much for the perfect image they projected to the rest of the world. It was all fake. A mirage. And it didn't take much for it to come crashing down.

Josie surreptitiously looks at her watch. Would it look odd if she made her excuses and left? Probably. Her tea's only half drunk, and Maggie's still chuntering on about the bloody trousers. Lily's sitting cross-legged on the armchair by the window, scrolling through her phone. She looks so much like her father it takes Josie's breath away. That's why it was so hard to...

'What do you think, Josie, love?' Maggie says.

'Sorry, what?'

'Which d'you think would be more useful, blue or black?'

'Oh, well, I spend my life in black, so I'd probably go with navy,' Josie says. 'Or why don't you cover all bases and buy a pair in both colours?'

Maggie's eyes light up. 'Now *there's* an idea. Why didn't I think of that? Thank you, Josie. I think you might just have the answer.'

It's another reason Josie's so good at her job. She thinks outside the box, looks at problems from a different angle. She is adaptive, creative. She's not afraid to question authority and, if it calls for it, bend the rules. Well, she smiles to herself, *break* the rules might be more accurate.

Lily unfolds herself from her chair and announces she's going upstairs. She nods at Josie as she passes. There is animosity there, Josie's sure of it. Has Lily sensed the undeniable spark there is between her and Jason? Or is it something else?

Josie can cope with a bit of jealousy, but if it's more than that it might prove problematic down the line. It's something to be aware of, anyway. She is keeping a watching brief.

There's no doubt Maggie's on side, and Lara's too wrapped up in Johnny and her work to pay much attention to Josie. Lara pretends Johnny's just a friend but any fool can see they have the hots for each other. Which is fine by Josie. It means Lara's focus is elsewhere.

And what about Jason? Her soulmate. He completes her, like the missing piece of a jigsaw puzzle. He always has, even when they were kids, knocking around on their Hackney estate.

Jason was her brother Rex's best mate. Three years older than Josie, it was inevitable, she supposes, that she was invisible to him. But if she nagged Rex enough, he sometimes let her hang out with them.

It wasn't puppy love, or a crush. It was the real deal, whether or not Jason realised it. And so, Josie kept tabs on him when his parents moved from Hackney to Bexley and he lost touch with her brother. She found out the location of Jason's first garage under the railway arches in Lewisham and watched proudly from afar as his business flourished.

When Josie was eighteen, she applied to join the Met. Rex had joined a couple of years earlier and Josie couldn't think of anything else she wanted to do. And she was good at it. Could probably have climbed through the ranks if she'd wanted, but she was happy staying under the radar, a rank-and-file PC. And keeping track of Jason was a cinch once she had access to the Police National Computer.

She dated other men over the years; she wasn't a nun. But no one came close to Jason. They weren't even in the same ballpark.

And so, when he moved out of London to the south coast, opening a classic car showroom in upmarket Tidehaven, Josie had simultaneously applied for a transfer to the local police force and started saving for her own classic car.

She turned up at JC Classics with butterflies in her stomach and a budget of five grand. At first, when Jason greeted her like a long-lost friend with a beaming smile and outstretched arms, she thought he'd recognised her from the estate all those years ago and she'd blushed to the tips of her ears. It was only when he gave his next customer the same effusive welcome that she twigged. He greeted everyone like that, and she was neither special nor memorable.

Not yet, anyway.

She ended up blowing her entire budget (and then some) on a postbox-red Fiat 124 Spider that broke down on the way home from the garage and has been nothing but trouble ever since.

But if life's taught her anything, it's that nobody's perfect.

When Josie had been working in Tidehaven for six months, she engineered a meeting with Jason at the Duke of Cumberland, the pub he, Trev and the rest of the mechanics frequented every Friday night.

She looked good. Jason was on the drunk side of tipsy. They had sex in the back of his Austin Healey, parked behind the recycling bins at the back of the pub car park. As she snuggled up on the slippery leather back seat for a post-coital cuddle, Josie believed all her dreams had come true.

And perhaps they would have, had Isabelle fucking Beckett not walked into the showroom a week later, draped over the arm of her rich boyfriend, stealing Josie's happy ever after from under her nose.

Bitch.

Jason and Isabelle were married with indecent haste. Josie retreated to lick her wounds. She watched and she waited.

Five years later, her patience finally paid off.

73

JOSIE

'Would you like a fresh cup of tea, Josie?' Maggie Beckett says. Her brow puckers. 'That one must be cold by now.'

Josie gives a small start. She'd been so lost in her thoughts she'd forgotten she was sitting in Maggie's front room listening to her prattling on about trousers, sequined tops and Christ knows what else.

Let's face it, Josie has nowhere else to be. Her cold, bland, rented flat, with its beige walls, brown carpet and mismatched furniture, holds little appeal. At least sitting here in Maggie's cosy living room she feels close to Jason. And there's always a chance he'll come home before she goes.

'Just a quick one.' She's about to hand Maggie her mug when she remembers herself. 'You stay there. I'll get them.'

In the kitchen, Josie fills the kettle, rinses out their mugs and, never one to miss an opportunity, has a quick rootle through Maggie's handbag, which is hanging on the back of a chair. Disappointingly, there's nothing to see of interest.

As the tea brews, her mind drifts to the day she discovered Isabelle Carello was having an affair with Curtis Frampton. Josie was the family liaison officer in a nasty child abduction case in which Frampton was the senior investigating officer. The arrogant twat had clicked his fingers at her at the end of a briefing and told her she was driving him into town. Josie would have liked to have told him where to go, but rank is rank, so she'd found the keys to a spare patrol car and had driven round to the front car park. She was ready and waiting when Frampton sauntered out of the station ten minutes later.

After she dropped him off, she parked a little further up the road and watched him in her rear-view mirror. To her surprise, he jumped into a waiting Volvo and embraced the blonde woman at the wheel. Josie memorised the woman's number plate before the car sped off.

And then, a gift. Josie still can't believe her luck. A quick PNC check revealed the car was registered to Mrs Isabelle Carello of Sea Gem, Chetwynd Avenue, Sandy Lane Bay Estate, Tidehaven.

Jason's wife was playing away.

An anonymous note was all it had taken to plant the seed of doubt in Jason's head. And Josie made sure she was at the Duke of Cumberland the next evening offering him a shoulder to cry on. Admittedly, she'd had to ply him with drinks and listen to him droning on for hours about how he feared Isabelle had betrayed him and how much he loved her, but Josie didn't mind, not really. She was playing the long game.

'It's funny,' she'd said, as she sipped her Diet Coke. 'You remind me of a lad my brother Rex knocked about with when we were growing up.'

'You're Rex's sister?' he'd slurred. He'd leant forwards and looked at her owlishly. 'Dammit, I can see it now. You have his eyes. Well, fancy that. Of all the pubs, in all the towns, in all the world, she walks into mine.'

And Josie's eyes had shone. Because the way he said it, their meeting in this backstreet pub on the wrong side of Tidehaven with its garish, swirly carpet and sticky tables, was meant to be.

He didn't need to know she'd been watching him, following him, all her life.

Her patience was rewarded with a knee trembler in the disabled toilet just before closing time. As Jason came in juddering gasps, the tears that had rolled down his cheeks washed away any doubts she'd had about being a revenge fuck.

Josie pours the tea and adds a splash of milk. She remembers how all her families take their tea: weak and milky; strong and sweet; so strong you could stand a spoon in it.

Her razor-sharp memory and attention to detail stood her in good stead when it became apparent Jason had no intention of leaving Isabelle.

'I'm sorry, Josie,' he said. 'You've been a good friend to me, but I think it's best if we don't see each other again.'

And Josie had said, 'Of course. I understand.' And she had let him hug her, glad to bury her head in his shoulder so he couldn't see the fury on her face.

And while she seethed and raged, she plotted.

Josie carries the mugs into the living room, and Maggie taps her phone.

'Jason's just texted. He's on his way home.'

Josie allows herself a small smile. Patience is a virtue. Everyone knows Rome wasn't built in a day.

She turned up at Sea Gem on the off-chance that night. Glimpsing Jason through the kitchen window was as much as she could hope for since he'd ended things between them.

Isabelle never closed the curtains. It was as if she wanted the world to see what she had. Look at me, with my designer kitchen and my art deco staircase and my perfect fucking family.

Josie sensed something was wrong the moment she peered into the brightly lit kitchen. She'd seen so many families implode in her years as a family liaison officer, she knew conflict when she saw it.

Jason was standing with his back to her, his knotted shoulders clearly visible through the thin fabric of his T-shirt. Isabelle was facing him across the huge kitchen island, her eyes shiny with tears.

'You're never here. You're always working, and I was lonely, Jase. I know it's no excuse, but it's the truth. I was bored and I was lonely and Curtis was there when you weren't.'

'You should have talked to me if you were unhappy.' Jason's voice rose. 'You should have helped me understand!'

'I know. But it's over now, I promise.'

'How can I believe a word you say?'

'I know I've messed up.' Isabelle was crying properly now, tears coursing down her cheeks. 'And Curtis, he's so angry. I'm scared, Jason, really scared.'

On the island a phone buzzed into life. The colour leached from Isabelle's face.

Jason frowned. 'Is that him?'

She nodded, glanced at the screen and looked up at Jason. 'He says he's coming over.'

'Now?'

She nodded, then cradled her face in her hands. 'Oh God, oh God, oh God. What if he does something stupid?'

'I won't let that happen.' Jason grabbed a set of keys from the island and made for the door.

'Where are you going?' Isabelle cried.

'I'm going to make sure that prick never comes near my family again.'

'You can't, he'll kill you!'

'Let him try,' Jason said grimly.

There was a scuffle as Isabelle tried to wrestle the keys from Jason, but he pushed her out of the way. Moments later the front door slammed and a car roared into life.

Isabelle ran out of the room and a light came on upstairs.

Well, well, well, thought Josie, as she crouched outside the kitchen window. Jason was on his way to Curtis Frampton's. Frampton was on his way here. And stuck between them, playing piggy in the middle, was Isabelle, who had cheated on them both. A plan was forming in Josie's mind, a plan so perfect, so *audacious*, she even scared herself.

Glad she'd had the foresight to park in the next road along, Josie jogged back to her car, opened the glove compartment and pulled out the latex gloves and paper overshoes she always carried with her, *just in case*, before retracing her steps back to the house.

74

JOSIE

Afterwards, Josie watched Frampton's old Austin Healey pull up on the beach behind the house with gleeful anticipation. How she would have loved to have been a fly on the wall when he walked into Isabelle and Jason's bedroom and saw his lover's still-warm body spreadeagled on the bed. Had he checked the children's rooms before he fled, or did he discover their deaths much later? She'll never know.

Josie left while he was still inside the house. She drove straight home, stripped off in the kitchen and threw her clothes in the washing machine and the bloodied knife in the dish-washer. She'd taken no pleasure in killing Isabelle. She'd acted out of necessity. She wasn't stupid – she knew she'd never win Jason's affections while Isabelle was around.

And the children? She had killed them because that was what a frenzied lover would do. They were collateral. Nothing more, nothing less.

Early the next morning, Josie slipped the photo of Jason, Isabelle and the children she'd taken from the house into her bag and drove to Beachy Head. Walking past the sign bearing the Samaritans helpline number, she wiped the photo clean of her prints and left it on the wiry grass as close to the edge as she dared.

As she drove into work, she congratulated herself on a job well done. Frampton would believe Jason had murdered Isabelle and the twins. Jason would think Frampton killed them. And the beauty of it was that both had means and motive. No one would ever guess her involvement.

As the days following the murders turned into weeks, and then months, everything played out exactly as Josie hoped. Curtis Frampton made sure he was part of the investigation team. Josie, the most experienced family liaison officer, became Maggie, Lara and Lily's FLO.

Frampton, terrified his colleagues might discover not just his affair but the fact that he was at the house on the night of the murders, hid any evidence that could conceivably incriminate him, from Isabelle's phone records to forensic evidence found at the scene.

Jason, prime suspect from the beginning, vanished. Josie hadn't bargained on that, but she was pretty sure he'd come back for Lily one day. She had waited for him once. She would wait for him again.

And then something happened that no one could have predicted. Lily announced to the world on TikTok that she'd started to remember what happened the night her mum and brothers died. It set in motion a chain of events even Josie couldn't stop.

Fearful the semiconscious Lily might have seen him in the house the night of the murders, Frampton panicked and had run her over. The guy was a detective chief inspector, and yet he couldn't tell the difference between a fifteen-year-old girl and a sixty-four-year-old woman. What an idiot. Josie would never have made such a schoolboy error, that's for sure. Even if he isn't convicted of the murders, he'll still do time for dangerous driving and, frankly, it serves him right.

Hearing a key turning in the lock, Josie's skin tingles, and she smooths her hair.

'All right, gorgeous?' Jason says, breezing into the room; Maggie titters, and Josie's insides swoop when he sees her and smiles. 'Hello, Josie, to what do we owe this pleasure?'

She beams back at him. 'I'm just keeping Maggie company.'

'I don't know what I'd do without her,' Maggie says.

'Amen to that,' Jason agrees, before flopping into the armchair Lily has just vacated. 'Don't suppose there's any tea left in the pot?' he asks hopefully.

Josie jumps up to make her man a cup of tea. Those eyes, she thinks, when he smiles his appreciation. She could happily drown in them.

And her heart skips a beat, because her shiny, happy future, the one she's imagined since the days she trailed around after Rex and Jase when she was seven, is within her grasp.

Everything is in place. The only obstacle she might have to address further down the line is Lily, but if the last ten years have taught Josie one thing, it's that anything's possible if you put your mind to it.

Absolutely anything.

A LETTER FROM A J MCDINE

Dear Reader

Thank you so much for reading *The Photo*, and I hope you enjoyed it! If you would like to keep up to date with all my latest releases, just click on the link below and I'll let you know when I have a new book coming out. Your email address will never be shared and you can unsubscribe at any time.

www.bookouture.com/a-j-mcdine

I had the idea for *The Photo* during a wet and windy week's holiday in North Wales. I hadn't even been thinking about books the morning the premise for the story popped into my head: what if a photographer saw someone in the back of one of her photos – someone who *really* shouldn't be there?

I let the idea percolate for a while, not least because I was in the middle of writing *The Baby*, and when it was time to decide who was in the photo – and why they shouldn't have been there – I let my imagination run wild!

I was keen to make my protagonist, Lara, a press photographer who left her job after a personal tragedy. Having worked on local newspapers as a reporter for over twenty years, I had great fun writing the newspaper and press conference scenes.

Once I had my protagonist and the inciting incident, I started writing. Four months later I had a very messy first draft on my hands and the polishing began.

The Photo is my seventh psychological thriller and is the most plot-driven book I've ever written. It also has the biggest cast of characters. Working out their motivations and how they interacted with each other was a challenge, and I hope I pulled it off.

The final plot twist came to me when I was about two-thirds of the way through the book, which isn't as strange as it sounds when you're a discovery writer like me. I would love to be one of those authors who plots every scene before they type a single word. Sadly, my brain just isn't wired that way!

Anyway, I hope you've enjoyed the result. If you have, it would mean so much to me if you could leave a review on Amazon or Goodreads. I'd love to hear what you think, and reviews make such a difference in helping new readers discover my books.

But, please, no spoilers!

That's all from me for now, but please feel free to drop me a line at amanda@ajmcdine.com, visit my website or come and say hello over on Facebook or Instagram.

All the best,

Amanda x

www.ajmcdine.com

 facebook.com/ajmcdineauthor

 instagram.com/ajmcdineauthor

ACKNOWLEDGEMENTS

A huge thank you to the wonderful team at Bookouture for helping me turn my unformed ideas into actual books, with much support and encouragement along the way.

Particular thanks are due to my editor, Billi-Dee Jones, whose advice is always on the money and whose suggestions have made this book so much better than it would have been without her wisdom and insight.

Thanks to my copy editor, Nicky Lovick, and proofreader, Jenny Page, for their eagle eyes and expertise.

A thousand thank yous to my readers and all the amazing bloggers who read, review and recommend my books. I'm so grateful to be able to make up stories for a living and I wouldn't be able to do that without the support of all you lovely people.

I would like to thank my husband and fellow author, Adrian, and our boys, Oliver and Thomas, for putting up with me when I'm lost in my own little imaginary world.

Finally, I would like to thank our three rescue cats, Minstrel, Amber and Charlie, who keep me company during the long hours I spend holed up in my writing cave. This writing lark would be infinitely less fun without them.

PUBLISHING TEAM

Turning a manuscript into a book requires the efforts of many people. The publishing team at Bookouture would like to acknowledge everyone who contributed to this publication.

Audio
Alba Proko
Sinead O'Connor
Melissa Tran

Commercial
Lauren Morrissette
Jil Thielen
Imogen Allport

Data and analysis
Mark Alder
Mohamed Bussuri

Editorial
Billi-Dee Jones
Nadia Michael

Copyeditor
Nicky Lovick

Printed in Great Britain
by Amazon